DANIELLE BINKS

the year the maps changed

Quill Tree Books
An Imprint of HarperCollinsPublishers

Quill Tree Books is an imprint of HarperCollins Publishers.

The Year the Maps Changed
Copyright © 2022 by Danielle Binks
Copyright © Map illustration Astred Hicks, Design Cherry

ISBN 978-0-06-321160-5

Typography by Laura Mock
22 23 24 25 26   PC/LSCH   10 9 8 7 6 5 4 3 2 1
❖
Originally published in Australia and New
Zealand by Hachette Australia, 2020

This is a work of fiction. All central characters are fictional, and any resemblance to actual persons is entirely coincidental. In order to provide the story with a context, real names of places are used as well as some significant historical events. A number of high-profile people are also referred to, but there is no suggestion that the events described concerning the fictional characters ever occurred.

This fictional story takes place in the Kulin Nation and is set on the lands of the Boon Wurrung people. The Boon Wurrung are the traditional people and custodians of these lands, from the Werribee River to Wilsons Promontory. I pay respect to their elders and acknowledge this land was taken by force and that the First Nations have never ceded sovereignty to their lands and waters.

For Mum and Dad, and Omi too.
I love you.

We are volcanoes.
When we women offer our experience as our truth,
as human truth, all the maps change.
There are new mountains.

URSULA K. LE GUIN

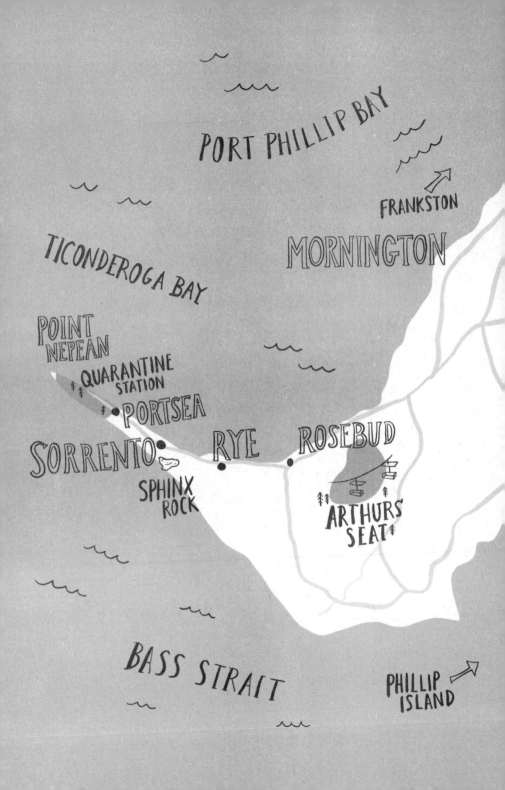

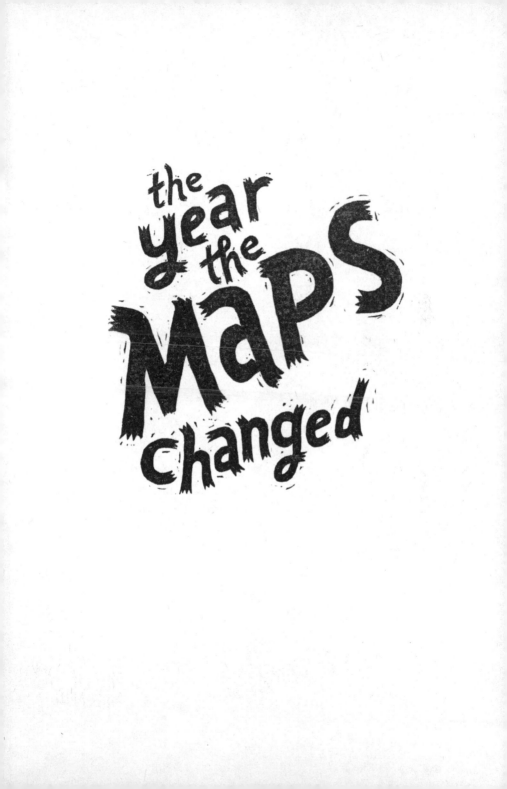

PROLOGUE

Maps lie.

Or at least, they don't always tell the truth. They're like us humans that way.

Mr. Khouri would say it's because they can't show us everything about a place or the people in it. Maps don't tell you about the ownership, genealogy, or history of an area. A map doesn't even really tell you where to begin or end—those ones with "Start Here" and "X Marks the Spot" are just that way in movies, or kids' menu coloring placemats. Really it's up to us—the people who live within the borders—to keep the truth and know the way.

And lately I've been thinking that it doesn't matter so much where you end up, if you can't remember how you got there in the first place. Like my pop would say: it's not the destination, it's the journey.

Remembering is like retracing my steps. There are so many different trails to this story and it's hard to know which one to take. But I need to lay down a way to see everything that happened this past year: the war, Nora, Operation Safe Haven, and the baby we couldn't keep.

I was eleven when everything started and twelve by the end. But that's another way that maps don't tell the whole truth—because it felt like the distance I traveled was a lot further than that.

1

MEMORIES LIKE MOUNTAINS

Arthurs Seat is the highest point of this mountain range here. It's named that because it looks like someplace else—it's got nothing to do with King Arthur and the Knights of the Round Table, like I'd always hoped.

Last year we learned that the Boon Wurrung people called the mountain Wonga and held corroborees—sacred dance ceremonies—lower down on the slopes called Wango—probably about where the parking lot is now.

From the very top of Arthurs Seat, you can see clear across the Mornington Peninsula, where we live, and over the whole bowl of Port Phillip Bay, from the tip of Point Nepean to the silver city of Melbourne winking in the distance. But if you want to go to Arthurs Seat and see all of that, you have to take the chairlift.

Luca first took me there when I was six, the year my mom died.

I was obsessed with great heights back then. I nearly gave everyone a heart attack one day when I crawled out of our neighbor Jed Trần's bedroom window and onto the slanted shingle roof. I was too chicken to go to the edge like I thought I wanted to, so I ended up sitting somewhere between the gutter and the window, like a flung Frisbee, until Pop called Luca to come and get me.

After Luca roared up on his police motorbike, he went and got the Trầns' old ladder from the garage while Pop kept calling to me from down below, telling me to stay put.

I could hear Jed's mom, Vi, somewhere inside too. She was giving her son an earful for letting me climb out there, and for not having the good sense to come get her the second he saw what I was up to.

By the time Luca finally crawled out to me, I was heaving my guts up with tears, but it wasn't because I was scared. It was hearing Jed's mother yell at him like that and remembering that mine never would again.

Well, Luca got me down and proved that fathers can yell at reckless children just as well as mothers can. Then he asked me what I'd been trying to achieve in the first place.

"I wanted to see her," I said.

"See who, Freddo? Maria?" He shook his head. "Your mama?"

I nodded.

"Heaven's *right there*." Then I pointed at the sky, that big endless thing. "I just wanted to see her again." Because that was all anyone said to me in those days: she was in heaven now, safe and sound and looking down on me.

I still remember the feel of Luca's polyester police shirt, and how it ended up smelling like salt and his aftershave once I'd cried into it for what felt like a decade. He explained a few things to me then, about heaven being more of an idea and less of a place, much less one you can climb to. But then he said trying to get a little closer to her wasn't such a bad idea. I'd just gone about it all the wrong way.

Luca took the rest of the day off. He told Pop that he was going to take me someplace special. "Our own little corner of heaven."

And then he did—the chairlift on the Arthurs Seat summit. The metal double chairs had a little canopy like an umbrella up top. They'd swing you down this 950-meter-long cable, starting 314 meters above sea level (the numbers were all written on warning signs at the ticket booth), with nothing for protection but a skinny metal bar across your lap as you went diagonally down the mountain.

And the view from up there . . . it's really something else. I remember thinking that I could touch the tops of trees with the soles of my shoes if I just swung my legs enough. And I remember knowing that my mom would have loved it up there with us.

Luca guessed what I was thinking. "Your pop says Maria used to love riding on this when she was younger." And then he kind of muttered, "But probably not quite this young."

It was true I was young for the ride. I think the lift operator had been a little nervous to let me on, but since Luca was still in uniform he'd sold us tickets and let us go anyway. I think Luca had been worried, too, because he'd kept one of his big hands on the collar of my dress the whole way, and I could hear him gulping when my swinging legs made the chair sway.

I was no closer to heaven that day and I'm not so sure I even believe in it now—the place or the idea—but I felt closer to Mom. And every year since, when Luca and I made our annual trek to the summit, I felt like I got closer still. We'd talk about Mom while we were up there, just the two of us, in a way that we couldn't with our feet planted firmly on the ground.

At least, that's how it used to be.

I have decided that memories are a little like mountains. You need to hike to the top and get some height—what Mr. Khouri calls perspective—so you can look down at how far you've come, and see all the people and choices that make up the map of your life.

2

THE GREATER THE HEIGHT

On the second to last Tuesday of the school holidays in January 1999 (in Australia, our holiday vacation extends through the whole month of January), we were snaking our way up the mountain: me, Luca, Anika, and Sam. And even though I must've made that climb a dozen times, I still got a little green around the gills, as Pop liked to say, when we lurched around corners. My stomach would go one way while the car went the other.

At least now that I was older I remembered to look straight ahead and not out the window as we went higher and higher up, because watching the drop always made my stomach heave. Don't ask me why, but I felt safer in those metal chairs swinging down the mountain than in a car as it hugged the bends.

Sam didn't know not to look, and I didn't bother

telling him. He was sitting behind Luca, who was driving, with his face practically kissing the window while both hands clutched the door handle. From where I sat behind Anika, I could see she was holding her handle the same way, knuckles popping.

"How are we all doing?" Luca asked.

"Good! Great! Are we nearly there?" Anika did not sound excited.

She's Luca's girlfriend, but he doesn't call her that. He'd say Anika was his "partner," like they're working on a school project together or riding around in his police car.

Sam is her son from her first marriage and he was ten when everything started—one year younger than me. He and Anika look like copies of each other. They have these dark-green eyes and pretty, long lashes, plus they both wear glasses. Only their hair is different—his is a short mop of dark-brown ringlets, and Anika's is long and springy-curly.

I look like my mom, too, or at least that's what Pop reckons—and he'd know, since he was her dad. I'm tall for my age and lanky, with blue eyes and floppy, fair hair with bangs. I even have light-brown freckles just like she did. Luca says they're like connect-the-dots on our noses.

We took another bend and I watched Luca reach over the center console and give Anika's leg a pat. He put his hand back on the wheel and said, "Just think about the view from the top—it'll all be worth it, right, Freddo?"

"Right. So worth it." But my voice sounded dry and crumbling, like a first-try pancake. Luca caught me in the rearview mirror and raised his eyebrows as though to say, *Play nice, be polite.*

Ever since Anika and Sam moved in with us two months ago, Luca has kept telling me to be on my best behavior. He'd say I had to mind my manners and be extra polite and welcoming because we're a family now. Which really didn't sound like any family I'd ever been a part of. It wasn't the way we used to be, when it was just Pop, Luca, and me. And even though I can barely remember the time before I was three—which is how old I was when Mom and Luca married—I was also pretty sure it wasn't that way when it was just Pop, Mom, and me either.

Anika tried to turn around and look at us kids, but her seat belt locked so she could only look at Sam, who was still staring out the window. "Are you getting excited, babe?"

He ignored her question. "How high up are we?" he asked, his words fogging the window.

"You should ask Fred! Her class came here last year on a field trip, isn't that right, Freddo?" Anika tried to look at me, but I just saw the side of her face and one of her cheeks bulging in a smile.

I hated the way Anika tried all my nicknames on for size. She still hadn't settled on one yet, and part of me just wanted to tell her to call me Winifred, but Luca might think that was impolite.

I was named after my nan—Pop's wife—who I never met. Fred is Pop's nickname for me, Freddo is Luca's, and Winnie was Mom's. I once asked Pop why they couldn't stick to one name for me, and he said he didn't know, but maybe they all wanted to have little pieces of me, all to themselves. Lately I'd been wondering what piece Mom took with her when she died, and I'd been thinking about the Winnie I would have been if she hadn't. It was something I wanted to talk about with Luca, when we were 314 meters above sea level.

Sam pulled me out of my thoughts by repeating his question. "So, how high up are we?" He turned away from the window to frown at me. "Do you even know?"

"I can't remember," I muttered, and went back to looking at the safe scenery of granite ahead.

Last year, Mr. Khouri had shown us a map of the area. It was full of lines and lines and lines wrapping around each other. He explained that it was a topographic map, and those lines were contours—a way to represent a three-dimensional surface on a flat piece of paper. He showed us how to read the lines to find valleys and hills, and how steep the slopes were; the smaller the circle, the greater the height. Around Arthurs Seat were all these tight circles and lines, and he

8

asked our class what they reminded us of.

"Yes, Winifred?" Mr. Khouri had said, like he couldn't believe how quickly I'd put up my hand.

"Like . . . fingerprints?"

"That's exactly right!" And then Mr. Khouri smiled. Full-on, full-blown *beamed*. At me. "That's correct, Winifred! Place is as much a part of your identity as your fingerprint or DNA. Little disturbances around where you live have these ripple effects that spread out and out and out into the lives of everyone, and everything around you."

Mr. Khouri was right about those disturbances. They started rippling that day we went driving up the mountain, and then kept spreading—and lately I've been thinking that maybe they're still going, even now.

It was the kind of morning where the sky was the same color as Port Phillip Bay; the whole world was blue on blue. And from the Arthurs Seat summit you could even see white sailboats bobbing in the water.

But as soon as we pulled into the parking lot, Anika jumped out and dashed to the toilets saying she thought she was going to be sick. Luca had followed her, and then came back to stand with us kids by the stone wall of the lookout.

"She'll be right, just those bends took her by surprise," he said.

Sam was playing with one of the coin-operated standing binoculars, gripping both sides and making *rat-a-tat-tat-tat-tat* and *brrrrrp!* sounds, like he was in a shoot-'em-up game at Timezone.

When Anika finally wandered over to us, her face was as white as those sailboats, her glasses were all steamed, and she'd tied her hair up into a messy bun.

"Hey, guys, I'm so sorry—that's not a very fun way to start our day."

Luca reached for her hand and squeezed it, and then they smiled at each other. Sam kept gunning boats behind us, and I rolled my eyes—which of course Luca caught and frowned at me for.

"I don't think I've got it in me to do the chairlift either," Anika said.

Sam stopped gunning and turned around, frowning hard at his mom. "But you promised!" he whined and pushed his slipping glasses back up his nose.

I tried not to smirk.

"I know, babe, and I'm sorry. But I'm just not up for it today."

Sam opened his mouth, about to whine more, but Anika cut him off. "Let Fred and her dad do one trip together, then when they come back Luca will do another one with you, okay?"

I looked away when Anika said that. She cleared her

throat and said quietly to Sam, "Let Luca and Fred have their time together first, okay?"

"Well, wait a minute," Luca said and held a hand up. "I've had plenty of goes on this thing—and this is Sam's first time, so why don't the two of you just ride together?"

Luca was looking at me when he said it, and I could see it all right there in his eyes—asking for one big happy family. *Play nice. Be polite.* I nodded my head and shrugged, then felt Luca's hand land on my shoulder, squeezing as he said, "Good girl, Freddo."

I showed Sam how to get onto the chairlift and lowered the thin metal safety bar across our laps. We waved to Anika and Luca as they watched us sail over the parking lot, and then we cleared the trees and took in the view of the whole peninsula—the dips and valleys, towns with houses like little boxes, and the long stretches of sand hugging the water. Our town was down there somewhere to the left of us too: Sorrento.

If you looked at a map of where we live, you'd see that the Mornington Peninsula is shaped like a fatter version of Italy—a Blundstone boot instead of a fancy high heel—and instead of kicking Sicily, we're putting the boot into the Bellarine Peninsula. In class last year, we learned that our town, on the toe of the boot, was named after the town Sorrento in Southern Italy (another place that got its name because it looked like someplace else).

I pointed this out to Sam but I didn't know if he was really listening. After a while there wasn't much left to say.

The seats in front of us were all full and we kept passing couples to the right of us making their way back up the mountain. I turned around a little to see that behind us was full up too.

"Don't do that!" Sam yelped.

I sat back around and looked at him. "Do what?"

"Make us move around. *Stop* it!"

I noticed his hands were gripping the steel bar in front of him, knuckles popping just like Anika's had been in the car on the way up.

"Are you okay?"

He closed his eyes. "Just stop moving so much!"

I sat back and tried to be still, even with my legs hanging out and dangling a hundred meters in the air. I listened to Sam take shuddery, shaky breaths beside me and watched his knuckles turn whiter on the safety bar.

"Why do you and Luca do this every year anyway?" he asked.

I looked over and saw his eyes were still shut behind his round, red glasses, so I couldn't just shrug his question away. "I was sad one day and he brought me here, and it didn't make everything better but it was . . . okay." I shook my head. "So now he always takes me in the last weeks of

12

the Christmas school holidays—just the two of us."

I wondered if Sam could hear the hurt behind my words, but he didn't seem to.

"Kinda like how my dad takes me to his first game of cricket every year," he said.

I'd met Sam's dad a few times in the last eight months since Anika and Luca had become a couple. His name was Ian and he seemed nice enough, except he lived all the way on the other side of the city and didn't come down very often to see Sam. He hadn't even been to visit since Anika and Sam moved in with us, and now he was away over the holidays with his new wife. They'd sent Sam a present from Queensland, but it arrived two weeks after Christmas—one of those Super Soakers. Sam had seemed disappointed. I think he'd been expecting something different, or else just wanted his dad to be there to give it to him in person.

Our chair was coming to the end of the downward loop, speeding up a little as the cable wrapped around a steel pole and pulley at the bottom of the mountain. A few people in front of us were hopping off there, maybe to go and explore along one of the hiking trails, but most people were like us, staying on and making their way back up.

Sam opened his eyes when we got to the bottom, and one of the chairlift attendants nodded at us when I didn't make a move to lift the safety bar and get off.

Instead our chair started making the climb back up, and that's when Sam said, "You're lucky that Luca does this with you." He took a shaky little breath. This part was scarier: climbing higher and higher up with your back to the plummeting view.

Sam kept talking, even as he closed his eyes again. "I mean, it's not like Luca has to do this kinda stuff, since he's not . . ."

He didn't finish but he didn't need to. When Anika and Luca started dating, the dad thing was one of the first that Sam asked me about. Or rather, told me about.

"Luca's not your dad, obviously," he'd said one evening when the parents had lumped us together after dinner. Like sticking us in the living room with old board games and no TV was going to make us fast friends.

I'd glared at him, and his face went tomato red—right to the tips of his earlobes.

He had meant that Luca and I look nothing alike. Luca's father was Italian, and he married Luca's mother when he migrated to England, before they decided to settle in Australia, where Luca was born. I never met Luca's parents, because they died before he married Mom. I've seen photos: he looks a lot like his father with the same kind, dark eyes. Luca is also tall but broad, with dark, olive skin and he wears his black hair in a policeman's buzz cut.

"I just mean he's not, like, your *actual* dad—right?"

14

"Luca *is* my dad" was all I'd said. Because I didn't think Sam deserved to know all the details of how Luca adopted me when I was three.

"So why don't you call him that?"

I used to. But I stopped a couple of years ago, after I figured out that he was about to be my father for longer than she had been my mom. I felt sick about that: like I was letting her down somehow. So I started calling him Luca, and then I was afraid that if I stopped, I'd have to explain why I started in the first place. I wonder if there's a worse feeling than knowing that no matter what you do, you'll hurt someone you love without meaning to.

But I didn't tell Sam any of that.

It might have been something I talked about with Luca that day, when we were up in the air and far away from how much everything had been changing on the ground back home.

But instead I was stuck up there with Sam, and his stupid heavy breathing and rude questioning. I started swinging my legs, a little at first and then—maybe even a little bit on purpose—in bigger back-and-forth sways that made the chair rock and tilt.

Sam's eyes flew open. "Stop it!"

"Oh, don't be such a baby," I said.

"STOP IT!" he screamed.

"Come on, this is the best part!" I rocked my legs just a

15

little more. "Try to touch the treetops!"

But then I saw the grown-ups in front turn around to glare at us, as well as a few passing on our side, so I stilled my legs—but the chair kept rocking anyway, tipping and tilting to my momentum.

"Fred!" Sam yelled again, and he threw his arms out like he was maybe going to hit me to get me to stop. I jerked away and that made the chairlift bob and sway even more, and because his face was suddenly so wet with tears and sweat Sam's glasses slipped right off his head.

He made a move like he could reach down and grab for them, so I tugged his arm away, afraid that he'd keep leaning and somehow go tumbling over the safety bar.

We watched his glasses plummet into the thick bush below, hitting a couple of branches of a gum tree on the way down, and all the while we kept climbing higher and higher up.

By the time we got back to the summit, Sam was crying in big gulps. I raised the metal bar and Sam jumped off before the attendant said to, and he nearly crashed onto his knees. Sam put his head down and kept running until he literally slammed into Anika and they wrapped their arms around each other.

I watched as Luca knelt down to Sam's height, and saw his face change while Sam told them what had happened.

"Get in the car" was all Luca said when I came up to

them. He wouldn't even look at me when he said it.

That trip home was so quiet. As our car crawled down the mountain I felt my belly sink lower and lower with us. I found a new worst feeling in the world when we reached the bottom.

3

BRIGHT AND TERRIBLE

Sorrento has always been the type of place where the houses have names, and ours was called Il Castello di Maria, for my mom.

Pop started building it the year she was born, and our family have lived here ever since. The name is a fancy Italian way of saying Maria's Castle, which was also kind of a joke. We were part of the Sorrento regulars, not the holiday-chasers—the house was a low weatherboard many roads over from the beach, about as royal as Arthurs Seat. And our surname was Owen, nothing Italian about that. Not until Mom married Luca, then she and I became Owen-Ricci.

When we pulled into the gravel driveway of Il Castello, Anika and Sam got out of the car but Luca told me to stay put. We watched them walk inside, Anika with an arm around Sam's shoulders, his head bowed. It wasn't until the front door closed behind them that Luca turned around.

"I'm so disappointed in you, Winifred."

"I know," I said, and I took the bottom of my T-shirt between my fingers, kept my eyes down, and concentrated hard on that little strip of fabric.

"Can you look at me?"

Luca always says that people have "tells" that give them away when they're guilty of something. It's his job to pick up on them, since he's a policeman—which means he knows exactly how hard it is to look someone in the eye when you've done the wrong thing. It's why my head felt like lead, and I needed to take a deep breath to meet his stare.

"What you did with Sam was inexcusable, but worse than that it was reckless and dangerous. One of you could have been seriously hurt!"

Reckless and *dangerous* were policeman words. *Inexcusable* was too—they all meant I'd been bad today, as if I'd broken something.

"It was an *accident*. I didn't even want to be up there with him in the first place!"

"What? I asked and you said you were fine—"

"*No*, I didn't! Today was *our* thing, and you just stuck me with him!"

"That's no excuse for *terrifying* the kid!" Luca's voice rose.

"I know that!" I practically screamed, and Luca's eyes widened in shock. I looked out my window. It was still only afternoon, but while everything had been sunny and beautiful before, now it all looked too bright and terrible.

"I'm disappointed in you, Winifred. Because I know you can be better and kinder than you were today," Luca said, and I felt my eyes begin to sting, "and because we're a family now, and you're going to be a big sister."

I laughed a little at that, but not because it was funny. "Sam is *not* my brother."

"I'm not talking about Sam." Luca was staring at me. "That's what today was about. We wanted to tell you together—you and Sam—that you're both going to be . . ." He faltered, and then the words just came tumbling out. "We're going to have a baby, Anika and I."

No.

No, no, no, no.

"Winifred? Do you hear what I'm telling you?"

I didn't want to look at him. I didn't want to know.

"Winifred?"

I unbuckled my seat belt, reached for the handle, and flung the door open. I ran inside, past where Anika and Sam were sitting at the kitchen counter, and not stopping when I heard Luca calling to me. I ran down the hall to my room and slammed the door.

4

RRC AND AN ALBUM OF MEMORIES

I apologized to Sam that same afternoon, and then about a hundred more times—but it was into next week and he still wouldn't talk to me. He had to wear his old, baby-ish pair of glasses with light-blue frames that pinched the bridge of his nose. Every time I saw them, I felt my shame pinching too.

In the last week of school holidays I went to visit Pop at the RRC—the Rye Rehabilitation Center—which was two towns away on the 787 Sorrento to Safety Beach bus.

I can't really remember it, but Pop used to live with us in the big house when it was just me, him, and Mom. But then Luca came when I was three, and Pop had an apartment built out back—a little boxy house with a brown roof, cream walls, and a ramp out the front. Inside it had a tiny kitchenette, living room, bedroom, and bathroom.

I once asked Pop why he didn't live with us in the big house. He said, "A castle can only have one king," and I still don't really know what that means. And I never even thought to ask why he didn't have his own house some-place else. I could never imagine him not being with us.

But then late last year it really happened.

Pop slipped in the shower and cracked two of his ribs. He didn't tell us—he just pretended everything was okay, even though he was limping a little bit. He came up to the big house for breakfast and dinner as usual and helped me with my homework every day after school.

But two days later, he couldn't get out of bed and we had to call an ambulance.

He stayed in the hospital for two weeks, and then he caught a bout of pneumonia and had to stay for four more. I thought he'd come back to his apartment after that.

But he couldn't. Luca said the fall had shaken him, and he wasn't as young as he used to be. He said it'd take longer for Pop to heal, so Pop moved into the RRC—but only temporarily. It's this big place that's not really a hospital, and not really a nursing home, but something in between. He even had to walk with a walker while his ribs were still recovering.

Luca said we'd go visit every weekend. But it was too hard to go from seeing Pop every day to only once a week. So Luca bought me a bus ticket and traveled the 787 with me twice to make sure I'd be okay. I promised not to talk to strangers and to let the RRC receptionist know when I arrived and when I was leaving, so he could call in and check on me. That's what it's like to have a policeman for a father.

Luca let me go there every Wednesday afternoon, plus every weekend he'd take me too. It still wasn't the same as having Pop back home, but at least it was something.

That afternoon I knocked on Pop's bedroom door and he called "Come in, Fred!" because he knew the bus timetable as well as I did by then.

Pop's room at the RRC smelled like English Breakfast tea and this cinnamon cologne he sprayed on himself every morning. It was how his apartment still smelled even though it was just sitting there empty in our backyard like a giant garden ornament.

"So did Luca tell you about the baby?" Pop asked me right away. He was sitting in a reading chair by the window, a paperback book open in one hand and his gray eyes focused on me.

"You knew!"

Pop and Luca spoke on the phone a couple of nights a week.

He nodded. "For a while now." And then he sighed when I gave him a hurt look. "It was not my news to tell you, Fred."

I slipped my backpack from my shoulders and went to give him a kiss on the cheek, and then sat cross-legged on the floor by his feet.

"You know, Maria—your mother—would be happy for him."

I frowned, and instead of saying something, I got up on my knees and reached over to Pop's coffee table, where his photo albums were stacked. He has a ton of them in a big wooden chest in his apartment, but the chest was too big for this room at the RRC, so he just took his two favorites with him: thick ones full of the last thirty years.

"You know it's true, Fred—" Pop started to say, but before he could get another word in, I'd flipped open one of the albums.

"Where was this taken?" I pointed to a photo of him and Nan that I really liked. It was in black-and-white, but you could still tell that the heels she was wearing were leopard print, and I thought she looked wicked cool in them.

Pop looked over my shoulder, squinting to see. "Queenscliff, for our anniversary one year," he said, and then he smiled.

I held up a photo of Mom next, from her high school days—her blonde hair was flicked out around her head, and she was wearing a school uniform with a short blue skirt and neatly tucked white shirt. The photo had this glow of the olden days.

"What was she like in high school?" I asked, pleased that Pop wasn't talking about Luca, Anika, or the baby anymore.

"She went on a tear—skipping school and going into the city every chance she could, hanging out with boys with bad haircuts." Pop sighed. "We lost Winifred the year before and it hit her hard."

Nan died of cancer when my mom was a teenager. When I was really little, I could never understand how Mom grew up without her mom around. I couldn't imagine how that could be—and then it happened to me.

"There was a lot I probably missed, but . . ." He shook his head a little. "You're lucky you'll have Anika around, to talk with about growing up and getting older. And things you maybe don't want to talk to your dad or me about . . ."

I rolled my eyes and reached for the second of Pop's albums. It was my favorite one, from Mom and Luca's wedding. The cover was this baby-blue leather with the words "Wedding Memories" in curly white writing. I opened the book up and there were the three of us—Mom, Luca, and me as a toddler—stuck down on the page, behind a sheet of clear plastic.

My mom was beautiful, even though she wasn't wearing a proper wedding gown like the ones you see in movies and on TV—just this simple flowing dress, in a buttery yellow color with little pearl buttons all the way down the middle. Her skin was lightly tanned, and her hair was twisted up on her head so you could see the small diamond earrings that Luca had given her. They used to belong to his mama and are waiting for me in his dresser for when I'm older.

Luca looked a lot younger then, probably because he had long black hair. He shaved it all off when he became a policeman. He wasn't wearing a tux or anything fancy in the photo either, just this crisp white shirt tucked into black pants. I had stuck a yellow daisy in a buttonhole on his shirt, right in the middle of his chest, so he'd match Mom. I fuzzily remembered picking it for him, and holding it up—him crouching down and helping me stick it through the buttonhole. . . .

He was holding me up in the photo, kind of in the crook of one arm and so my head was level with his, and Mom was standing on his other side, her arm hooked around his middle.

"We look really happy here."

"Because you really were," Pop said.

And I believed him. Even if I couldn't really remember how happy we were, I felt better because Pop still did.

"Why didn't you get married again after Nan died?" I asked. When I was little, I was so worried about Luca falling in love; but I figured that because Pop hadn't, there was a good chance it would always just be the three of us.

"It was different for your nan and me. We had a life-time together and there was never going to be anyone else. But with Luca and Maria . . . it wasn't fair, they should have had more time."

I whispered the next part, and Pop had to lean down a little to hear me: "Do you think he still loves her?"

I didn't need to say who. Pop knew I meant Mom.

"Fred, you should know that it's very easy to be both happy and sad at the same time, and it's possible to love two people at once, and miss someone so much even while you move on without them," he said, and sighed. "And yes, I think he still loves her. That's a good question to ask Luca, so you can hear him tell you so."

But I knew I wouldn't. Because it was also possible to want to know an answer so badly, but still be too scared to ask the question.

5

THE GOOD WITH THE BAD

Anika drove us to school on the first day of term.

Normally I'd walk or ride my bike, because Sorrento is so small it only takes about ten minutes to get most places. I'd tag along with Jed and his older sister, Lily. But she started high school this year and needed to take the bus to Rosebud, so it would be just Jed and me. And Sam, too, I guessed. Especially since he'd started talking to me again.

But that day Anika wanted to drive Sam and me to wish us luck. Then she was heading to her job cleaning the big holiday houses around Sorrento.

Anika kept a whole lot of supplies in the trunk of her car, and every day she went off to clean fancy houses that had views of the beach. They belonged to people who only lived in them for three months every year but wanted them to be clean year-round. I thought it was silly.

"Are you excited for your last first day, Fred?" Anika asked while we were stopped at the only traffic light in town.

She meant because it would be my last first day of elementary school, as I went into sixth grade. For Sam it was just another first day, starting fifth.

"I guess?" I said, but I could feel Anika looking over at me and smiling the way she does, a little smile trying to be gentle and get more words out of you. "Lots of kids have swapped out to do sixth grade at the same place they'll go to seventh grade," I said, and then I gave a big huffy sigh to blow my bangs out of my eyes. "A bunch of them who started out in kindergarten with me at PNP have gone, and that sucks."

Point Nepean Primary—PNP—is named for the Point Nepean National Park, which is just down the road from us. There are only three elementary schools in Sorrento, and PNP is the oldest and smallest, facing the water at the bottom of Ocean Beach Road.

"Mr. Khouri is your favorite teacher, though, right, Freddo? So that's something, at least." The light went green, and Anika turned onto Ocean Beach Road. "Maybe he'll be your favorite teacher too, Sam!"

Pop had this saying that *you take the good with the bad.* I never really understood it, but I came closer to getting it when we found out that some of Sam's fifth-grade class-mates and my sixth-grade classmates would be smooshed together in a composite classroom that year. They combined our sixth- and fifth-grade classes because there's not enough of us students in either, so they needed us in a multi-age classroom to make a whole.

The good was that Mr. Khouri would be my teacher again. The bad was that not only was I stuck with Sam at home, but now I'd be lumped in a classroom with him too.

There were twenty-three of us in the Skeleton room. Really it was "Skelton," after one of the first European settler families in Sorrento, but we all thought Skeleton was cooler. When we arrived on that first day, Mr. Khouri had hung a paper skeleton on the door, making it official.

Aidan McMillan laughed. "My dad thinks this composite class is a conspiracy I made up because I just don't want to tell him that I've been held back a grade."

Keira Thomas raised her eyebrows at him, and Aidan narrowed his back at her, saying, "Obviously not, my dad's just nuts."

I don't know how it is at bigger schools, but when you live in a small town like Sorrento and attend a tiny elementary school, you kind of have to stay friends with everyone. I've known Aidan and Keira since kindergarten, same as all the other kids at PNP. But while Keira and I used to play together a lot in second and third grade, we hadn't so much lately—until her closest friend, Sandy, left to attend Rosebud Primary this year. Aidan and Jed have always hung around in the same big group—they play soccer together at lunchtime most days.

But they're not best friends or even that close, not like Jed and me.

I don't think Aidan even knew that Jed's real name is Trung Văn. Jed's just a nickname he got because his dad was a big fan of those old *Star Wars* movies. His family grew out of the "Jedi" joke and call him "Văn," but at school the name Jed had stuck.

Except for with Mr. Khouri, who insisted on calling out Jed's full name as it was written on the roll, and then asking him what he'd prefer to be called.

"Jed is fine, sir," he said.

"But—who's Trung?" Aidan asked, and I rolled my eyes.

So while it was true that we all knew each other, it was also true that we hadn't always been close, and we had never really hung out as just the four of us. But this year it was all different, and I didn't yet know if it would be a good different or bad.

6

MAPS DON'T ALWAYS TELL THE TRUTH

One night over dinner Sam asked, "What'll its name be?"

He meant the baby.

"We can't decide that just yet, babe—we've got to meet them first." Anika smiled at Luca, then back at Sam. "Before you were born, you were this close to being called Benjamin." She held her index finger and thumb up in a pinch. "Until your father and I met you and just knew that you were definitely more of a Sam than a Ben."

Sam picked up his fork but only moved it around his plate. "No, I meant . . . what'll its *last* name be?"

I looked up from my own plate because I was curious about that too.

Anika and Sam's surname is Murray because that is Sam's dad's last name. I didn't know what Anika's was before she married.

My name had been Owen, same as Pop, until Luca came and Mom and I became Owen-Ricci. But this baby was no Owen and that name—my name—wouldn't mean anything to it.

"We're not sure yet, mate," Luca said. "We'll have to have a think about it."

Then dinner went back to being quiet.

But I started to think how names are important—and what Mr. Khouri had told us last year about Uluru, up there in the Northern Territory.

That's what it had always been called, until some guy came along and decided to name it after someone else—a politician called Sir Henry Ayers. Uluru became Ayers Rock, but not really—because that name didn't mean anything, no matter how many people wrote it down that way in books or on maps.

"Maps don't always tell the truth," Mr. Khouri had said, "and sometimes maps are used to give power or take it away—just look at Africa."

He pulled down the Collins World Map from where it was rolled up above the blackboard. Sure enough, there was Africa, right in the middle.

"Africa is often drawn to seem smaller, or roughly the same size as North America, when it is in fact *three times* the size. . . ." Mr. Khouri stepped to the side of the map, picked up a piece of chalk and drew the shape of Africa, like an elephant's ear, only so much *bigger* than on the map.

"But why would they make Africa smaller?" someone asked.

Mr. Khouri put the chalk down and clapped his hands clean, powder swirling for a second as he looked between us and the Africa he'd drawn.

"Well, the most famous map we use today is just one type—called a Mercator projection. It was the standard projection for easy navigation, but it was also made during an era when certain empires tried to hoard all their power, and to take it away from other nations, so it suited them to make Africa seem smaller than North America. . . ."

"So why do we learn it then, sir?" Aidan asked, screwing up his nose. "If they're all *wrong* like that?"

"A very good question, Mr. McMillan." Mr. Khouri rolled the map back up, but he didn't answer Aidan's question. The bell rang and everyone bolted for lunch—except for me. I hung back for a bit.

"Why, sir?" I asked.

Mr. Khouri shrugged. "What can I say, Winifred? Sometimes maps are used to take power away from people, along with their land and language. And sometimes they help to change history—or erase it."

"That doesn't seem fair," I said.

"No, it doesn't."

7

SIT WITH US

A few weeks later Jed asked, "Should we invite him over?"

We were sitting on the rocks underneath the big pine tree at the edge of the playground—this cluster of five big fat sandstone boulders that had been cut in half so they were smooth on top and made good tables and seats. Every year it was the unspoken rule that only the sixth-grade kids got to hang out at the rocks.

I looked where Jed was pointing and then quickly turned away.

"Fred, do you—" Jed started again, but I shook my head no.

Jed, Aidan, Keira, and I were sitting together, while most of what was left of the sixth grade were playing foot-ball on the playground. Sam was sitting by himself on a low bench outside the brick classrooms, on the other side of the playground.

"It's cool if you want to go get him," Aidan said, as he bit into his sandwich. He kept talking as he chewed. "If it's just him it's not too bad—but the other babies can't come over." The "babies" was what Aidan wanted us to call the fifth graders.

Anika and Sam moved to Sorrento two years ago, and Sam had been at PNP that whole time. But I never paid him any attention, not even after Anika and Luca met at one of the parent-teacher evenings and started going out. I guess I kind of remembered him playing with other kids in his grade, but older kids don't pay attention to younger ones, so I didn't know for sure.

Keira rolled her eyes. "Stop pressuring her!" she said to Aidan. "Do you think if you were stuck in a classroom with your sisters, you would want to hang out with them at lunchtime too?"

I didn't correct Keira about Sam being my brother, but only because she made a good point. Aidan had two younger sisters—the twin terrors, we called them—in third grade.

He shuddered and shook his head at Keira, but then looked back to where Sam was sitting. "I dunno, maybe I would if they looked *that* pathetic?"

I remembered Luca's words from a few weeks earlier,

after the awful thing I'd done to Sam at Arthurs Seat. He had said he knew that I could be better and kinder, like it was a choice.

But being better and kinder is like being *one big happy family*—it's one thing to say it, another thing to be it.

"He walks with us to school and home every day. That's enough," I said. "He doesn't need to sit with us too."

Mr. Khouri was quiet and serious and young—easily the youngest teacher at PNP—but he acted like he was older than my pop.

The best thing about Mr. Khouri was the trick he used to get us all to quiet down. He'd make just one of his bushy black eyebrows arch up—the right one—which was something we all loved, because it reminded us of this guy from the World Wrestling Federation called "The Rock."

When Mr. Khouri did the eyebrow arch, it was a sign to get serious and pay attention. By the time his eyebrow went down again, we'd have stopped fidgeting, and the room would be silent.

"Geography is not just about flags, maps, and compasses, or naming capital cities," Mr. Khouri was saying, and I stopped the work I was doing on tectonic plates to listen. "What geography is really about is human beings, and how we spread across the Earth's surface. How what we do affects the physical features of this planet and its atmosphere, and how the Earth affects us too."

Then Mr. Khouri clapped his hands so loudly it made us all jump a little in our seats. "Okay, fifth graders—I want you to make a fist and then grab a pen with your other hand."

All us sixth graders remembered this from the year before, and we watched as the fifth graders did exactly that—made fists and reached for their pens.

"Your wrist is a valley and your knuckles are mountains and hilltops. I want you to start by drawing a small circle around the top of each of your knuckles, then a circle around each of those circles, and then slightly bigger circles around those ones, and keep going. Until the lines make their way down from the mountains of your knuckles to the valleys of your wrists."

When they finished, everyone laid their hands flat on their desks.

"What you've just made are 'contour lines,' sometimes called 'level lines,' which join points of equal height above sea level." He pointed to the map stuck to the board behind him. "A topographic map is illustrated with contour lines that show valleys and hills, and the steepness or gentleness of slopes—the smallest point being the highest."

I looked at the fifth graders one table over and saw them all staring at the snaky lines on their hands.

Mr. Khouri asked, "What do the lines look like?"

And then a voice from the back said, "They kinda look like ripples."

I whipped around to follow the answer, and my eyes went straight to Sam. He slowly lowered his hand and pushed his new black-framed glasses up his nose.

Mr. Khouri clapped again. "Thank you, Samuel—that is a brilliant observation!"

I turned back to the front and found Mr. Khouri's eyes on me. "Maybe there's more than one budding geographer in the family?" he said and smiled.

I felt my face heat up, but I didn't know if it was anger or embarrassment or both. And I didn't know why it all annoyed me so much.

Mr. Khouri went back to pacing, holding his hands out wide while he talked.

He stopped at the front of the room. "And here's the thing—we don't rely on maps to tell us where we're going, so much as where we've been. Because where we live has such an impact on who we are, and who we will be, that it may well be the thing that defines us more than any other."

Then Mr. Khouri put his hands behind his back and cleared his throat. "You might have been hearing some things on the evening news, or read about them in the paper—I expect you all, particularly the sixth graders, to read and watch the news regularly." He paused for a second, and I frowned—there was something wrong with

Mr. Khouri's voice. It sounded off, somehow.

"We are very lucky to live where we do. Not everyone in this world is as fortunate. . . ." And then he stopped again, shook his head, and brought his hands back around to clasp in front of him. "Right! Where were we? Back to volcanoes for some and mountains for others—the difference between crust and magma!" And just like that his voice was back to normal.

8

A CONSPIRACY IS A SECRET

"Your dad thinks you being in a composite class is a conspiracy, and you think your dad coming down to check that you're in a composite class is a conspiracy?" Jed asked.

"I'm telling you, it's definitely a conspiracy against *me*," Aidan said.

"You are *so* paranoid," I said, sighing.

"My dad thinks that just because you're paranoid it doesn't mean they aren't out to get you."

"Who's out to get you and what's a conspiracy?" Sam asked. He'd been walking a little ahead of us but stopped and turned around.

I rolled my eyes. "It's a secret."

"Don't be annoying—just tell me!"

And I had to bite back the words I wanted to say,

the ones that weren't nice or polite and would get me in trouble with Luca if Sam ratted me out—which he would.

The three of us caught up to him and turned onto the winding street, at the end of which were Jed's and my houses.

"Well? Are you gonna tell me?" he demanded.

I opened my mouth, but Aidan gently nudged me.

"No, Sam—a conspiracy *is* a secret," Aidan said. "It's when a bunch of people come together and plan something that nobody else knows about and they make up all these lies and secrets to cover it up."

Aidan surprised me sometimes. He was soccer-obsessed and could be spiteful, like insisting on calling all the fifth graders "babies," but then he'd do something nice that reminded me he was a big brother to two younger sisters. He had a patience for Sam that no amount of politeness gave me.

"So it *is* still a secret, technically," Aidan finished.

"Like my mom being pregnant?"

We all stopped walking, and I spun toward Sam, my face aflame and fists clenched. My heart was about to beat right out of my chest.

Jed's hand landed on my shoulder, and he pulled me back a bit. "Fred, you can't . . ."

Aidan looked from me to Sam and back again.

42

"That wasn't your secret to tell!" I yelled.

And then I watched Sam's eyes fill with tears. He screamed right back at me, "It's my secret more than yours!" He raced off ahead of us, his backpack bouncing as he ran to the end of the street and our house. My house.

At dinner I was surprised that Sam hadn't said anything about that afternoon, and that Anika and Luca hadn't either. I was so certain he'd tell on me, even though I wasn't sure what for. He'd been right, the baby *was* more his sibling than mine—which meant it was more his secret to tell.

"You're being awfully quiet tonight," Luca said as he washed our plates. "Everything okay at school, Freddo?"

I shrugged and kept on drying.

"Oh, are we already onto the surly teenager routine, then?" But he smiled when he said it, and gently bumped his hip into me, until I pretended to smile back.

"Where are you going to put the baby?" I blurted, without even knowing the question was on my mind. "Where will it sleep?"

Luca paused for a second, but then he picked up the pace again and shrugged. "Not sure yet, but I was thinking of maybe building a kennel for it in the backyard?"

I rolled my eyes when he laughed at his own silly joke,

but then he said, "We don't know, Freddo. It'll definitely be a squeeze once it's older. Actually . . ." He dried his soapy hands on the hand towel and turned to me. "Anika and I were thinking—and we'll have to talk to Jeff about it too, since it's still your pop's house—maybe we'd look at converting your bedroom into two rooms?"

I whipped my head around to stare at him.

Luca held up his hands. "Whoa! It's just preliminary discussions at this point, Winifred. Nothing is set in stone!" That was another policeman word: *preliminary*. No matter what the dictionary said, it meant that Luca wasn't just *thinking* about doing something. It was *definitely* going to happen.

"But that's Mom's room!"

The peeling paint, squeaking floorboards, some of the books on the shelf and even the faint smell of lemons from the tree planted outside the window were all my mom's from when she was my age.

"I know, I know it was, Freddo. But it's your room too. And it might really help us all out. . . ."

I could feel my eyes getting watery and I blinked them quickly, not wanting to cry.

Luca reached out and gently moved my bangs out of my eyes, then made as though he was going to bring me in for a hug—but I stepped back and lifted my forearm up to my head and rubbed my eyes quickly on my sleeve.

"I mean it, Freddo! Nothing is certain yet. We'll talk about it some more and . . ."

"Fine." I threw the hand towel down, still with half the dishes to be done. "I've got homework to do."

9

WORLDLY POSSESSIONS

One night in March, there was a baby in barbed wire on the TV.

Luca wasn't working late for once, so after dinner we were sitting with him and Anika on the couch, waiting for the news to be over. The news always felt like the longest ad between better shows.

Sam's sweaty-socked foot was touching my bare leg because he knew it annoyed me, and I was about to start kicking him again when suddenly Anika moaned and said, "That poor bub!"

The way she said it, I had to look over and see.

And there was a baby in barbed wire, right there, on the TV.

There were mountains and blue sky in the background and this baby boy, in a blue onesie and socks, being held by many hands. He looked so calm, like it was all normal—but there were barbs on the fence, and his chubby legs looked like they were about to be cut by one of them.

The newscaster spoke. "A photojournalist has captured the happy moment as members of a Kosovar family displaced by the war are reunited at a refugee camp in Kukës, Albania. The youngest member of the family is being passed through a barbed wire fence to greet his relatives on the other side, who were thought lost, or worse, deceased."

The footage changed and the newscaster said, "The military action being undertaken to stop President Milošević's army marks the first time that the North Atlantic Treaty Organization—NATO—has gone to war."

"What else is on?" Sam whined, but nobody listened.

A city skyline came on the screen—for a second it reminded me of the view of Melbourne from high atop Arthurs Seat—and then the whole place lit up in a blinding flash of light.

"Geez . . . would you look at that," Luca said, the words rumbling out of him.

The next image was of rocks and dirt and then the camera zoomed out and I realized it was showing us where the skyline had just been.

They'd dropped a bomb on that city, and now parts of it were just . . . blown away.

"While the NATO bombings are said to be in aid of civilians trapped by the fighting between the Kosovo Liberation Army and Yugoslavian security forces, many have criticized Western and NATO intervention, and highlighted that without authorization from the UN Security Council, the bombings are illegal."

We kept watching as a new video showed hundreds of people, maybe thousands, walking along a muddy path. They were all walking in a line, following each other—I didn't know where they were going.

While they walked, they cried.

Some were carrying children, while others had bags that were spilling over.

"NATO's involvement has support from world leaders—most vocally from US president Bill Clinton, UK prime minister Tony Blair, German chancellor Gerhard Schröder, and Australian prime minister John Howard." The reporter paused and that image of the baby in barbed wire came back before they continued. "But NATO's peaceful intervention has also resulted in hundreds of deaths and created thousands more refugees and displaced persons. Those still able are now walking across the border into Albania, carrying all their worldly possessions in their arms and on their backs, as they flee Serbian forces and the unsanctioned bombings. . . ."

"What is this world coming to?" Luca asked, but he

didn't expect an answer from anyone.

Anika rubbed the bump of her belly as she blinked back tears, then she said, "Change the channel."

And so we did.

10

LITTLEST RIDGE

t was on the news nearly every night.

Those people were still walking to nowhere with all their worldly possessions. They showed a clip of two teenage boys carrying an old lady between them—their grandmother, maybe?—as they walked along a train track, with a long line of people behind them. The voiceover said they were crossing borders, trying to get away from the bombs that were dropping day and night.

Other times it showed our prime minister, John Howard, saying the bombing that was happening was badly needed. He got up in front of flashing cameras and said it was a war for "genuinely humanitarian purposes," whatever that meant. But he also said that Australia couldn't help those people who were victims of the bombings.

And I went to bed one night, still thinking about the

baby in barbed wire and how that photo had looked scary, but the truth was happy—kind of. And I wondered how that could be. In school Mr. Khouri had said *a picture is worth a thousand words*, but I didn't think it could equal so many questions too.

And I couldn't stop my brain from thinking about the other baby—the one that would be here and living with us before the year was out.

Then on Sunday, Luca said, "We've got something to show you two."

We were sitting at the dinner table having dessert when Luca went and got his wallet and pulled out a square piece of paper. He slid it across the table to Sam and me, and then reached for Anika's hand.

It was a photo of a cloud at night.

There was blackness around the edges, and the fuzzy gray cloud in the middle, all swirling and unfocused.

When I looked up, Anika and Luca were smiling at me and still squeezing hands. And I stopped eating my ice cream, because I suddenly got a sinking feeling and brain freeze.

"What does this mean?" I asked.

Luca's smile was so big. "It's a boy!"

Then I realized what the photo was: not a cloud, but a baby! It was from an ultrasound, a scan to see inside Anika's tummy.

"What's it called?" Sam asked, and Anika shook her head.

"Well, what do *you* think we should call it?" she asked, looking between Sam and me and still squeezing Luca's hand.

Sam swallowed a spoonful of ice cream, then spoke.

"I thought you said not to give it a name yet?"

Anika rubbed her belly with her free hand. "Not a proper name, no, but a nickname for now. Just so we can stop calling it 'it.'"

Sam scooped more ice cream and seemed to take a long time thinking on this, and we all watched as he polished off the rest and then wiped his mouth with the back of his sleeve, adjusted his glasses, and declared he had no ideas.

Anika rolled her eyes and then poked her tongue out at him, and Sam did the same back. I couldn't help but smile.

Then I cleared my throat and said, "Drumlin."

Luca looked to me and smiled, "What's that, Freddo?"

"Just something we learned about last year, but maybe it's silly. . . ."

"Now, hold on! Drumlin, drumlin." Anika said the word like she was trying it on for size. "What is it then?"

"Littlest ridge," Sam said, and I turned to him, surprised. "They're these little hills that show where glacial flow goes. . . ." He turned a little pink, like he was embarrassed. I was surprised that he'd remembered all that from class.

"Littlest ridge, I like that," Anika said.

And then, like it was the most normal thing in the world, Luca placed his hand over her belly, the whole span of his hand covering the little bump underneath her T-shirt.

They smiled at each other and Anika said, "Meet Drumlin—a temporary name for a soon-to-be baby."

Sam got up from his seat and went to Anika's other side, reached out his own hand—so much smaller than Luca's—and said the name again and again. "Drumlin, Drumlin, hello there, Drumlin. . . ."

They were like a picture. A look-up-the-definition-in-the-dictionary, kinda perfect picture of one big happy family.

And I suddenly felt lost—a little out of frame, or off the map completely.

11

NO-MAN'S-LAND

The following week, Jed invited me over for dinner because his mom, Vi, was making my favorite beef and noodle soup called phở.

His dad, Khoa, was in Sydney on business—he did something with computers that I don't think even Jed really understood—but Lily was home and ignoring us as usual. She was upstairs in her room while Jed and I were downstairs playing Nintendo 64 when Vi's car pulled up. The two of us went to help her bring in the groceries.

"Thank you for having me over, Vi," I said.

"That's okay," she said. "You know you're always welcome here."

Vi once told me her name meant "small" or "pretty" in Vietnamese and it suited her. She owned a hairdressing salon in the middle of Sorrento, which was always busy.

"Is your sister upstairs?" Vi asked Jed.

Jed and I were back on the couch. Jed murmured something and bounced where he sat. We were playing Super Mario 64, and every time Mario had to jump onto a floating brick platform, Jed jumped a little too—he couldn't help it.

"Văn, are you listening to me?"

He rolled his eyes, but only because she couldn't see. "Yes! And yes! She's on the phone with her *boyfriend*!"

We heard a cupboard door slam and then Vi was picking up the phone on their kitchen wall, saying, "Huệ! Huệ! Who is this? . . . Oh, hello, Melissa—yes, Lily has to get off the phone now. Goodbye!"

The same way Jed was Văn at home, his sister was Huệ—which means lily in Vietnamese. Her full name is Ngọc Huệ Trần. I never wondered how they could go by so many different names and not get confused, since I was Winifred, Fred, Freddo, plus Winnie once too.

Jed laughed next to me, and I poked him in the ribs. "What?" he said.

"You're a cheeky boy!" Vi called to him, but not like she was actually mad.

The radio crackled behind us as Vi switched it on and started humming along to some oldies song while she cooked.

The music stopped and a voice came on: "We have

breaking news out of southeast Europe."

Vi turned the volume up and went back to chopping something crunchy.

"Some eighty-five thousand people are trapped in a muddy no-man's-land along the border of Kosovo and the Republic of Macedonia, with no access to food, medical assistance, or shelter, as they seek refuge from the ongoing conflict in the former Yugoslavia, and NATO bombings in Serbia. . . ."

The sound of Vi's chopping had stopped, and Jed had paused the game.

"The UN high commissioner for refugees has submitted a formal request to the Australian government for aid and assistance, while the US has continued to urge their allies to make similar provisions in offering safe haven."

The sound of Lily's footsteps running down the stairs carried over. When she got to the bottom she started to say, "Mẹ, that was so embarrassing—" but Vi shushed her as the newscaster kept talking.

". . . Prime Minister John Howard has reasserted that the government will not offer asylum. Immigration Minister Ruddock said . . ."

Then a different voice came on, a recording of a man saying, ". . . flying planeloads of refugees into Australia would not be an appropriate response."

Vi said something under her breath and then she

switched off the radio. Jed unpaused the game and went back to Mario, but his heart and thumbs weren't really in it anymore.

Lily wandered over and sat sideways on one of the armchairs, her legs hanging over the side. The screen door opened and shut behind us as Vi went outside.

"She's having a smoke," Lily said.

My eyebrows went up. "Didn't she quit?"

Lily shrugged but Jed said, "She did, but that stuff stresses her out." He threw his head back slightly, toward the kitchen and the radio. "I think it reminds her of when she was a kid."

I knew there'd been a war in Vietnam, where both Jed's parents were from. I knew that Pop had missed out on something called the draft—when the government forced young men to go and fight. Jed's mom and dad were our age and growing up in Vietnam when the war was on, and then they came to Australia with their parents once it was over. Jed's parents didn't know each other when they came here—they met when they were older and living in the city, studying business at university. But after their first meeting, they swapped life stories and figured out that they had actually lived only a few towns apart in Vietnam, and that both their families were evacuated on planes to Australia within just a few days of each other. I guess when you hear a story like that, it must be fate that you're meant to be together. Or something.

"I think it's a bit crappy that our government won't help."

I blinked at Jed's swearing. Lily swore all the time, and Vi was always threatening to wash her mouth out with soap—but Jed was quieter.

"Yeah, I mean I don't know what's going on—but it totally sucks," I said—wincing at my awkward attempt.

Vi came back inside and bustled around the kitchen again.

"You kids going to set the table or what?" she called out, and we got up.

She did not put the radio back on.

12

BOUNDLESS PLAINS

Sam was going to his dad's for the first week of the Easter holidays. They spoke on the phone most nights, but you could tell from the way Sam was constantly going on about it that he was excited to spend time with his dad— and I was pretty happy that he wouldn't be around for a bit.

On the last day before Easter break, Anika drove Sam and me to school because she had a doctor's appointment after. Her belly was so much bigger than it had been in January, and now her driver's seat was pushed back to make room for her bump and her arms stretched out more to meet the steering wheel.

It had been raining so much that the gutters of our school overflowed and the water seemed to roar down like rapids outside the window. It was the start of April and warm outside, so the classroom became sticky from the damp and the heat. Or maybe that was just from the questions that we had burning inside us.

After recess Jed stuck his hand up. "What about the national anthem?"

Mr. Khouri could say a lot with his eyebrow arch. This time the eyebrow seemed to say, *Go on, continue.*

"It's like, we have to sing it every week in assembly—but does it even mean anything?"

"What line are you thinking of specifically?" Mr. Khouri asked the question like he already knew the answer.

And Jed probably only meant to speak, but after so many years singing the anthem, his voice came out with a sing-song lilt—like the words wanted to rise up. "'For those who've come across the seas, we've boundless plains to share.'"

The sound of us agreeing with him was a hum, low and sure.

"You're right," Mr. Khouri said. "Those words are in our national anthem."

"Are we just supposed to sing them but not believe in them?" a fifth-grade girl asked.

Mr. Khouri leaned forward in his chair at the front of the room, put his hands on his knees, and looked at us.

"I think that's something each of you will have to ask yourselves," he said. "What is the purpose of a national anthem, and what does it mean when a country refuses to live by its traditions?"

He wasn't like other teachers we'd had or other grown-ups we knew. On the first day of term he'd written the words *Not all those who wander are lost* at the top of the blackboard, and they were still up there, looking down on us.

Back on that very first day of school he'd said he hoped the words would remind us that it's okay to follow your curiosity, even if you don't know exactly where it will lead—and that the point of life was not to have all the answers, but to never stop asking questions.

And then during the school holidays the prime minister said he'd bring the refugees to Australia. Just like that.

The newspaper Luca left on the kitchen bench one morning had a photo of John Howard on the front page and a caption saying he'd told a bunch of journalists that an affluent country like Australia needed to be seen to be generous. And I wondered if that was the same as "we've boundless plains to share."

He said they'd start arriving the following month, in May. But he didn't say where they'd stay. It seemed like good things were finally happening, but Pop's old words came back again—when the good was here, it meant the bad was still coming. . . .

"Fred—are you still going to the movies?"

Sam was at his dad's on the other side of the city. Luca was working most days, as usual. But the houses that Anika cleaned had people in them for the holidays, so she was home—and getting rounder every day.

"Freddo?"

Anika knocked on the bathroom door. "Fred, honey—are you okay?"

I was supposed to be meeting Keira and a couple of other sixth grade girls at the Athenaeum on Ocean Beach Road. We were going to go see this film, *10 Things I Hate about You*.

"Fred, are you okay in there?"

But something had happened, and I couldn't go.

"I'm going to open the door, okay?"

Anika's tummy came first and then she poked her head in too.

"What are you . . . ?" Anika seemed to take everything in—me standing at the sink and crying, wearing my new white peasant top, but with a towel wrapped around my middle like a sarong, and my denim shorts in a heap on the floor. With a giant bloodstain on the crotch of them.

"Hold on a second, babe."

When Anika came back in, she closed the door gently behind her and took a seat on the closed toilet lid. She was holding a square bit of plastic.

"You're probably my one opportunity to do this, so I

want to get it right," Anika said, and I looked over to see her eyes were shiny and she was smiling. I didn't know what she meant until she rubbed a hand over her stomach. She meant that Sam and Drumlin were boys, so she wouldn't get to do this kind of stuff with them.

"They're lucky," I huffed.

"Yeah, it can be a pretty lousy deal."

Anika turned to the roll of toilet paper and ripped me some squares, handed them to me so I could wipe my eyes.

"Do you have any pain?" she asked.

I shrugged and said, "A little."

"Is it so bad that you want to lie down?"

I shook my head.

She took a deep breath. "I'm very honored that I get to talk you through this, Fred—it's not as big a deal as some people make it out to be, but it's still pretty special and *nothing* to be afraid or ashamed of."

"I feel gross," I said, and then I started crying again, because I suddenly thought how much I wanted my mom for this.

Anika opened her arms, but I didn't want to go to her, so I turned the tap on and splashed water on my face, and she handed me a washcloth to dry it.

"I don't want to go today," I said.

Anika nodded. "That's okay. You don't have to, but . . ." She sighed again. "I don't want you to feel like you have to

63

hide away or have anything to be embarrassed about. And I don't want you to get it into your head that you can't do anything on the days you have your period."

I felt my face blush furiously when she said that.

"And hey! I've seen the ads for this movie you're going to see. Personally, I wouldn't want to miss seeing that actor's smile on the big screen for *anything*!"

She reached up and brushed my bangs out of my eyes. "Everything's going to start changing a little faster now, Fred—but you're still you. Don't miss out on the things you really want to do, okay?"

And it didn't sound so bad when she put it like that.

13

EXCULPABLE

Term two started. On the news, no one knew where the refugees would go, even though there were bombs still falling and people still fleeing.

At school, Mr. Khouri said geography was done. The sixth graders were moving onto outer space while fifth grade studied marine life. But he let me borrow his big world atlas—the ninth edition of *Times Atlas of the World*, to be exact. He said to take it home for a bit and keep wandering.

Sam came home from his dad's, too, but he was different.

"Hey, *Winifred*!" A voice shouted at me from across the playground shortly after we were let out for lunch.

I spun around and yelled, "What?"

Ben Sturgess was calling to me from the middle of the

playground. "Isn't that your brother?"

I'd been walking around the perimeter with Keira, from the rocks to the shop on school grounds that sold snacks. Ben jogged over to us, pointing behind him to the back fence.

I was thinking about ignoring him, because I did not have a brother. But it only took me a second to see what he was pointing at, and then I started running.

"I'll get a teacher!" Keira yelled somewhere behind me.

From the corner of my eye I could see Aidan and Jed at the rocks. They stood up, watching me run across the playground. I knew they'd follow me to the back fence, where a gang of kids had Sam cornered.

"We thought you weren't coming back," one boy said with a sneer.

One of them poked him in the shoulder. "Come on, say it again!"

Another attempted to hook their foot around his ankle, trying to make him trip over.

"What'd you call us?"

A tall boy—I think his name was Lachie—was grinding his fist on the top of Sam's head. I could see Sam's eyes were watering behind his glasses, and he was biting down on his bottom lip to keep from crying out.

"Oy! *OY!*"

I'd never had to break up a fight before, so I just called

out what I'd heard the teachers say when kids were acting up. I even put a deep voice on, to sound like our PE teacher, Mr. Harvey.

"STOP IT!" I roared. I stepped into the circle of kids and started pulling on their arms, trying to get them to move away.

"Are you serious?" Lachie looked from me to Sam and back again. "You need her to look out for you? Are you pathetic or what?" He flattened his palm and pushed hard on Sam's head, shoving him away. Sam tripped and fell to the ground, losing his glasses on the way down.

Jed and Aidan ran up then. Jed bent to pick up Sam's glasses—luckily unbroken—while Aidan reached out a hand to help him up.

"What is your problem?" I said, and then I threw my hands out and pushed Lachie.

He stumbled back. "He started it!"

I turned around in the circle of fifth graders. There were ten of them, mostly boys but a couple of girls, a mix from our class and Mrs. Watts's.

When one approached Sam and started yelling in his face again, Jed got between them. He put his hands up and didn't touch them, but kept stepping up until they moved back.

"Tell them what you said, *Samuel*!" Lachie was practically screaming. "Tell them what you said!"

I pushed him back again.

And the whole time Sam just stood behind Aidan, holding his glasses loosely in one hand while he raised his other arm and wiped his face on his sleeve.

"What is going on here?"

We all turned around when we heard Mr. Harvey's voice—for real—and saw him striding toward us, with Keira at his heels.

"What did Lachie mean?"

Sam shrugged and slid down even farther on the couch as we waited outside the teachers' lounge.

"He said you started it, Sam—what was that about?" Another shrug.

"I thought Lachie was your friend? Didn't Anika say you should invite him over sometime?"

Sam turned his face away, so I huffed and blew my bangs out of my eyes.

There were still a few minutes left of lunchtime. Mr. Harvey had given the fifth-grade kids trash duty as punishment—and Jed and Aidan, too, just for being there—but none of them wanted to say what the fight had been about, so he'd sent me and Sam to sort it out with Mr. Khouri.

I huffed again. "I swear, if this is a fight over something stupid like *Tazos* . . ." Those plastic discs that came free in packets of chips had started a craze in all the lower grades.

"It is, isn't it? You got into a stupid fight over—"

"Shut up," Sam whispered.

"Excuse me?"

He turned back to me. "I said *shut up*! You don't know anything, and you don't even care, so stop acting like you do!"

I was about to put him in his place when the door to the teachers' lounge opened wide, and then Mr. Khouri was standing there, clearing his throat and brushing crumbs off his shirt. "Mr. Harvey tells me there's been an altercation," he said, and it wasn't a question.

Mr. Khouri stared at me and then Sam. "Either one of you want to tell me what happened?"

Neither of us said anything.

"Right, well. I am told that you laid hands on a fellow student, Winifred?" I opened my mouth to defend myself, but Mr. Khouri had already turned back to Sam. "Mr. Harvey didn't see anything directly, but he has his suspicions that Winifred did so in defense of you, Samuel—is that true? Did someone hurt you today?"

Sam didn't say anything.

Mr. Khouri lifted a hand to rub between his eyes. "We do not condone bullying or intimidation of any kind at this school—you both understand that, don't you?"

Sam and I nodded.

"Winifred, defending a fellow student is commendable, but physical altercations are not entirely exculpable. I trust you know what that means?"

I nodded. It was another Luca policeman word—meaning to clear from a charge of guilt or fault. If I *wasn't* exculpable, it meant I wasn't about to be free.

"Winifred, every day this week after you've finished eating your lunch, you'll come see me to assign you menial cleanup tasks around the school. You'll do that for one week instead of playing and hanging out with your friends at lunchtime. Let's see you give back to your school community as atonement. And Mrs. Watts will be supervising punishment for the fifth graders involved."

Mr. Khouri eyed us both carefully and then nodded toward the door. "I'll permit you to enjoy the rest of your lunch."

I made a move to leave, but Sam spoke up. "I'm doing it too."

Mr. Khouri raised his "The Rock" eyebrow as if to say, *Pardon me, Mr. Murray?*

So Sam said it again. "Detention—I'd like to do it, too, if that's okay."

"I'd much rather you told me what the fight was about, or who was bullying you at lunch. . . ."

I couldn't believe it when Sam stared him down. Just

zipped his lip and kept looking straight ahead.

Mr. Khouri sighed. "Okay, detention for both of you then."

We thanked him and left.

The note about my detention was burning a hole in my backpack. I imagined it as a lump of molten rock, sizzling at the bottom of my bag. Sam was striding ahead of Jed and me—it sure didn't seem like he was worried or weighed down.

Jed and I stopped at his driveway and I said, "Sorry you got in trouble."

Jed shrugged. "No big, so long as the kid's okay."

The kid hadn't even bothered to say goodbye to Jed or thank him for today—I looked over and saw the screen door bang as he went into my house.

"It was pretty cool," Jed said, when I looked back at him. "The way you ran over there and rescued Sam." He smiled and gave a little shrug. "He's lucky you were there to help him." I could feel my face burning up as Jed kept smiling at me, so I rolled my eyes and punched him— lightly—on the upper arm. He grabbed it and pretended to wince in pain.

"It was pretty cool how you and Aidan helped too," I said, and then I started walking backward, toward my house. "You're a good friend." I watched as Jed opened the door to his house, and then I yelled, "And I'm lucky to have you too!" I heard his door slam, but I didn't want to see if he'd heard me, so I spun around. And that was when I saw it.

Luca's police car was tucked all the way into our driveway—down the side of the house so it was hidden from the street.

He was supposed to be at work, and would only come home if . . .

I bolted.

I crashed through the door and followed the sound of voices to the living room. Luca and his partner, Senior Constable McNeal, were standing over Anika as she lay on the couch, and Sam crouched in front of her.

"Dad?"

He looked up when he heard me and lifted an arm that I quickly wrapped myself under. I breathed in his cologne and the faint smell of leather from his duty belt, which was pressing painfully into my hip as he squeezed me.

"I'm fine, everyone—stop fussing!" Anika groaned.

Sam had burrowed his head into his mom's side, and she was gently stroking his hair with one hand and her rounded tummy with the other. Her glasses were pushed atop her head, and her whole face looked a little gray.

"What happened?" I whispered, and Sam lifted his head, his glasses all askew, to hear Luca explain.

But instead Luca huffed and said, "If Anika would let us call an ambulance for her, we could find out!"

"Don't be ridiculous, I'm fine—" Anika started to say.

"You're not!"

I was surprised at how sharp his words were.

"This is ridiculous, Anika—you need to see a doctor!"

"And I will. I've got an appointment for tomorrow—I can wait that long!"

Senior Constable McNeal—Penny—came to stand beside me and ruffled my hair as a hello. I'd known Penny for as long as she and Luca had worked together. She was the only woman among a handful of officers at the Sorrento Police Station.

She was a little shorter than Luca, and a few years younger than him too. I only knew because she always called him "old man," which could either make Luca grin or grimace, depending on what mood he was in. Penny had dark-red hair the color of ketchup straight out of the bottle and had worn it the same way for as long as I'd known her: perfectly straight to her shoulders when she was off duty, and bobby-pinned into a bun when in uniform.

"The ambulance station is just one little radio call away," Penny piped up. "They can be here, check you out, and hopefully give you the all-clear in twenty minutes flat!"

Anika replied by throwing her a weak smile. "Really,

I'm fine—I just overdid it at work today!"

"Enough that you called the station for me!" Luca roared.

Sam stood and looked up at Luca in a way that reminded me of him staring Mr. Khouri down earlier. But seeing Sam stick his bottom lip out seemed to ease something in Luca, and he slowly stretched his hand out and laid it on Sam's shoulder.

"If you're sure the dizziness has passed . . . ?" Penny started to ask, looking to Anika again.

"I am, I am!" she agreed, and then she threw her forearm over her eyes and kept speaking. "It's just normal pregnancy stuff! All I need is a long bath, a good nap, and to see the doctor tomorrow."

Luca nodded and then collapsed onto the other couch, cradled his face in his hands, and let out a deep sigh.

"A cup of tea for everyone—how does that sound!" Penny said, and then she nudged my shoulder to come help her.

I watched while Penny moved easily around the kitchen. She'd been here a thousand times before. Her stiff leather boots squealed against the linoleum, and her leather duty belt jangled as she turned toward a cupboard. I once told Luca that he was like Harriet the Spy with that duty belt, and he said I wasn't too far off; it held his gun in its holster, radio, handcuffs, plus a key, mini first-aid kit, a little flashlight, baton, and a whole bunch of other stuff that made a clattering sound when he walked. But he said it made him ready for just about anything.

I didn't realize I'd been staring off into space until Penny waved a hand in front of my face, and I finally handed her the milk for the tea. Then she really looked at me and frowned.

"Hey, kiddo," she said, and gently nudged me again. "It'll be okay—it was just a scare. Anika's done this all before, she knows what she needs."

But I couldn't shake the feeling that those ripples had started spreading again.

14

BE

That night when the news came on, I changed the channel quickly. I couldn't stomach seeing the people fleeing again. Too much had happened that day, and I didn't have enough room in my brain for them.

Anika didn't end up having dinner with us; she only wanted toast in bed, while Luca, Sam, and I quietly ate the tuna salad that Luca had made.

When he finished, Sam asked to be excused, and then it was just Luca and me.

"That was a bit of a scare today," he said.

I shrugged. "Yeah, but Anika's okay, right?"

"She seems to be now." He leaned forward and put his elbows on the dinner table, looking at me carefully. "I'm sorry if you were worried when you saw our car."

I shrugged again, but I also suddenly felt too warm. "It's okay."

Luca shook his head. "I used to come home during the day all the time, in the patrol car—just to say hello, or for lunch, or to check on you and Maria. . . ."

He did. For most people, a police car in their driveway only meant bad news, but when I was growing up it just meant Luca was home. Until one day when it meant something worse.

"Hey, do you want to talk about . . . ?"

"I got detention!" I blurted, to stop Luca from saying anything else.

His eyebrows shot up. "What? Winifred—excuse me?"

I looked down at the table. "It was silly, there were these kids. . . ." I didn't want to mention Sam or get him in trouble, so I said, "Um, they were sitting in our spot on the rocks so I pushed one of them—accidentally!—and Mr. Harvey saw, so Mr. Khouri gave me detention for two weeks."

Luca collapsed back in his seat, brought his hands up to his face, and dragged them down, before looking at me again. "This had better not be the beginning of a pattern with you."

"What?"

He shook his head. "First what you did to Sam on the lift, now this. . . ."

"I didn't mean to! That was ages ago, and I said I was sorry—"

Luca pushed his chair back roughly and gathered

up our plates. When he chucked them in the sink, they crashed so loudly it made me jump.

He gripped the bench with both hands, his head bowed. "We don't need this right now."

"I know, and I didn't—"

He spun around. "I don't want to hear you say that you didn't mean it or you're sorry! You're going to be a big sister soon, for crying out loud, Winifred! I expect more from you." Luca took a deep breath. "I just need you to be *better*."

Be happier. Be kinder. Be better. Be a big sister.

Be, be, be, be.

"I'm trying," I whispered.

"Try harder."

15

BRINGING THEM HERE

The first planeload of refugees from Kosovo arrived in Sydney at the beginning of May.

The prime minister was there to meet them at Sydney Airport, and it was all over the news—footage of John Howard shaking hands and high-fiving little kids, hugging these grandmas with kerchiefs on their heads.

There were four hundred people arriving at first, but everyone said there were thousands more still coming. The news said that in the end, Australia would take in four thousand Kosovars from the 840,000 who were refugees.

It looked like we would share a small part of our boundless plains, after all.

That same weekend, Luca got a phone call asking him to come into the station on his night off—they said it was for an emergency town meeting. And maybe it's because

I'm looking back on it now, but I think we could all feel it then—the ripples spreading again.

I'd been feeling the ripples in the weeks before, while I'd been burning up with shame being in detention. It was like every piece of rubbish I picked up was a reminder that I'd let down my favorite teacher, and that I needed to try harder for Luca. Except I didn't really know what I was supposed to be trying harder at . . . maybe not disappointing him so much anymore?

It was even worse at the end of the second week of detention, when Mr. Khouri had Sam and me clean out the art room.

"Whoever made this was seriously disturbed," I said, gently poking at a wet clay head whose mouth was carved open in a screaming "O."

Sam barely looked up from where he was sorting through kids' old paintings on a drying rack.

I was light-headed from the smell of the methylated spirits that I was using to clean out the disgusting sinks caked with old paint, so I sat down for a moment.

I was getting used to silence from Sam. We'd both talk to Jed on the way to and from school, and then at home we went to our separate rooms.

On that last day I finally asked what I'd been wondering ever since Sam stared Mr. Khouri down outside the teachers' lounge.

"Why did you want to have detention anyway?"

Sam shrugged as he kept sifting through the drying racks. "Didn't seem fair not to."

"I don't get it. Those kids were picking on you. You didn't do anything wrong. . . ."

Sam's face went bright red—his biggest tell—and his eyes quickly darted away from me.

"Did you? Sam?"

"What do you care?"

I shrugged and started scratching at a deep cut on the wooden table I was sitting at, digging my fingernail into the rough groove. "I don't care, really. So maybe that's the best reason you should tell me: because I won't make a big deal about it."

Sam didn't speak, so I heaved a sigh and went back to the sinks, pulled the disgusting rubber gloves on, and got back to scrubbing.

"You didn't tell my mom about Lachie, or anything?"

Over my shoulder I said, "I didn't, actually—you're welcome!"

He sighed behind me, and then said, "Thanks—for that day."

I didn't turn around, because I didn't know what to say. It wasn't that I'd been doing as Luca asked, trying to be a better person and maybe a big sister. It was something I couldn't explain. When I'd seen Sam cornered, my feelings took over.

"Lachie hates my guts," Sam whispered.

I still didn't turn around.

"I did something last term, and now he hates me."

"What did you do?"

He huffed. "Told him that this town sucked and they could all get lost and go jump because I was never coming back. . . ." He took a deep breath. "Because I was going to go live with my dad."

At that, I spun around.

Sam shrugged, and I watched as he started fiddling with some leftover butcher's paper, tearing it into strips. "But then—that didn't work out."

"Anika wouldn't let you?" I asked.

"Dad didn't want me to. I asked him over Easter, but he said . . ." He shook his head but didn't finish that sentence. "Doesn't matter. He doesn't want me."

The bell rang then, making us both jump a little, and I was glad. Kids started filing in, and there was no time for me to tell Sam that I was sorry, or ask why his dad said no, or even what Anika would have done if he'd said yes.

We both just let the bell tell us that nothing more needed to be said.

Luca came home from the town meeting late. I heard the floorboards creaking as he came through the front door, and then the sound of Anika in the living room with the TV still on, waiting for him.

"What was that about?" she asked.

Since there was now stuff worth overhearing, I'd grown good at sneaking. If I opened my door a little, I could see from my bedroom to the living room opposite, where Luca crashed down on the couch as Anika muted the television.

"What? What's that face, Luca?"

He was shaking his head. "They're bringing them here."

"Who?"

Luca leaned forward, running his hands back and forth over his scalp. "Four hundred of them—to Portsea."

"Babe, what are you talking about? Who's coming?"

He sighed and said, "Refugees from Kosovo. The ones who have been on TV."

I felt my stomach drop from the shock of Luca's words, like I was on a roller coaster.

Anika said something under her breath that I couldn't hear, and then Luca was leaning back, looking up at the ceiling like he couldn't believe it.

"Where in Portsea?"

"The Quarantine Station."

"What? That's . . . that's in the middle of nowhere— that's Point Nepean!"

Luca threw up his hands. "Trust me, I know! We tried explaining to them, but it's all been arranged." He laughed, but not like it was funny. "Apparently they wanted to keep

83

it under wraps. The optics aren't great, they said."

"Who? Who said?"

"Some lackey from the minister's office came down to tell us. . . ."

Anika shook her head. "Wait, when is this supposed to be happening?"

"Next month. They'll be bussed in from the airport." I heard Luca take a deep breath before he said, "They'll be coming straight from a war zone."

16

ROSEBUD

Over the next week, I kept waiting for Luca to tell me about the refugees coming to Point Nepean. But he didn't, not even when we watched the evening news and saw refugees arriving in America too. The newscaster said how good it was that America had decided not to put the Kosovars on a naval base in Cuba anymore, because it wouldn't have been right to lock them up like that.

Instead, the footage showed refugees flying into an American airport and being greeted by First Lady Hillary Rodham Clinton before being driven to a place called Fort Dix, New Jersey. They showed American people welcoming the refugees. One even held a sign up that said "Mirësevini në Amerikë," which the journalist said meant

"Welcome to America" in Albanian.

Still, Luca said nothing until the following Wednesday. I was pushing open the doors and leaving the RRC after visiting Pop when Luca pulled up in his squad car.

My arms broke out in goose bumps as I watched Luca open the door and step out in full uniform. As soon as he saw my face, he strode over, holding his hands up and saying, "Whoa, whoa—everything's okay, Freddo!"

"Anika's all right?" I asked, then gulped, "Sam? Sam got home okay?" I'd asked Jed to walk him home, same as I did every Wednesday, but suddenly I panicked, imagining that something had happened between school and our house.

Luca's face changed, but just a little—enough that only I would notice. His brown eyes grew sad, and then smiled to fold it away again. "No, no—nothing like that!"

"What are you doing here?" I asked, maybe a little meanly. But he'd scared me by showing up suddenly and making my mind jump to bad news!

Luca reached forward and lifted my backpack from my shoulders, slung it easily over one arm, and motioned for me to walk toward his squad car.

"I had something I needed to do in Rosebud, at the hospital. The meeting wrapped up early, so I thought I'd swing by and pick you up from Pop's, give you a lift home."

When we got to his car he turned and looked down at

me. "Plus I thought you and I should probably have a little chat. . . ."

"How's Jeff?" Luca asked as we pulled out of the RRC parking lot.

"Okay."

"And how was school?"

"Fine."

"Learn anything interesting today?"

Mr. Khouri had taught us this theory that 250 million years ago the Earth looked very different and had only one continent—a supercontinent called Pangaea, and one ocean named Panthalassa. And—the theory goes—that huge continent eventually broke apart, creating all the landmasses and oceans we have now. Even today the continents look like they could fit together like puzzle pieces. Mr. Khouri showed us how the east coast of South America and the west coast of Africa follow the same curve from millions of years ago.

But I didn't tell Luca any of that. Instead I said, "Not really."

He let out a long sigh while I kept staring out the window at the bay.

"We haven't been getting along so well lately, have we, Freddo?" he asked.

When I didn't say anything, Luca kept talking. "What

I mean is, I know a lot's been changing. Ever since your pop left, then with me and Anika, and her and Sam moving in." He gave another deep sigh. "And the baby coming."

I got this tingling feeling—like a sneeze was coming and about to make my eyes water—so I kept watching out the window.

"I've been thinking a lot about Maria too," Luca said, and I nearly stopped breathing. "Thinking about how much I miss her and how much I love her."

I looked over at him then, watched him watching the road.

Luca kept talking. "I wanted to know, Freddo, if you've been thinking about your mom a lot lately too?"

I gulped down a lump in my throat and pressed my fingernails painfully into my palms as Luca went on.

"That's why I wanted us to have a little talk today." He glanced quickly at me and then back to the road. "I know you had a scare the other week when Anika wasn't feeling too well—we all did! And when you saw my patrol car . . . but you did the same thing today when you saw me at the gate." He paused, and then a little quieter he said, "You were expecting the worst, I think?"

My mouth felt dry, and I opened it just to close it again. I didn't know what to say.

"Freddo, it's okay. You can talk to me—about anything! But especially if you've been remembering what happened with your mom, and scared it could . . ."

There was so much I wanted to say. I wanted Luca to know that I missed her, but I was worried I was forgetting her, and maybe that made me a bad daughter. I wanted to say that sometimes trying to remember her was like following a map without a compass: you're bound to get lost.

Instead I was quiet for a long time and finally Luca sighed again. "We need to get better," he said. "Better at talking to one another and being honest with each other. Don't we?"

He looked over at me, and I forced myself to nod and to swallow down all the things I hadn't said.

He adjusted his hands on the steering wheel, seemed to grip it a little tighter. "Something kind of big is going to happen around here over the next few months, and it's my job to help out with it. So I'm going to be busier than normal, and I need you to step up and take on more responsibilities."

"You mean, because of the refugees who are coming?"

Luca was silent for a long time, then he huffed out a breath and said, "How on *earth* do you know about that?"

I turned a little toward him, as much as my seat belt would let me. "Don't be mad, but I heard you and Anika talking the other night. . . ."

"You were *eavesdropping*?"

I looked down at the hem of my school shirt and started

pleating it nervously. "I'm sorry—but you were just saying how I could talk to you about anything! And . . ." I looked up at him again and shrugged. "I want to talk about this."

Luca glanced at me. "I don't appreciate you sneaking like that, Winifred. You won't do it again, is that clear?"

I nodded once.

"This is confidential information—do you know what that means? It needs to be kept secret. If you tell anyone, I'll be very disappointed and won't trust you again, is that understood?"

I nodded again and Luca sighed once more.

"Yes, they're coming here—some of the Kosovar refugees from the evening news."

"That's a good thing, right?" Luca didn't say anything, so I prodded again. "In class we talked about how the national anthem says we have *boundless plains to share* and Mr. Khouri said that was right, and . . ."

Luca waved my words away. "Yes, it's a good thing— but it won't be easy."

I kept looking at him and Luca shook his head. "These people will have been through a lot, Freddo. Where they're coming from, and what they've seen . . . it's worse than most of us could ever imagine, and we've got to look after them." He shrugged. "I'm not so sure we're well equipped to do that over here, or where they'll be staying."

"At the Quarantine Station on Point Nepean?"

Luca looked at me sharply, then back to the road. "I mean it, Winifred, you can't tell *a single soul* about this."

I nodded again.

"Yes, at the Quarantine Station. It's run-down and very isolated. That's why they built the station at Point Nepean in the first place. Because there were no towns nearby and it would be hard to escape."

In class when Mr. Khouri pinned up the map of where we live, he showed us how Point Nepean was the most westerly point of the Mornington Peninsula. We'd been there on field trips just about every year of primary school—we'd seen the limestone cliffs and the old cement artillery batteries at Fort Nepean. Point Nepean was mostly a skinny strip of cliff edging out into Port Phillip Bay, and behind it was all thick bushland making up the national park. But we'd never seen the Quarantine Station before. The first I knew there was one was when I overheard Luca say so to Anika the other night. . . .

Luca kept talking. "The old authorities wanted to keep the immigrants coming into Victoria away from everyone else, until it was clear that they weren't bringing illness and disease with them. That's what it means to 'quarantine' someone."

"It wasn't a very nice place?" I asked.

He shook his head. "No, quarantining had to be done for the safety of everyone, but I doubt it would have been a nice place, or a very happy way to come to a new country. And then for a long time, until only a few years ago, the army took it over and made the station a cadet school and teaching hospital, for soldiers in training."

"Like the police academy you went to?"

Luca nodded again. "Just like that, but the army's version."

I figured that was why we'd never been to the station on school field trips—the army was busy using it all this time.

"And they're going to make the refugees stay there?" I asked, scrunching up my nose.

"They are. It won't be very comfortable, and it hasn't been used since the army left. . . . It's also probably not a great idea that a place that used to house military personnel and still has some leftover army equipment is going to be home to people who are fleeing a war zone." I saw Luca's hands tighten on the wheel again.

"How will you help them?" I asked, because I knew straightaway that's what Luca would be doing. It was his job as a policeman to help people.

"The government has official people who'll be in charge of this thing, working with the Australian Red Cross. But it won't be enough, so they need volunteers from town too."

"That's you?"

He nodded again. "I've said I'll do what I can—but

only until the baby comes. They'll need volunteers who understand that these people—these refugees—have been through something terrible and seen awful things back home." He looked over at me and then back to the road, just as we drove past the sign for Rye. "That's why I came to Rosebud today. It has the closest hospital and will be the first one we take refugees to if they need medical care. There may be a lot of them, so the hospital staff will have to work very hard to help out. Since I know a lot of the staff there, I offered to help coordinate."

"So, lots of other people have volunteered too?"

"Some have, yes." Luca frowned. "It's also possible that not everyone in town will like the fact that these refugees are coming here."

"How do you know?"

"I just do, Freddo. I just do."

I slumped down in my seat, trying to keep track of all the questions I had bubbling over in my brain. But only one kept rising to the surface, so I took a deep breath and asked it. "How long will they have to stay there for?"

Luca drummed his fingers hard on the steering wheel. "That's the thing—nobody knows. . . ."

17

THE HELPING HAND

Anika came into my room that evening to say good night. I put aside the book I was reading by the light of my lamp, as she sat on the edge of my bed, her tummy poking out from underneath her T-shirt like a tight, smooth drum.

"Luca told me about the conversation you two had today," she said.

I was lying in my bed, watching her hands make slow, gentle circles over her belly. And then she reached one of those hands out to smooth my bangs from my eyes.

"He said that you heard us talking the other night. . . ."

I didn't know if she was asking me, but I nodded my head anyway.

Anika tucked my hair behind my ear and then took her hand back, and I almost told her to keep going—to keep playing with my hair, smoothing it out and touching me. But I didn't.

"That was a lot for you to keep all to yourself," Anika said, and I was worried for a second that she was going to tell me off for sneaking. But instead the next words out of her mouth were "I'm so sorry, Winifred."

I sat up a little and frowned at her. She smiled back, but sadly, so it didn't reach her eyes.

"I'm sorry that you didn't think you could come to us sooner—to your dad or me—and talk about it. That's a very big secret to keep, all locked up inside. . . . But I'm glad you felt like you could talk about it today with Luca. And I just want you to know that I'm here, if you want to talk some more."

I nodded, but before I could say anything else, Anika's eyes got wide, and she smiled—for real that time.

"The baby's kicking," she said.

I looked down at her belly as she lifted her T-shirt up, and sure enough—even with just the light from my lamp and the hallway coming in—I could see where the skin on her stomach seemed to bounce, just a little bit, from the movement within.

"Do you want to feel?" she asked me.

I didn't speak, just reached my fingertips out to the spot where the kick had been. But then Anika gently took my wrist and laid my hand flat.

"He reaches for the warm spot where your hand is. . . ." she explained.

Soon enough there was a shove against my hand, and I snapped it back as Anika laughed quietly.

"It's okay, he's just saying hello," she said, and I put my hand back.

We sat like that for a little while, me feeling him kicking and Anika smiling. After a few minutes Drumlin stopped, and Anika said he'd probably gone back to sleeping.

I slipped down in my bed again and watched as Anika heaved herself up and moved to the door.

But just before I switched off my bedside lamp, I called out quietly to her.

"Yes, Fred?"

"Do you think it's a good thing?" I asked. "That they're bringing those people here?"

Anika had the door halfway closed, but she paused at my question.

"My mom used to say that you have two hands: one to help yourself, and one to help others. So yes, I think it's a good thing." Then she sighed. "Though sometimes I wonder if the hand we use to help others moves a bit slower and with a little less purpose than the one we use to help ourselves."

And with that, she closed the door.

18

OPERATION SAFE HAVEN

n the first few days of June, the refugees would start arriving in Point Nepean.

It was on the news every night. We'd all started watching a little more quietly, paying closer attention. Just like Luca had said, about four hundred of the refugees would be coming to the Quarantine Station in the national park, overlooking Ticonderoga Bay.

They'd be flown from the emergency camps outside of Kosovo, land at Melbourne Airport, and then be driven on dozens of buses down to Point Nepean.

"Guess the cat's out of the bag then," Luca said, and Anika reached for his hand.

The government had also come up with a name for their plans to bring the refugees here: *Operation Safe Haven*.

One morning in class, Keira asked Mr. Khouri what

the word *haven* actually meant and what it would mean to have a safe one nearby.

Fifth grade had been practicing synonyms, and Mr. Khouri said that's what *haven*, *refuge*, and *sanctuary* were—all synonyms for the same thing. A safe place.

Then Sam stuck his hand up to ask if *refuge* and *refugee* were connected.

Mr. Khouri nodded. "They both mean, in a round-about sort of way, 'to flee'—to seek safety elsewhere, because your life is in danger."

Sam stuck his hand up again, and Mr. Khouri raised his eyebrows, telling him to go on.

"I know there's a war on, and that's why they're coming here, but . . . what is the war about?"

We were supposed to be discussing fractions, but it felt like the whole school—even the entire town—just wanted to talk about Operation Safe Haven.

Mr. Khouri eventually sighed and put down the chalk he was using to draw pie charts on the blackboard. He grabbed his chair and dragged it to the front of the room, and then sat down before us. The words *Not all those who wander are lost* were still staring down on us, and I guess Mr. Khouri was going to let us do some wandering around the questions we had for him.

"I don't really know what the war is about, Samuel—it's very complicated, but it basically started when the state that used to be called Yugoslavia started to break up into different countries. . . ."

Mr. Khouri paused before he went on. "Yugoslavia was created, in a way, after World War I, but back then they called themselves a kingdom, and after World War Two they changed again—to a federation made up of six republics and two provinces. They had a president called Tito who was very powerful, but after he died the different parts of Yugoslavia started fighting. . . ."

He leaned forward in his chair to put his elbows on his knees. "A few years ago, some of those republics started breaking away—they didn't want to be part of Yugoslavia anymore, they wanted to be independent. Be their own country."

"What's so bad about that?" Sam asked, and Mr. Khouri shook his head.

"Nothing bad about it, except for some leaders who thought they were losing control and getting only a little bit of power instead of a lot . . . and those who didn't like the way the new countries were forming or the new maps that were being made; some people felt like they would be outnumbered if they broke away from the larger territories."

"Outnumbered by who?" someone asked.

Mr. Khouri sighed again. "The different religions and ethnicities—the people—within all the different territories of Yugoslavia."

"Is that what the war in Kosovo is about?" I asked.

"It's partly that, yes; we're told that another country called Serbia is trying to claim control over Kosovo, to make it its own. And Serbia doesn't want a particular group of people to live there anymore—those who are called 'ethnic Albanians,' which is why Kosovar Albanians are mostly the ones seeking sanctuary. . . ." Mr. Khouri said.

"I still don't get it," Sam said. "Why can't they just live together? Why did they have to start a war?"

"Lots of reasons that don't make much sense if you really get down to it, which is true of all wars, really," Mr. Khouri said. "But one reason is that the entire region— called the Balkans—has a very long and complicated history, going back centuries, and some people remember that history very differently. It could also be that Kosovo happens to be a majority Muslim country, and Serbia is mostly Christian . . . and I guess they don't like that they each have different ways of doing things. And then it's probably that a whole lot of powerful countries that are not even part of the Balkans are trying to take control of the situation and get involved in things they don't *really* understand."

Mr. Khouri stood up again. "Mostly I think a lot of this started because a whole bunch of people thought that maps are what make a country. But we all know—fifth and sixth graders—that that's not how geography works, is it? Remind me: What is geography *really* about?"

"Human beings," I whispered, and then a little louder when Mr. Khouri raised an eyebrow at me. "Human beings, and how we move across the Earth's surface."

Mr. Khouri nodded. "And human beings can rarely be contained simply by drawing lines on a piece of paper, forcing them together or tearing them apart now, can they?"

Someone else stuck their hand up, but Mr. Khouri waved them away. "I know you all have a lot of questions, and you're very curious—and that's a good thing! But it's early days yet. We'll have a lot more time to talk about this, I promise. But no more today, okay?"

Mr. Khouri went back to the board to pick up where we left off with fractions and pie charts. Which just made me think how wars sounded like someone was always trying to cut countries into pieces, and people were fighting over who got the biggest slices.

19

A WELCOME SIGN

The refugees arrived in the middle of the night.

That evening, Luca was getting ready to drive out to help greet them and get them settled. I wanted to go, too, but Luca kept telling me it wasn't possible.

"How come? All those other times on the news there were people waving and saying hello when they arrived. . . ."

All the primary schools in Sorrento had gotten their students to make signs. On big pieces of poster paper we'd used markers or paint to write the message "Mirësevini në Australi!"—Welcome to Australia!—again and again.

Luca turned around and smiled sadly at me. "I know, but they've flown in too late tonight, and the Red Cross wants to get them checked off and settled into the barracks as soon as possible. . . ."

When Luca was all ready to go, he stood behind Anika,

bent down and kissed her forehead, and then offered his hand to rub her giant belly. Then he reached over to Sam and ruffled his hair.

"You be careful, babe," Anika said, and Luca replied, "Always."

He came back to me and crouched just a little so we were at eye level. "Freddo, I promise I'll tell you everything that happens as soon as I get home—and I'll ask about when a welcoming party can get together and go out there . . . but I need to be going now, okay?"

I nodded once, then got an idea—I held a finger up for Luca to wait for me, and then I dashed into my room.

When I came back he was at the door, pulling a woolen beanie over his buzz cut and grabbing his keys. I thrust the rolled-up poster paper at him.

"What's this?" he asked, taking the fluorescent orange scroll from me.

"A welcome sign—we were making them in school," I said. "It's not finished yet—I haven't added the glitter— but maybe you could hang it up somewhere?"

Luca smiled down at me, then tucked the roll of paper under one arm as he bent to kiss my forehead too. "I'll see what I can do."

I was woken by a knock on my door. Luca opened it a crack and I sleepily waved him in, then he lay down beside me like he used to when I was kid, leaning his back against the headboard, throwing an arm over my pillow, and carving out a place for me by his side.

"Did you hang my poster up?" I asked, and then yawned.

Luca squeezed my shoulder. "I did, in one of the girls' dorm rooms—I'm sure they'll love it."

"Were there lots of people there?"

"So many people, and it was so dark. All us volunteers had to point our cars toward the entrance and pop our headlights on so people could see the way once they stepped off the buses."

"Were they scared?"

Luca shifted, and I could feel the cold denim of his jeans through my blanket—it must have been freezing out there.

"I think they were tired, mostly."

"Were there many kids?" I yawned again, then closed my eyes as I listened to him.

"Yes, there were a lot of kids . . . plenty are teenagers, mothers were carrying babies and toddlers, and there were a few who were the same age as you and Sam." I blinked my eyes open to look up at him, but he was staring off at the far wall. He seemed to be thinking very deep thoughts.

"Just little kids in these big, bulky jackets that people had donated. Some of them were carrying donated toys, too, and had small backpacks—but that was it. That was all they had. Everything they managed to take with them when they ran."

"Were there cameras there? And newspeople?"

Luca seemed to shake himself, then he looked down at me and frowned. "No, none that I could see."

"So you won't be on the TV tomorrow?"

"Tonight, Freddo—it's the next day already—and no, I very much doubt that you'll be seeing my ugly face on the TV."

"Can I come out there with you next time you go?"

"We'll see." Then he squeezed my shoulder again. "It's so far away, Freddo; in the middle of nowhere surrounded by all that bushland and those cliffs. . . ."

I was getting sleepy again. I didn't think it was time for me to get up, so I closed my eyes for a second.

But I must have drifted off, because when I woke up again Luca was gone—and I had to get ready for school.

20

AXIS

The Earth moves at about thirty kilometers per second. That's nearly 110,000 kilometers per hour. We just don't feel any of it because the speed stays the same.

You only feel motion if your speed changes, you see.

Mr. Khouri said to think of it like the Earth was a car we were all traveling in. Then imagine if that car accelerated or braked all of a sudden—that's when you'd feel it. The Earth would be thrown off its axis and we'd either be flung back in our seats or sent flying through the windshield. . . .

That's how it was in the days after the refugees arrived—like we were braking and moving in slow motion. Or maybe it just felt that way because we were frozen in those wintry June days, feeling like our feet were ice blocks and our noses were about to drop off.

106

I kept wondering about the refugees over at Point Nepean—what they were thinking of Australia and the peninsula, overlooking it all from up on those limestone cliffs, and feeling the blustery winds coming in off the bay.

"Dad thinks they're still protesting," Aidan said one lunchtime, a few days after Operation Safe Haven had started.

It was cold, but not raining. We were all outside, bundled in our sweaters and jackets. Aidan, Keira, Jed, and I were sitting on the rocks as usual—except Sam was with us too. Jed had waved him over one day after the fight with Lachie and our detention. And every lunchtime since, Sam would quietly follow us to the rocks and sit with us, but also a little apart. He never said much, unless Jed or Aidan asked him a question. I was too tired to fight about it, either with Sam or Jed.

"What do you mean, 'still protesting'?" Keira asked.

Aidan cupped his hands around his mouth and huffed into them to warm them up—he'd forgotten his gloves and beanie again. "They're shoving clothes down the toilets so they back up and stuff. They're just doing it so they'll get moved to fancy hotels instead."

It wasn't the first I'd heard of protests at the Quarantine Station. The local newspaper had run a story only a few days after the refugees arrived with the headline:

The story said that on the night they arrived, some of the refugees had gotten back on the bus that brought them and refused to get off again until better accommodations were found. The newspaper ran a two-page "vox pop," which Mr. Khouri explained to us meant "Voice of the People" when Aidan brought the newspaper in to show our class.

They asked a bunch of locals from up and down the peninsula what they thought of the refugees being here and their protesting. And Aidan's dad—"Bill McMillan: forty-one, café owner, Sorrento"—had been one of the people whose voice was heard. And what he had to say was this: "Beggars can't be choosers, can they? If they are, then it means the whole deal is suspect."

Whatever that meant.

Luca had been furious about the article. He'd been out the night before volunteering at the safe haven again and was reading the paper during breakfast the next morning. "Can you believe this?" he said to Anika, who'd been leaning against the counter, sipping orange juice.

Luca swore under his breath. That had Sam and I quickly turning to each other, and Anika raising her eyebrows at us and shaking her head.

"The paper has completely mangled what happened—

or else made it up!" Luca said. "They're making out like it was an organized protest, as though the refugees were spitting in our faces. . . ."

"What happened?" Sam asked. "I mean—what *really* happened?"

"There was a family with a grandmother in a wheelchair, and when they found out that the shared bathrooms and toilets are nearly five hundred meters away from the dorms, they got the translators to explain that she wouldn't be able to use them." Luca rubbed a hand over his head. "The translator told the officials—who said they couldn't do anything, and it was either this or . . . nothing."

"What did they do?" I asked.

Luca started rolling up the newspaper. "Whatever the refugee family could to get some help for the poor woman—they didn't want to see her soil herself in the middle of the night because she couldn't get all the way to the toilet in time, and the bathroom doorway wasn't wide enough for her wheelchair anyway!"

"Wait—are the kids supposed to use those toilets in the middle of the night too?" Anika asked, a frown forming. "That would scare the bejesus out of me in that creepy place! Imagine asking a kid Fred's age or Sam's to go wandering around outside in the middle of the night to find the toilet."

Luca stood up so quickly that the chair fell down

behind him. He strode over to the trash can, lifted the lid, and shoved the newspaper in, down deep.

Anika was rubbing her belly with one hand, and when Luca came over she reached her other hand out to gently touch his back.

"You know what the government reps said to all that?"

"Babe—" Anika started to say.

"They said it was a 'totally unreasonable' complaint and suggested they could send the family back to Kosovo if they were 'dissatisfied' with Australia. Can you believe that?" Luca sighed. "They gave the family a bedpan, and between that or going back to the bombings, they chose the bedpan."

At the rocks that lunchtime, it was Sam who spoke up. "That's not true!" he said. "Luca's been there and he knows what's happening, and he says none of that is true!"

Aidan held his hands up, like he was surrendering. "It's what my dad said. He thinks they're ungrateful and kicking up a stink just because they can."

"Luca said . . ." Sam started again, but I shook my head at him and his mouth snapped shut.

"Luca said the toilets and bathrooms there are really old," I began instead. "They're not shoving clothes or anything else down the toilet—it's just that the plumbing's all rusted and hasn't been used in ages, and now suddenly hundreds of people are going to the loo every day and it's all backing up."

"Ew, that's disgusting—I'm eating!" Keira whined, and she delicately put her salami sandwich back inside her lunch box.

"Luca would know better than your dad does," Jed said to Aidan, and I looked over at him with grateful eyes. "Luca's the one who's been volunteering there nearly every day."

Aidan shrugged. "Whatever. I'm just telling you what my dad heard."

Jed shrugged too. "Sam and Fred are telling you what their dad saw."

Sam and I looked at each other then, and I didn't know if it was Jed calling Luca our dad, or appreciation that he'd stuck up for us. But for a second, Sam and I shared a private smile, just between us. And it made me feel light, and maybe even happy.

But then chasing that thought away was the memory of what Luca had said before: that some people in town wouldn't like the refugees coming here. That seemed true enough now.

21

SAY HELLO

The war officially ended in June, around the time we first saw some of the refugees in town.

Our government was giving the refugees an allowance—Luca said it was like pocket money. Twenty dollars a week for adults and five for children, to buy things like clothes, toiletries, travel fares, and extra food. The officials in charge at the safe haven had started arranging a private bus service so the refugees could come into town and have a look around—and spend the money they were given.

A whole bunch of shops on Ocean Beach Road did things to celebrate and make them feel welcome. The Athenaeum Cinema's sign said: "Refugees Welcome: Monthly Free Movie." The local bakery made Anzac biscuits especially, and offered them free to anyone from the safe haven who popped in. Mac's Cycles bike shop even started a bike share: refugees could pay five dollars to borrow a bicycle for a week, so they could get to Sorrento and back to the Quarantine Station, about forty minutes' ride away. Aidan's parents' café—the Pram Stop—was just about the only shop on Ocean Beach Road that hadn't put out a welcome sign.

But we didn't see any refugees in town in those first few weeks.

Luca said it was partly because they were scared. The government had told them that if they left the safety of the haven, it couldn't guarantee protection and support, and so the refugees stayed right there, afraid to leave.

And then, only weeks after they arrived, news broke that the war was over.

"NATO has called off its eleven-week air war against Serbia following the beginning of the withdrawal of Serb troops from Kosovo," the newscaster said.

Sam looked from the car radio to Anika in the driver's seat. "Does that mean they're going home? Even though they've only just got here?" he asked.

"It's not quite as simple as that," Anika said. "Both sides may say it's over, but it might not be—there's still a lot of violence over there, and military everywhere, plus there's also not a whole lot for these people to return to. No law and order, destroyed homes . . ."

We were in the car that Tuesday after school, heading to

113

the supermarket while Luca was volunteering again. Sam and I had taken turns telling Anika what Mr. McMillan had told Aidan—about how the refugees could have gone home weeks ago, but they wouldn't because they had a good thing going here, and would bleed Australia of all our good intentions.

We saw Anika rolling her eyes in the rearview mirror, and we heard her mutter something under her breath before she cleared her throat to talk to us properly. "That's all well and good for Aidan's father to say, but I'm sure he'd feel differently if it was *his family* choosing between staying here in safety or going back to a bombed-out city that could still come under attack."

Anika put the turn signal on and swung us into the car park, but before we got out of the car, she awkwardly tried turning her big body in the seat to look at Sam and me. "Don't go telling Luca every bit of word-vomit that comes out of Mr. McMillan's mouth, okay?"

Sam and I smirked when Anika said that, and she did the same. "I know, I know—you shouldn't disrespect your elders. Especially not your friend's parents, understand?"

Sam and I both nodded.

"But Mr. McMillan can . . ." Anika sighed and fidgeted in her seat. ". . . He can be a bit of a gossip and run his mouth without caring what other people think, or how they'll react or even what the full story is."

114

Then a little quieter, Anika added, "I can just imagine what he thinks of me and Luca."

But I didn't have to imagine—I knew. I knew because Aidan was forever inviting Jed and Keira over to his house after school, but never me. He didn't make a big deal about it, but I'd asked Jed the other day why Aidan never asked me to hang out, too, and Jed's neck had gone bright red and he'd scratched at it while avoiding my eyes.

"What? What did Aidan say?" I asked. "Did I do something wrong?"

Jed shook his head. "Nah, nothing like that. It's just . . ."

I yanked on the strap of his backpack then, making him stumble and stop short with me so I could raise my eyebrow at him. (Or try to—I wasn't as good at it as Mr. Khouri.)

"All right, all right!" Jed huffed. "His dad reckons Luca and Anika having a baby together isn't . . ." Jed waved his hands, trying to find the words. "Isn't a good thing— because they're not married."

I didn't know what to say to that. So I'd stalked off, and made Jed run to catch up to me. Sam was way ahead of us by then, and I made Jed swear not to say anything. Which he hadn't.

Standing in the supermarket aisle I was still lost in my thoughts of what Anika had said, and the gossip that

Aidan's dad was spreading, when Sam suddenly tugged sharply on my sleeve.

"What?" I said, and turned to him—only to see exactly what he was staring at: a little girl about his age, standing in the middle of the cereal aisle with her mouth hanging open and eyes just as wide.

She was one of the refugees from the safe haven.

For one thing, she wasn't in uniform even though school had just got out—instead she was wearing a black tracksuit top and bottoms, and really old, scuffed runners, and her brown hair was sticking out all over, like she needed a haircut and a brush. For another, she was excited to be at the supermarket—one of the most boring places on Earth.

Three more people rounded the corner—two women wearing headscarves and another little girl in a matching tracksuit who looked like the first one's little sister. The adults seemed a little . . . worried? But the two girls were practically vibrating with excitement and then they started dancing—right there in the aisles.

They grabbed each other's hands and started twirling and spinning and giggling, until they twirled and spun a little too fast and knocked over a display of cereal boxes. One of the women scolded them immediately, grabbed one of each girl's wrists and told them off until they looked like they were about to cry.

"Sam, Fred—go help them."

I turned around when Anika said that, but she wasn't looking at the refugee family or the mess they'd made—she was turned toward the other customers in the supermarket, who had stopped what they were doing and were frowning at the family or shaking their heads as they walked away.

"Now, please!" Anika said.

Sam and I hurried over. We both smiled awkwardly while the women kept talking in hushed, angry words to the two girls. The girls stared at us, their eyes still round and curious as we crouched down to stack the boxes back up.

Anika walked up with our cart as the family of four kept talking in whispers. "Hello. Meerdeeta!"

Suddenly all four of them were looking at Anika—first with those same round eyes of shock and then it was like a light went on, and the two adults broke out in big smiles.

"Mirëdita!"

"Mirëdita!"

They each said it, then the little girls squirmed out of the hold one of the women still had on them, to shyly come over and start helping us stack the cereal. Sam and I quietly and a little sheepishly said "Meerdeeta!" trying to copy what everyone else had said.

The little girls giggled at us and kept stacking.

"I'm—I'm sorry, that's all I know," Anika said to the two women. "Hello—Meerdeeta!"

The two women spoke rapidly to the children, and the

older one with the sticky-out hair looked at Anika over her shoulder. "Thank you, we are sorry," she said, the words rolling off her tongue with tumbling *r*'s.

Anika, Sam, and I all must have looked at her in shock because she giggled again, and then they all said something else rapidly.

"Little English," one of the women explained, pointing to her own chest. And then she smiled down at the girl and said, "More English."

"Do you learn in school?" Anika asked the girl, who stood up once the stacking was done. The display wasn't as fancy as before, but at least all the cereal boxes were off the floor.

The girl nodded.

"And what's your name?"

"Merjeme," the girl said.

"And who's this?" Anika asked, nodding and smiling to her little sister, who was now standing shyly behind Merjeme and peeking around her shoulder.

"Arta."

"Merjeme and Arta, it's nice to meet you!" Anika said. "This is Fred and Sam." She pointed at us in turn, then she smiled at the women. "And is this your mother and . . . ?"

"Mëma," Merjeme said, pointing to one of the women. "Emta," she added, pointing to the other, and then turning back to smile at us.

"Your mother and . . . aunt?" Anika guessed, and Merjeme nodded proudly.

"Well, tell your mëma and emta that we hope to see them around town too."

As soon as Anika had finished speaking, Merjeme was quickly translating. Her mom and aunt smiled so widely at all of us, it made me smile back wider too.

"Falemenderit!" the aunt said, and Merjeme translated: "Thank you."

We left them in the cereal aisle, and once we were far enough away Sam asked, "Can we tell Luca what happened?"

Anika smiled. "Yes. *This* we will tell Luca about."

22

WHEN THE TIME COMES

That Wednesday, I told Pop about the refugees.

"And Luca goes there after work sometimes—just to help out," I explained. "Mostly he says they want people to talk to, test their English out on, and show them how to play Aussie football."

"Shame you couldn't give those poor souls my apartment to stay in," Pop said.

"But—you'll be needing that when you come back."

We'd just got word that after six months, Pop would finally come home in the first week of July. His ribs were healed up and he'd swapped his walker for a cane to get around.

"Of course, of course," Pop said. "I just meant if I *wasn't* needing that old apartment out back . . . one of them could have had it."

It was true, and something I asked Luca about a few nights later, over dinner: why we had a perfectly good granny apartment sitting empty while all those refugees had to stay in a run-down old quarantine station with toilets that were overflowing and heating that wasn't always working.

"Plus, Mom. You clean all those big houses that are empty now over winter," Sam added. "They should have just let the refugees stay in them since no one else is."

I could tell Anika and Luca were a little impressed and surprised by Sam's words.

"That is true, yes," Anika said. "But the government wanted the refugees all in one place so they'd be easier to look after. And it's a very big favor to ask of people, letting strangers into their homes." She took a sip of water and cleared her throat. "And anyway, there's not much room in Pop's apartment right now."

I put my knife and fork down and looked between them. "What do you mean?"

I watched Anika's cheeks turn a little red. "Well," she started, "we didn't think you'd—"

"It's where we've been storing the baby's things," Luca interrupted. "Out of the way until we're ready to set it all up." I hadn't been inside Pop's apartment for months; it was bad enough staring at it from the back porch or kitchen window, knowing it was sitting there empty and waiting for him, same as me.

"But—you have to get rid of them," I said, and then frowned when I thought how that must sound. "I mean— you can't keep them there! Pop's coming back soon, and he'll need his apartment."

I thought I saw Luca shake his head at Anika, only a little—but maybe I imagined it. I was stuck on knowing that Pop's apartment, which he needed back, was full of things for Drumlin.

The next question on the tip of my tongue was where the baby would stay when the time *came*. Luca beat me to it.

"And speaking of," Luca started to say, and I felt my stomach drop. "Anika and I have been thinking, Freddo, that maybe we should switch rooms with you for when Drumlin arrives. . . ." Luca raised his hands the second I opened my mouth to protest. "I know, I know! But what was fine when it was just me in the back room isn't going to work so well when it's me *and* Anika *and* a crib. And your room . . ."

"Mom's room!" I snapped, and Luca sighed.

"We've talked about this before, Freddo," he said, "that it would be more convenient for the three of us. It's the only one that's big enough."

"We're still working out the logistics, though!" Anika said, and then she and Luca frowned at each other and each raised their eyebrows, in a way that would have made Mr. Khouri proud.

"Nothing is set in stone," Anika finished, and smiled tightly at me.

Luca shook his head. "But it really would be for the best and help us all out."

"I thought you said we had to talk to each other more!" I said, and I shoved my chair back from the table. "But you've already decided without asking me, haven't you?"

Luca sighed and rubbed his hand over his head. "I'm sorry, Freddo—but we have to start making these decisions and getting ready for when . . ."

"The baby comes—I *know*! But Pop's coming home first, so you have to move all that *junk* out of his apartment—"

"Winifred!" Luca snapped.

I blew my bangs out of my eyes and asked to be excused.

"I think you'd better, yes," Luca said, and he shook his head at me.

As I walked away I heard Sam offer his room for the crib, and Anika said that was very generous of him—even if his room was too small. And that just made me slam my door a little bit harder.

23

HOLD ON

had a nightmare that we could barely hold on. Me and Anika, Pop and Sam, and Luca, too . . . all of us lying flat on the ground and trying to claw into the dirt while the Earth spun madly on, like it was the Tilt-A-Whirl ride at the Royal Melbourne Show.

Or as if somebody had stomped on the accelerator, to make the Earth spin off its axis.

I woke up in the middle of that night, covered in sweat and calling for Mom. I hadn't done that since I was little, right after she died. Pop said I used to have fevered dreams and I'd wake up having forgotten she was gone, and then I'd cry and cry and cry for her until he or Luca rocked me back to sleep, hugged in their arms.

That night, though, I knew something else had woken me—and then I heard it again, coming from down the hallway.

A kind of whimpering. When I listened closely to the dark, I realized it was coming from Anika and Luca's room.

At first I thought it was Drumlin—but it was too soon. I sprang out of bed and opened the door, and then I heard the crying more clearly.

Light spilled from underneath their door, and I was moving toward the thin strip of light when Sam's door opened next to me, and he stood there with his curly hair sticking out in all directions, rubbing his glasses-less eyes.

"What . . . ?" he started to ask, his voice slurry from sleep.

Just then, Luca's bedroom door burst open, and I squinted from the sudden bright light.

Anika was hunched over, cradling her stomach with both arms, and her legs wide apart. Luca had an arm wrapped around her shoulders and guided her out of the room. He was wearing a thick sweater over his pajamas, while Anika had one of Luca's big work windbreakers on, clutched over her rounded belly and going just past her knees.

Luca gently closed the door behind them, cutting off all light until he flicked the hallway switch. Anika whimpered again—the sound that had woken us—and Luca looked up, right at me.

"We're going to the hospital," he said, and then he and Anika started walking.

"What?" Sam asked again, his voice sharper now. "What's happening?"

125

"Take Samuel and go next door, tell Vi what's happened. . . ." Luca said, while he and Anika shuffled down the hall.

"Mom? Mom!" Sam reached out to touch her as she passed him, but I pushed to keep him behind me, and he didn't struggle.

"Fred, get the door!" Luca yelled.

I quickly looked to Sam, who had started crying. "Stay here, I'll be right back!" I whispered.

And then I ran down the hall in my socked feet, moved around Luca to flick the locks and hold the door open for them while Luca half-carried Anika down the couple of stairs out the front.

He pressed his car keys into my hand, and I ran ahead to unlock the door and hold it open for her while she gently lowered herself in backward, her hands locked around Luca's forearms. I gave him the keys back and he dashed around to the driver's side.

I hung off Anika's passenger door once Luca's had slammed shut. The little interior light in the car was all there was in the darkness, and it let me see Anika's face. It was wet from tears and sweat and looked so strange with her glasses all crooked. She just kept looking down at her belly, her arms wrapped around herself and kept crying while Luca spoke next to her.

"Get Sam, go next door, I'll call as soon as I can,"

he said, and then I was slamming Anika's door shut and walking down our driveway, shivering in the cold night as I watched their headlights trail down our street and then disappear around the first bend.

I swear I only stood there for a second or two, listening to my breath all ragged as it came out, like I'd just run cross-country . . . and then I turned around and ran back into the house to find Sam standing at the end of the hall, in the middle of Anika and Luca's doorway with his arms hanging limp by his sides as he looked into their room.

I walked slowly toward Sam and stopped behind him to see what had him shaking like that.

There was blood on the sheets.

So dark it was nearly black, and pooling right where Anika slept.

And then I was grabbing Sam by his shoulders and hauling him back, turning the light off again and swinging the door shut.

"Put your shoes and a coat on. We're going next door!"

And to my surprise, Sam did exactly that.

24

NEARLY IMPOSSIBLE

'd spent the night on the floor of Lily's room—not sleeping—while Sam stayed in Jed's room. In the morning Luca called Vi to say everything was okay. Anika was tired and sore and staying in the hospital to make sure Drumlin wouldn't try to come again before it was time.

When I'd asked to speak to Luca, Vi said he had to go, and she hung up the phone. I asked if Sam and I could go to the hospital, but Vi said we had school and that Luca had insisted we go.

"I think Sam's very shaken up," Vi said, and I leaned forward and looked sideways to see Sam wiping his snotty nose on his pajama sleeve as he sat next to Jed at their kitchen table. "I think school would take his mind off things, and you keeping a close eye on him today would be good."

Vi drove us and even hopped out of the car to talk to Mr. Khouri in private. That was kind of embarrassing but also made my chest feel a little lighter. She gave Sam and me a kiss on our foreheads, same as she gave Jed, and I tugged on her arm as she turned to leave.

"Vi . . ." I whispered, so Sam wouldn't hear. She crouched down to me. "Anika and Luca's bed. There was all this . . ." But I couldn't say the word *blood*; it just wouldn't pass my lips. And I didn't know how to explain that I kept imagining Anika or Luca coming home to see it all, the sheets still black and ruined, and that we couldn't let that happen.

Vi tucked my bangs behind my ear and smiled kindly. "Luca told me. There's no need for you to worry," she said, "I'm going to pop home now and take care of it—I've got your spare key."

It was the weirdest thing to sit through assembly and PE, and Mr. Khouri talking about prime numbers and active verbs, and how the Summer Olympics were coming to Australia the next year.

And if it was nearly impossible for me to concentrate on anything, I don't know how Sam must have felt when it was his *actual* mother and more-his brother stuck in the hospital two towns over.

Jed must have told Aidan and Keira what happened, too, because nobody asked any questions—they just

129

seemed to *know*. It also meant that when the bell rang at the end of the day, nobody—not even Mr. Khouri—said anything about me and Sam bolting for the door without bothering to stack our chairs away or make sure our tables were tidied.

Luca was waiting at the gate. He'd changed out of his pajamas into normal clothes, so he must have been home. He was wearing about a million frowns and looking so tired, it was like he'd shrunk overnight somehow. I ran right to him and his arms opened the same as always, so I just held on for a minute—and then one of his arms lifted and Sam was hugging him, too, and I didn't even mind.

We walked through the front doors of Rosebud Hospital, and the nurses directed us to something called the Green Wing, a side of the building where they kept all the families and babies together. Even the ones that weren't born yet.

I was glad that Luca kept a hand on my and Sam's shoulders, and turned us down all the right corridors. The smell of the hospital—too clean and cold—was making me dizzy, and I was relieved when we finally got to the Green Wing and a nurse showed us the way to Anika. She was sitting up in bed and already had her arms opened wide, as if she'd heard us coming.

Sam ran to her and fitted himself under her arm and

around her big belly, taking care not to disturb the tube that was stuck in her hand and running to a machine by her bed.

They stayed like that for a minute, and I could hear Anika murmuring muffled words into Sam's neck that had him nodding his head and crying a little bit. Luca and I hung back by the door. I grabbed my elbow with my opposite hand and shifted on my feet, wondering if Luca should've just brought Sam and left me at home.

But then Sam was stepping back and Anika was waving us over. Luca and I stepped forward as she adjusted her glasses and patted down her wild and curly hair. And then I was standing there, and she gently cupped my head in her hands and rubbed her thumbs under my eyes to wipe away the tears.

"Drumlin can have my room, we can share," I said, and I didn't even know those words were there until I had blurted them out. Anika shook her head and kept cupping my cheek.

"Hey—that's not why this happened," she said.

I started to speak, but Anika shook her head again and looked right into my eyes. "This wasn't because of anything you or any of us did. It was just . . . what happened, okay?" Anika looked up and behind me, and then Luca was hugging me to his side, and I don't remember what happened next, except we stayed together for a little while in that white room, where it was just the four of us and the sounds of the hospital all around.

"It's not so bad—I get all my meals cooked for me!" Anika said eventually, and we all smiled a little too wide, just because we could.

"When are you coming home?" Sam asked, and Anika ran a hand through his shaggy hair.

"Not for a while, baby," she sighed. "The doctors want to keep an eye on me and Drumlin." She rubbed her belly, like she was making sure he was still there.

"When will I see you then?" Sam asked, and his voice got a little wonky, like he might cry again.

Anika looked up at Luca, who was running his hand over his head, a worry line forming between his eyes. "I'll need to be home with the kids, so the station will give me daytime shifts. But I don't know when I'll be able to get them here during hospital visiting hours. . . ."

"We'll get the bus after school," I said. "And then during the day over the holidays."

Anika looked from me to Luca and back again.

"Freddo, I don't know. . . ." Luca started.

"It's *one* town over from Pop, and I'll be catching the bus here for school next year anyway!"

"Mom, I want to—please?" Sam whined, and I felt bad for him.

Anika stroked his hair again and smiled tiredly up at

Luca. "I'd like that."

Luca nodded. "All right, all right! But you need to be careful, okay? I mean it—no talking to strangers, and you come straight from school to here and home again, understood?"

He could never not be a policeman.

Eventually the nurse came around to check the tube that was running out of Anika's hand and to say that visiting hours were almost over.

"You're going to be all alone," Sam said.

Anika shook her head. "No, of course not! I've got Drumlin, for one thing." And then she rubbed her belly again. "And I do have a roommate—I just haven't met her yet." She nodded her head toward the drawn curtain behind us, which was hiding another bed that must have been empty just then.

"That's time, I'm afraid!" said the nurse, and we had to say goodbye. I thought it'd be hard, but just as we were leaving, Drumlin started kicking. All three of us ended up laying a hand on Anika's belly and feeling his flutters, like he had wings in there or something.

25

HERE BE DRAGONS

Cartographers from long ago used to draw dragons, sea monsters, and other made-up creatures in the unexplored territories on maps. It was their way of warning that there could be danger in the unknown, and it's where the phrase "here be dragons" came from.

If this story was a map, this is where the dragons would go. Because after Anika and Drumlin went into the hospital and we didn't know when they'd be back, it felt a little like we were off the map, in uncharted waters.

Sam and I didn't talk on the bus to the hospital. I let him take the window seat, and he sat the whole way with his forehead pressed against the glass. It reminded me of that day we went up Arthurs Seat, all of us, and I thought how long ago that was.

Anika was lying on her side in bed, and the curtain

behind her was still drawn closed, except this time we could see the shadowy outline of someone on the other side.

"Hello, my darlings," Anika said, her voice coming out a little croaky. She put an arm around her stomach as she slowly and awkwardly moved herself up a little on the pillow.

Sam went to her side but didn't make a move to touch her. She had a few more tubes stuck in her hand and running to a machine by her bed, and another that was tucked down her nightgown and stuck to her chest.

"You just missed Luca and Penny," Anika said, looking at me. "They popped in during their shift."

I nodded but hung back by the door, watching as Sam sucked on his bottom lip, pushed his glasses up his nose, but still didn't try to touch his mom.

"How was school today?"

"Good," Sam said. "Mr. Khouri let us take a nap in the nurse's office."

Anika frowned, but then smiled it away before Sam could see. "That was good of him, you've had a big couple of days. Were you tired during class?"

Sam shrugged and kept looking down at his feet.

"Pull that chair up behind you, Samwise, and tell me good things," Anika said. He pulled the chair a little closer and sat. To me, Anika added, "Fred, there's a chair here on the other side, come grab it."

So I slowly walked into the room and went around to the other side of Anika's bed, while she took Sam's hands and he quietly started telling her about his day.

The partition between Anika's and the other patient's sides of the room was like a shower curtain—thin white plastic. I could only make out their shadow, but as I bent down to drag the chair over, I heard the soft sound of them crying.

Whoever it was sounded like a woman. She was trying to take deep breaths; I could hear her struggling to breathe and cry and making little sniffles in between, and I desperately wanted to pull the curtain back and see, but all I could make out from her shadow was that she was lying down with her head burrowed into the pillow, trying to muffle her cries.

"Fred?"

I jumped a little when Anika whispered my name, and when I looked over to her and Sam, she frowned and motioned for me to come away.

"Should I . . . ?" I started to ask, but Anika shook her head.

"She's been like that all night and day," she sighed, and then moved herself again to get more comfortable in bed.

"Is she all right?" I whispered.

Anika looked over her shoulder and then back to us,

shaking her head again. "She's from the haven."

My eyes must have gone wide in shock, because Anika explained, "I tried talking to her last night, but I don't think she knows much English, and my Albanian isn't exactly great."

"But—why is she here?" Sam asked quietly.

"Same as me," Anika said. "She's having a baby."

26

ONE PART OF THE WORLD

That night, Luca burned the garlic bread he'd made to go with the spaghetti Bolognese and then he burned his wrist trying to yank the tray out of the oven. He got frustrated by Sam's math homework because the long division was different from the way he was taught in school, and he got a phone call after dinner asking him if he could volunteer at the safe haven that weekend.

And then right before bed, Sam's dad called and asked to speak to him—but Sam shook his head and refused to take the phone, so Luca had to apologize and say he should try again tomorrow.

"It's been a long day, Freddo," Luca said, when he came into my room that night, and pretended to collapse face-down on my bed.

I swiveled around from my desk and put down the

book I was reading for school. I still felt heavy and tired after today, the same as Luca looked, but for a little while at least, the story was taking my mind off everything.

It was *Playing Beatie Bow* by Ruth Park and I liked it a lot. It was about this girl who lives in Sydney and time-travels back to the olden days, before the Harbour Bridge was even built. The girl was so far from home yet she was still right there, even though nothing looked the same and everything was changed. I thought I knew how she felt, having her world turned upside down and inside out like that. And I was thinking of asking Mr. Khouri if I could show a map of the two Sydneys that Abigail sees, from long ago and during her time, as part of my report instead of doing another boring plot summary.

Luca sighed as he turned himself right side up and arranged my pillows behind his back. "I've been very lucky to have your pop around all these years, Freddo. I didn't realize how much until today." He gave me a weary smile. "Your taking Sam to see Anika was a really big help, though. Have I thanked you for that already?"

I rolled my eyes but smiled anyway. "About a million times."

"Well, I mean it. You think you'll be okay to keep taking him, even over the holidays?"

I nodded, and then spun a full circle in the swivel

chair. When I came back to face Luca I said, "She's sharing a room with one of the refugees. A woman from the safe haven."

"Ah, I wondered if she'd mention that."

"I didn't think about it," I said. Luca raised a questioning eyebrow and I explained. "That people would still have babies and things, even when there's a war on. I didn't think any of the refugees would be in the hospital because of that."

Luca nodded. "The world doesn't really stop just because there's tragedy happening in one part of it."

"Do you know who she is?" Luca shook his head, so I said, "She was crying when we went there today, and Anika said she was last night too."

"Anika told me the same thing."

I sighed. "I wonder if she's all alone, or if it's just her and the baby. . . ."

Then Luca was pushing himself off my bed and running his hands over his face, like he could wipe the tiredness away. He came over to me and bent down to kiss my forehead. When he straightened, he said, "You and Anika have a lot in common, you know that?"

"How?"

"She wondered the same thing and asked me to see what I could find out."

"Did you?"

He nodded. "It's just her. She didn't come over with any other relatives." Luca headed for my door, but turned back to add, "Her baby's due in November, so she might be there awhile."

27

THE LADY IN THE GARDEN

And then we were officially free and on winter holidays. It was fine at first, but being home for holidays was so different without Anika or Pop around, and after one day on our own, our excitement turned to mush.

"Maybe she'll say she can come home today," Sam said, when we'd just passed Blairgowrie on the bus.

"Yeah, maybe," I murmured—but I didn't really think so.

We got to the hospital and headed to Anika's room. This time as we walked past the hospital's atrium, the glass-walled courtyard garden for patients and visitors, I looked in to see who might be sitting on the wooden benches and enjoying the garden.

It was just one lady that I could see, sitting there in a loose white hospital gown. She was looking off at one of the far corridors behind the glass, while making gentle circles over a belly that wasn't nearly as big as Anika's, but still very round. She had long black hair in a braid that was thrown over her shoulder. And I don't know why, but I thought she looked so sad sitting there, still as a statue except for her hands making those circles. . . .

"Mom?"

Sam's voice snapped me back, and when I looked, I saw that he was running toward Anika. She was walking slowly, hanging on to a metal pole that was wheeling beside her and connected by a tube.

He skidded to a stop in front of her and then she reached a hand out to ruffle his hair, but he didn't dare touch her—she looked worse than she had during our last few visits, all swollen and sore, wincing as she turned to head back to her room. Maybe because walking around was tiring her out, but I could tell Sam was disturbed by how sick Anika looked, how fragile.

When we got there Anika sat on the bed, slowly wriggled back and then heaved her legs up after her.

She was out of breath, and I handed her the plastic cup from her bedside table. She drank quickly and then seemed to breathe a little easier.

"Thank you, my dears," she said, and smiled at both of us. Then she focused on Sam. "Luca tells me you refused to talk to your dad again last night?"

"Don't have to if I don't want to," he said, but I think he regretted the words when he saw the look Anika gave him.

"Fred, honey—would you mind giving me and Sam a minute alone?"

"Sure, I'll just—" But Anika was already snapping at Sam to sit down, so I dropped my backpack by the bed and hurried out.

I only stayed in the corridor for a second before I decided it was too busy and wandered back toward the atrium.

I pulled the heavy sliding door open and stepped inside, breathing in the smell of earth and green. Some kid sitting on a patch of grass started bubbling with laughter while a couple watched from one of the benches that were placed around the courtyard's perimeter.

The lady with the long black braid was still there, too—only now she was hugging her belly the same way Anika did, like she had to hold on.

I wandered over to the last empty bench and spaced out for a bit, watching the kid on the grass play until his parents said it was time to go. I realized the dad was wearing a bathrobe, and he looked so sad as they gathered the kid up and walked out.

Then the place was quiet, with just the lady and me. And in the quiet I thought about my mom. I wondered if this garden had been here when she had me, and if she sat around rubbing her belly the way Anika and that lady did or brought me here all bundled up. I wondered if she started calling me Winnie from the first day, and what she'd think of me now.

"Ne-deem! Ne-deem!"

My head snapped up and my eyes were instantly drawn to the woman—no longer as still as a statue, but wobbling to her feet and clutching her belly with one hand, while holding the other to her back.

"Ne-deem! Ne-deem!"

Her face crumpled in pain and I made a quick decision to run straight to the glass wall and bang on it for help. A nurse and a doctor came sprinting down the corridor while I waved urgently and pointed to the woman behind me.

I turned around and went back to her, but didn't know what to do. She grabbed my upper arm to steady herself, wincing again from the pain.

"Ndihmë!" she said, and then a whole lot of words spilled out that I didn't understand.

"Mirëdita, mirëdita." I whispered the only word I knew, and the woman kept staring at me, still gritting her teeth and with eyes watering, but for a second I thought she looked . . . relieved. And a little less scared.

"Coming through!" the nurse called. She was followed by a doctor pushing an empty wheelchair, and I moved out of the way as they helped lower her into the chair.

I hurried behind them as they pushed her toward the doors, and I listened to the woman keep talking in that language I didn't know. The doctor and nurse didn't know it either, but it must have been Albanian.

"Can we get the translator back here?" the doctor asked, and then they were out the door and rushing through the swinging doors to another ward.

I stood there, just staring down that hallway.

"Fred!"

I looked over and there was Sam, standing with his backpack on and holding mine in front of him, while pushing his glasses up again. "The nurse said visiting hours are over."

I nodded and walked to him, took my backpack, and had one last look down the corridor, where the woman had been wheeled away.

"You look weird," Sam said.

"I'm fine!" I snapped. "Let's go."

28

ON WINTER HOLIDAYS

Jed and I never knew what to do in the first days of holidays, especially in winter. And especially because we lived by the bay. You can hardly do anything at the beach, and the winds off the water make everything that much colder.

Mr. Trần was still in Sydney, Vi was working at her hairdressers shop, Luca had day shifts, and Lily didn't want anything to do with Jed, Sam, or me. But Vi and Luca insisted that they wanted us out of the house and not stuck on the couch playing video games every day.

All I really wanted was to visit Pop and then the hospital to find out how that lady in the garden was, and if her baby was okay. Hospital visiting hours didn't start until four p.m., so I still had to find something to fill my day. And Sam's, since I was in charge of him while Anika was away.

I didn't say anything to Luca or Sam about the lady or what had happened. I felt like without knowing if she was okay, it wasn't fair to tell them more sad stories, so I kept that one to myself. Just in case.

The three of us could hang around town, so long as we stuck our heads in at the police station or the hairdressers occasionally to let Vi, Luca, or Penny know we were okay.

In the end, Aidan, Jed, Keira, Sam, and I decided to finally pull our bikes out from our sheds, shake the cobwebs from our helmets, and go riding round town to find something to do. That was how we came across a whole gaggle of refugee kids, and Mr. Khouri too.

Keira's house was only one road over from PNP. After we collected her, we were riding back past the school when we saw a whole bunch of kids in the front playground and a big bus parked in the teachers' lot.

We screeched our bikes to a stop just outside the chain-link fence, hopped off our seats, and gawked at them—all these kids our age who looked pretty much just like us, although the words we could faintly hear coming from them definitely weren't English.

There were about forty or so kids, running around and giggling or else standing and talking to each other. Some of the girls were trying to do handstands against the brick wall of classroom 1B, while a bunch of boys were putting their thumbs over the drinking fountains to squirt each other with water.

"Weird, watching other kids go to school while we're on break," Keira said.

And then I spotted them—holding each other's hands and twirling, just like we'd seen them doing a week ago at the supermarket.

Merjeme and Arta.

The sisters looked just the same, except their tracksuits were blue this time and it looked like they'd had their hair brushed. Once they stopped twirling I thought I saw the younger one, Arta, look our way, so I lifted my hand and waved.

"What are you doing?" Aidan asked.

I shrugged and kept waving, and then Sam followed where I was looking and did the same thing.

Aidan slapped a hand to his helmeted head like he couldn't believe us.

The two girls eventually waved back but didn't come over—then some other kids standing near them must have asked what they were doing, so they started pointing at us.

"Hey, isn't that Mr. Khouri?" Jed said, nodding toward the front office.

We watched as he stepped outside, along with my old second grade teacher, Mrs. Vines. Both were carrying clipboards and wearing these yellow-and-white vests with little red crosses over their hearts and the word VOLUNTEER in black letters across their backs.

Some adults I didn't recognize followed, two of them wearing bright-yellow sweaters with the words "Albanian Community Volunteer" in bold black letters across the chests, and then a few more people wearing the Red Cross vests.

"Mr. Khouri!" Sam called.

Aidan huffed again and pulled down Sam's arm when he went to wave. "The whole point of being on holidays is to *not* be at school and *not* talk to teachers!" he hissed. "Quick, let's get—"

But it was too late; Mr. Khouri was already walking over and smiling at us with his eyebrows raised.

"Mr. McMillan—are you such a fan of school you couldn't stay away?"

"Ah, no, sir," Aidan murmured. "We were just riding by and saw . . ."

Mr. Khouri looked behind him, at the volunteers who had started calling out kids' names and having them line up against the side of the classroom.

"What are they doing today?" Keira butted in. "Is it regular school stuff like what we do?"

Our teacher turned back to us. "Math is pretty universal, so we're doing some of those regular lessons. And then we are teaching basic English phrases today. Most of them know quite a bit though some leave a lot to be desired."

"What do you mean, sir?" Jed asked.

Mr. Khouri sighed. "Apparently *The Simpsons* is quite popular in Kosovo, and everyone is very proud to say 'Eat my shorts,' no matter if the occasion or context calls for it."

"Have they not been going to school all this time, sir?" Jed asked, and Mr. Khouri shook his head.

"No. A few teachers have been hired or else volunteered to teach regularly at the haven, but it's—err—not the most ideal of classrooms." He shrugged. "So I suggested that we take advantage of our vacant school over the holidays and let them learn in the lap of luxury."

Sam laughed as Mr. Khouri swept his arms out to take in our little brick school by the sea. And then someone blew a whistle behind him and Mr. Khouri said he had to go.

"You're welcome to stop by again if you want," he said. "These children are very curious about all of you."

"About us?" Keira pointed at herself.

He nodded. "All of you local kids—they think you live in paradise. In fact, I'd say they're more curious about you than you are of them."

Then Mr. Khouri's eyes seemed to light up, and he opened his clipboard folder to unclip a piece of paper that he rolled up and passed through one of the diamonds of the fence. He motioned at Aidan to take it, which he reluctantly did.

"I'm going to start posting these around town, but since you're here . . ."

We each let our bikes go and crash to the ground so we could crowd around Aidan and read over his shoulder. It was a flyer with a pretty terrible drawing of a soccer ball, net, and stick-figure goalie that read:

ALBANIANS vs. AUSTRALIANS

Sign up for a friendly game of community soccer at the Safe Haven: Sunday 1 August

Under 18s and Over 18s matches

"The haven would like to organize a friendly game of soccer in a few weeks' time, and we're looking for players to fill out a local side," Mr. Khouri said.

Aidan started rolling the paper back up, but Jed snatched it from his hand to read more closely.

"Would you consider putting your talents as goalie to good use?"

I looked up to see Mr. Khouri's eyes trained on Aidan. Jed and a bunch of other boys played, too, but only for fun during lunch—Aidan was in junior leagues and easily the best soccer player at PNP for his age group, and maybe even the whole of Sorrento.

Aidan scratched under his chin where his helmet strap

sat and shrugged. "I don't think my dad will let me, sir."

"Will you at least ask him?"

The sound of a whistle came again and Mr. Khouri apologized and said he really had to run. We watched him jog back inside while we picked our bikes back up.

"Maybe it'd be cool?" Jed looked to Aidan as he handed him back the flyer.

Aidan scoffed at that, then got back on his bike and flicked his pedals to get his feet in position. "Eat my shorts!" he called as he was pushing off. We all had to pedal hard to catch up with him.

But I noticed that he'd tucked the piece of paper into his jeans pocket.

29

THE WAY IT WAS

Pop came home that first week of winter holidays, and I thought everything would go back to the way it was before his fall.

Luca and I got a banner from the two-dollar shop that said "Welcome Home" in sparkly letters and hung it on the front door of his apartment. Luca hadn't managed to clear out all of Drumlin's stuff, but Pop said he didn't mind.

At Pop's first night back at the dinner table, Sam just kept staring at him. I knew it was because he'd never seen anyone quite so tall and imposing. Sam's jaw unhinged and he cranked his head back to get a good look at him. I think it's also because Sam's not used to grandparents being around, the same way I'm not used to mothers anymore—and Pop is a lot to get used to, I suppose.

"I'm sorry it's not quite the celebration you were hoping

for," Luca said, nodding at the dishes piled up in the sink and the letters and bills pushed to a heap at one end of the table. "Things have been a little hectic since Anika . . ."

Pop waved him away and bit into his pizza, which we'd ordered especially from the best place in town. Once he'd swallowed his capricciosa, Pop said, "I remember what it was like. Don't you worry—you're doing fine."

I looked down at my plate, but suddenly couldn't take another bite of my barbecue chicken pizza. I forgot sometimes that Pop and Luca are similar and for all the worst reasons. Raising kids by themselves because the people they loved . . .

Except Anika wasn't gone, just at the hospital—she and Drumlin were off getting better and ready to come home again.

"I might hit the hay," Pop said, grabbing for his walking stick.

"Are you all right, Jeff? Will you need any help tonight, um . . ."

Pop waved him away. "Wiping my bottom and blowing my nose? Not yet, son—not yet!"

Luca blushed, and then Pop was giving Sam a little salute with his fingers to his forehead, which Sam copied in return.

"Fred—walk me back?"

Pop and I walked down the garden path to his

apartment, which was finally lit up again—like a little lighthouse at the back of our garden.

I ran ahead of Pop and held the door open for him as he limped in. Luca, Sam, and I had cleaned the place as best we could—got rid of the cobwebs that had formed in the corners and pushed Drumlin's stuff behind Pop's couch. Only the pram's box was sticking out.

Pop went over and lowered himself into his reading chair, closed his eyes, and let out a long "ahhhhhh" as soon as his butt hit the seat.

"Luca is run off his feet," Pop said, his eyes still closed.

I wandered into the room, getting used to seeing Pop back where he belonged.

"He's okay," I said, "but I think he misses Anika."

"Well, he loves her," he said. "And how are you and Sam?"

"We're fine."

"Are you? You're certainly getting on better than I remember. . . ."

I shrugged.

"Could it be that you don't hate him as much as you thought?"

I frowned at Pop. "I never said I *hated* Sam."

"You didn't need to, Fred."

I walked over to Pop's bookcase and looked at his shelf of well-thumbed Stephen King novels; all those cracked spines and wrinkle lines on the covers, musty pages and the puffy bold typeface of his name that I liked to trace with my fingertip.

"He misses his mom," I said, as I pulled one of Pop's favorite books off the shelf. It was called *Different Seasons* and it was thick and yellowed with age, many of the pages bent from Pop's dog-ears.

Pop once told me that the world splits into two types of readers: those who bend the corner of a page to dog-ear when they read a book, and those who use a bookmark (and maybe there's a third kind who choose not to read, period—but he couldn't figure them out). Luca was the bookmark type. But Pop believed that dog-ears in a book were like laughter lines on a face—signs of love. All the books on his shelf had cracks and creases, and pen marks in the margins of his favorite stories, like rivers and roads leading to the best bits, the parts he wanted to remember.

"I think you miss her too," Pop said.

I put the book back but didn't know what to say to Pop that wouldn't hurt him. Mom was his daughter, and Anika wasn't mine to miss.

"I'm happier now that you're home," I said instead. And then to change the subject I asked, "Will you take Sam and me to Farrells one day these holidays?"

Pop opened his eyes and smiled—Farrells Bookshop in Mornington was the best around, and ever since I was a little kid, Pop had been taking me to the corner bookstore for a special treat every school holiday and plenty of weekends too. Any chance we could get, really. But between Pop's fall and his stay at the RRC and everything that had been happening, it was a while since we'd been. I bought this book called *A Series of Unfortunate Events: The Bad Beginning* last time we were there. I hadn't got around to reading it yet, but it sounded like a good story.

"It wouldn't feel like proper holidays if we didn't go to Farrells," Pop said, and I smiled.

30

HER NAME IS NORA

When we got closer to Anika's room, we could hear the TV blaring and voices trying to yell above the sound.

"Please, miss—you're disturbing the other patients. . . ."

"Let her keep it on, it's just the volume! She doesn't understand. . . ."

"Ju lutem, ju lutem!"

"Don't cry! We just want to . . ."

Sam and I stood in the doorway and blinked at the scene before us.

There was a TV hanging in the center of the far wall— so both patients could watch—and it was turned to the news channel, with the sound of the weather report echoing around the room.

Anika was sitting up in her bed, a mountain of pillows

behind her, and she was trying to calm down the nurse who was over by the other bed. The nurse was waving her hands around and trying to get the remote control from the lady who was sitting up and refusing to hand it over.

It was the lady from the atrium garden, the pregnant one.

"Please, miss—it's too LOUD!" the nurse was saying, raising her voice on the last word as though to explain herself better, while pointing at the TV and shaking her head.

The lady's hair wasn't in a braid today—it was out and wild, long down to her back and raven-black. She kept shaking her head and making her hair sway every which way. The nurse tried to pluck the remote control from her hands, but she clutched it to her chest, and I realized she had tears rolling down her cheeks.

"Ju lutem," the lady said again, holding the remote closer to her chest.

"For heaven's sake!" The nurse threw her hands up and spun around. Her eyes widened when she saw us. "I'm fetching security," she said, and then marched out of the room.

Anika threw her own hands up, and then did a double take when she saw us too.

"Quickly—go help the poor woman!" she said, looking at me.

I turned to see where the nurse had gone, but Anika waved her hands and said, "No, no. Not that Miss

160

Trunchbull! Go and help poor Nora!"

I looked over at the lady, but she wasn't paying attention to me—her eyes were glued to the TV.

Anika snapped at Sam, "Keep watch! Stall the security guard if you see him!"

I walked toward the lady. The blankets were kicked off and pushed down around her, and she was wearing only her long white hospital gown, which stretched tight over her belly.

Her skin was olive, darker than Luca's, which Mom used to say was "Mediterranean." She was a grown-up, and maybe even the same age as Anika, but I couldn't really tell. What I did notice was how being scared made her seem so much younger, and how strange it was to see an adult look so lost.

Anika had said her name was Nora, so when I got to her bed that's the name I said—quietly at first and then a little louder to be heard above the sound of a TV ad.

Her eyes—wide, tear-filled, and the color of milk chocolate—stayed fixed on the TV.

"Mirëdita," I said, trying to remember the way Merjeme had said the word for *hello* the other day.

And then I got an idea.

I reached a hand out slowly and placed it lightly on Nora's shoulder—she jumped a little but still wouldn't look at me, not until I very seriously said, "Eat my shorts."

She turned her head then and blinked at me, and I smiled back—a little sheepishly—and shrugged.

"The nurse is back, she's got a man with her!" Sam said from the doorway.

I took my hand off her shoulder and put it out, palm up. "Please."

She blinked at me again, and I thought I could see her realizing she recognized me from the atrium.

"We'll keep it on, I promise!" I said.

She looked down at the remote and placed it gently into my outstretched palm, and then seemed to sag against the pillows behind her.

I quickly aimed the remote at the TV and turned the volume down.

"Give it here!" Anika said, and I spun around to hand it to her. "Close the curtain," she added, and I did just that, hiding Nora just as the nurse and a tall security guard walked into the hushed room.

Anika pushed her glasses up her nose and held the remote control up triumphantly. "All sorted, as you can see!"

The nurse stuck her hands on her hips and harrumphed, while Sam stood smirking behind her.

When she and the guard left, Anika gave a sigh of relief and leaned back against her own pillows.

"Us pregnant ladies have to stick together, isn't that

right, Nora?" She looked over at the curtain, but there was only silence and stillness from that side of the room.

"Mom . . . ?" Sam started to ask.

"Let's leave her be," Anika said to me, and then she motioned us back closer to her bed.

Anika put the remote down on her bedside table, then she closed her eyes and started rubbing both hands over her belly, taking deep breaths.

"Is she okay?" Sam asked.

Anika shook her head, eyes still closed. "She gets upset when the TV is turned off, but then she cries whenever the news is on."

"How come?"

Anika opened one eye to look at the two of us, and then closed it again. "I think she wants to know what's happening over there."

"In Kosovo?" Anika nodded.

"But—the war's over, there hasn't been much on the news . . ." I started to say, and it was true. Mostly it was stories about the safe havens now, and how the refugees in Australia were coping, or—according to some people— protesting and being ungrateful, and when they should go home.

"I think that's the problem." Anika opened her eyes and reached for Sam's hand for support while she adjusted the pillows behind her back. "I think it's the not knowing that scares her the most."

We talked a while longer before we heard, "Time's up, I'm afraid!" and the nurse was back, sticking her head into the room and, I thought, smiling a little meanly at the three of us.

When she left, Anika rolled her eyes. "Okay, my darlings—until next time!"

And for the first time in ages, I watched Sam hug his mom—actually get his arms as far around her as he could, and I watched Anika squeeze her eyes shut and hug him back.

There wasn't any room for me, so I stepped away and headed to the door. I looked back at Nora's shadow behind the curtain, then Sam joined me and we walked away, the sound of the TV volume going back up and echoing behind us.

31

A PATTERN OF ROUTINE

Animals don't need maps, but they follow them anyway—even if they don't know it. They go where they need to eat and breed, chasing the seasons. And even though they don't follow any direction that's written down, they know the way—called migratory patterns—and they never change.

Humans do the same, I guess—except we call repeated movement "routine," which is what Luca, Sam, and I had over those holidays.

Pop still couldn't drive, so Sam and I continued to catch the bus to see Anika by ourselves. Pop also didn't come up to the big house as much. He said the garden path seemed to have grown longer while he was away, so he spent a lot of his time in the apartment by himself.

"Give him time, Freddo," Luca said one morning,

when Pop hadn't come up for breakfast.

"How much time?"

"As much as he needs."

Luca went to work and saw Anika whenever he got a moment during the day. I took Sam to Rosebud so often that I swore I could see the 787 bus timetable when I closed my eyes at night.

At the hospital it was always the same—Anika in bed or trying to walk the hallways, Sam getting better about hugging her tighter, and Nora's curtain always drawn, the TV a low hum in the background. I hadn't seen her in the garden for days.

During the week, Jed, Sam, and I hung out, sometimes with Aidan and Keira too. We rode our bikes to the Athenaeum Cinema on Ocean Beach Road, at Sorrento Park on Hotham Road, or at the skate park near our school.

Sometimes Keira and I would break away from the others and do our own thing together. Once upon a time we would have played with our Barbies or endless rounds of having our fortunes told with cootie catchers. But those school holidays the two of us wandered up and down the pharmacy aisles debating the better Lip Smacker flavor— Berry Jelly Donut or Candy Confetti—before going back to Keira's house, where her mom always seemed to have a fresh batch of honey joys or chocolate crackles ready for us to eat on the floor of her bedroom.

"Do you miss being an only child?" Keira asked me one cold afternoon when we'd left the boys to their brain freezes and Slurpees at the skate park. We'd already had what she called a "deep and meaningful" about what my period was like, since I'd confessed to her that mine had come months ago and she was still waiting for hers. I was both relieved and not when she changed the subject.

I shrugged and chewed the gooey honey joy still in my mouth before answering. "Sometimes," I said, and then I thought about it some more. "I have to wait a lot longer to use the bathroom in the morning now."

Keira scrunched up her nose and I laughed.

"I mean, there's just a lot less space and a lot more people."

She nodded like she understood. "But it's kinda like you've got this *instant* family now, right? Must be so bizarre for you!"

I opened my mouth, about to say that Pop, Luca, and I were *always* a family, and Anika, Sam, and Drumlin just made us a bigger one. But instead I popped another honey joy in my mouth so I wouldn't have to answer her.

Keira was an only child—the only other only child in our year, and it was the thing we bonded over when we first became sometimes-friends.

"Do you ever think that Luca and your mom would have had a bunch of kids, if your . . ." Her cheeks flushed.

"You *totally* don't have to answer that! I just meant it's weird to think how much everything has changed for you, you know?"

I nodded, but I also knew that she meant how much things had changed between us, too, and how we weren't the same anymore.

And then I suggested we pull out our old cootie catchers and spend the rest of the day trying to see what would come next, just by choosing the right combination of colors and numbers and following the old familiar patterns.

32

WHALES IN THE ATRIUM

Nora was sitting in the atrium garden for the first time in a while when Sam and I visited after school. Out from behind the curtain and in the open air again.

"You go," I said to Sam, and I stopped at the door to the atrium. "I'll be there in a minute."

Sam looked at me and tried to raise an eyebrow, but he was no Mr. Khouri.

She watched me as I walked in. There were a few other people in the garden that day. Another pregnant woman wearing the same green bracelet as Anika and Nora, for Green Wing, and visitors in regular clothes, who were pointing up to the ceiling and admiring the hanging plants.

Nora had her usual long white gown on, plus the same style of slippers that Anika wore. Her hair was braided again, and today she was wearing an old, battered brown corduroy jacket that was so big on her she'd had to push the sleeves halfway up her arms.

I walked to where she was sitting and she looked me up and down.

"Mirëdita!" I said, and I was proud of how good I'd got at the greeting.

She frowned and then replied quietly "Çkemi," which sounded like "she-kemay."

I motioned at the bench seat beside her, and she nodded slightly, so I dumped my bag off my shoulder and sat down. She turned a little to face me, and I tried to ask how the baby was.

I pointed at her stomach and then shrugged my shoulders like a cartoon drawing of a person wondering—hands raised as if I were carrying two dinner plates. She kept frowning at me.

I knew two words in Albanian by then—and one of them I'd only learned a few days earlier when Luca told us the story of a field trip he'd been on with the haven kids one afternoon. I shrugged again and said, "Mirëdita, balenë." I was about to try to explain that it was all I knew, when Nora's eyes narrowed.

She turned around and looked at the other pregnant lady across the way. The woman was just leaving, and when Nora turned back to me she seemed so angry, with an even deeper frown on her brow.

"Why do you call me whale?"

I felt my eyes go wide.

"Balenë," she said, "is *whale*."

A blush started at my throat and spread like a rash to my cheeks as I stammered, "I—I know! I'm sorry, I didn't mean . . ." I shook my head. "It's just the only other word I know in Albanian, and I learned it the other day, and . . ."

"Where did you learn this word? This whale?"

Her voice was deep and steady; her accent seemed to curl around the *e*'s and *r*'s beautifully. I couldn't believe she was talking to me.

"There were whales! In Port Phillip Bay the other day!" I said, and I couldn't stop my voice from rising awkwardly at the end of each sentence. "My dad—you might know him? He's a policeman who volunteers at the haven. His name is Luca? Well, he went on this ferry ride with all these other volunteers and kids from the haven to show them the whales and he said the kids kept leaning over the railing and saying 'Balenë! Balenë! Balenë!' He said they were so excited. . . ." My voice got smaller the more I talked, until finally I finished by saying, "So now I know *hello!* and *whale* in your language."

"Good morning" was all Nora said.

"Ummm. . . ." I wondered if maybe her English wasn't so good after all.

She rolled her eyes at me. "Mirëdita is *good morning*,"

she explained. "Çkemi is *hello*."

"Oh!" I could feel myself blush again. "Then I've been using that wrong."

She nodded once.

"I wanted to ask how your baby was, but I didn't know how. . . ."

At that, she opened her mouth and then closed it again, pulled her big brown jacket closed over her belly and shrugged. "Fine, thank you," she said with very proper, clipped words.

She turned away from me, and I figured she didn't want to talk. We were the last ones left in the atrium, and it suddenly felt too quiet and small, so I nodded and stood up, swinging my bag onto my shoulders.

"Thank you," Nora said.

I turned back to her.

"The other day," she said quickly, like she was bored of having to still talk about it. "Thank you—for the help."

When I just kept looking at her, she sighed. "And for the television. Thank your mother for helping me. . . ."

"Oh, she's not my mom," I said quickly.

Nora raised her brows, and I couldn't help but babble on. "She's Sam's mom. Sam? The boy who I'm normally with? He's Anika's son, but she's not my mom."

"Më fal—sorry," she said. "Do thank *Anika* for me."

"You could thank her yourself. I think she'd like to talk

to you. Does she even know you can speak English?"

Nora raised a hand. "No, I do not want to talk."

A silence stretched between us and I shrugged again. "I better go say hi to Anika," I said.

Nora nodded once, and I turned to leave. I'd only gone a few steps away when she called out, "Is good."

I turned back to see Nora had pulled her jacket open a little and was rubbing her bump with one hand. "The baby is good—but . . ." She waved her other hand, while she searched for a word. "Impatient."

"Oh yeah, so was Drumlin."

"Drumlin?"

I started walking backward. "Sam's brother," I said. "Anika's baby."

Nora frowned, and then she called out to me one last time, "Si te quajnë? What is your name?"

I stopped at the door. "Winnie," I said over my shoulder, and then I smiled to myself. "My name is Winnie."

THE MILLENNIUM BUG

Khoa Trần—Jed and Lily's dad—finally came home from Sydney in the middle of July.

He'd been away for months, working for a big company that was worried about Y2K, or the "Millennium Bug." People on the news said that all the computers in the world had problems reading four-digit years that didn't start with a *one* and would fail when the year switched from 1999 to 2000. They were predicting dramatic stuff like planes falling out of the sky on New Year's Day.

This company in Sydney was worried that they'd lose all their money, so they'd hired Jed's dad's computer business to come in and Y2K-proof their operating systems—which had taken months.

"Well, for one thing, it means I've got some computers to offload now," Khoa said to Luca one night over dinner.

Vi had taken pity again and invited us over.

"Oh yeah?" Pop swallowed the delicious pork Vi had prepared. "How many are we talking?"

Khoa leaned back in his chair and smiled so big his cheeks went round. "Ten of them. This firm wanted all new *everything*, so they threw out perfectly good tech for fear it had been corrupted by the bug."

Khoa rolled his eyes like he couldn't believe it.

"So I said if they really didn't want them, I'd be happy to take them and cover shipping costs to bring them down here—they arrive this week."

Vi dished out more pork on everyone's plates, then waved her fork in Khoa's direction. "Oi, just tell him already!"

Khoa finally spread his hands wide and said, "I thought the haven could take them, yeah? I can come by and set them up so those people can get online. . . ."

Then it was Luca's turn to sit back in his chair. "Khoa, that would be *amazing*! All they ever ask for is access to computers so they can search for their families back home. The ones at the library get booked so quickly, and the queues for them are ridiculous. . . ." Luca shook his head. "The internet cafés eat up their allowance in no time too. Setting up a free computer bank for them to use would be a *godsend*!"

Khoa nodded. "This is what I thought!"

"This is what *I* thought!" Vi said.

Khoa waved at her. "Yes, yes—it was my lovely wife's idea first!"

Jed, Sam, and I smiled at that, and even Lily only faked it when she pretended to gag as her parents kissed.

"When the haven is finished with them, we can donate them to the kids' school and the library," Khoa said, once he and Vi had pulled apart.

Luca nodded. "I'll have a talk to the Red Cross people— see if we can't get this thing set up before the week is out." He took a sip from the wine Vi had poured for him. "I'm warning you, though, Khoa, I don't know what the wiring at this place is like. If you try plugging in ten computers, it could blow their fuse box!"

Khoa waved him away. "I'll come in, I'll set up."

"Will you need help, Bố?" Jed put his fork down and sat up straighter.

Khoa looked closely at his son, deep in thought. Eventually he nodded once, then glanced at Luca. "He's good with the setting up." He clapped a hand on Jed's shoulder. "Can I bring him along, do you think?"

As soon as he'd said it, Sam and I were opening our mouths to plead to come too. Vi and Lily rolled their eyes in the exact same way, and Luca waved his hands to quiet us.

"Maybe. Let me think!"

He looked between us, and I hoped Sam was making an effort to pull the same pleading face I was.

Luca sighed. "I'll have to get permission. . . ."

"But if they say yes, we can come?"

Luca nodded.

34

THE GREATER GOOD

We went on a Thursday, after school.

We were so excited that we told Mr. Khouri during lunch. While he was eating a sandwich at his desk, we crowded around to tell him.

"Are there still graves and stuff?" Sam asked. "From the pirates and people who died there?"

I'd tried explaining what the Quarantine Station was to Sam, but from the look on Mr. Khouri's face, I hadn't done as good a job as when Luca had explained it to me.

"Your knowledge of local history is woeful, Mr. Murray—and clearly I am to blame," he sighed. "It wasn't pirates but immigrants who died there. From things like typhus, smallpox, cholera, measles, or influenza—especially after the Spanish flu pandemic."

"So, there were no pirates?" Sam asked. He sounded

a little disappointed.

"No pirates. But do you know how they used to discover that a diseased ship was coming into the bay?"

We shook our heads and Mr. Khouri put down his sandwich.

"An immigrant ship coming into Port Phillip Bay was cause for a lot of excitement back in the day. It meant new people arriving and cargo and supplies being distributed. Locals used to dot the shoreline, waving in welcome. And if the ship carried armament, the crew might set off a round of gunfire to celebrate. But the sight of a plague ship was very different. . . ." Mr. Khouri paused, and I swear we all leaned in closer to hear him. "There would be no one on deck and no gunfire. It was more like a ghost ship. A signal that things were not as they should be was the sight of the health officer rowing out from the station and then climbing onboard for an inspection."

"Then what happened?" Sam asked.

"If the ship had death and disease, they'd raise a yellow flag to signal plague and for locals to stay away and not to expect the supplies anytime soon. And then everyone onboard would be ferried from the boat to the shore. If you were found to have a disease, you went off to the isolation ward—right next to the morgue. Your bedding and luggage might be burned, boiled, or disinfected, your clothing gassed to kill any insects and disease. . . ."

"And that's where the refugees are staying?" Jed sounded like he couldn't believe it. "Where that all happened?"

Mr. Khouri nodded once in response. "It was all necessary, of course. It staved off countless more deaths, but . . . new immigrants didn't have much say in it all. It was for the greater good."

I was thinking of what Mr. Khouri had said while Luca drove Sam and me down Point Nepean Road. I wondered if it was for the greater good again, that the refugees were kept out this way.

Once we got past the town of Portsea I couldn't understand where we were heading. We were deep into the Point Nepean National Park, with thick bushland on either side of the winding road and nothing much to see for long stretches.

And then we took a turn and got to a clearing, a sign pointing the way, and a driveway leading to a hilltop.

Luca parked his car and we all got out. Sam and I stood in place and looked up at the Quarantine Station.

"Is it everything you hoped it'd be?" Luca joked, but his words weren't funny.

It was just a lot of buildings plopped down on a huge property facing toward Ticonderoga Bay, with a little cliff dropping down to the beach.

There were five two-story blocks with railings and staircases along their sides, which Luca said were the barracks. Shower and toilet blocks were way off in the distance, and then a lot of squat huts. Luca said the low houses with chimneys were administration buildings, and we had to go there to sign in.

A sour-faced man asked Luca a bunch of questions about what we'd be doing, and insisted we sign our names on a clipboard—and then Jed and Khoa came through the door, and Luca had to explain it all again.

While Jed and Khoa signed in, I tugged on Luca's arm.

"What, Freddo?" he huffed.

"Can we look around?" I whispered, and blushed when the sour-faced man seemed to narrow his eyes at me.

Luca nodded once. "But don't go far, and be back here in fifteen minutes, tops!"

Jed, Sam, and I burst through the door and ran to the middle of a great expanse of grass. The winds off the bay pummeled our cheeks, whipped my hair around my head, and made my teeth chatter.

"What is this place?" Jed asked, and then we all turned in circles to get a good look at everything.

There were refugees leaning on the railings of one of the barracks. We knew they were refugees because they were all different ages and weren't wearing the volunteer vests. They looked down at us curiously and we waved. It was too cold to be outside, and we figured that was probably why the place seemed to be deserted.

"This way?" Jed asked, and pointed to one of the two-story barracks buildings. Sam and I didn't say anything; we just followed him.

We'd only taken a few steps when Merjeme appeared. She burst through the door of one of the low buildings behind us and ran full pelt at us.

"Umm—should we be scared?" Jed whispered, and Sam laughed.

"Hello, hello, hello, hello!" she started babbling when she got to us.

"Çkemi," I said, remembering how Nora had pronounced it. Jed and Sam turned to look at me in amazement.

Merjeme clapped once. "Well done, very good!" she said, her accent thick and her voice delighted.

She took my hand and started pulling me toward another barracks building. I turned my head to see Sam and Jed shrug at me and begin to follow.

"You come, you come," Merjeme said when we got to the bottom of the staircase that ran down one side of the two-story building, leading to the balcony. And then she was racing up and the metal stairs clunked and clanged with her tread.

Jed put his hands on the railing and gave it a shake,

then gulped a little at the way it gently swayed.

"She did it okay," I said, raising my eyes to where Merjeme was now hanging over the balcony and waving to us.

So I followed her—but walking—and I heard Jed and Sam coming up after me.

When we got to the top, Merjeme took my hand again and pulled me along toward a wooden door that was ajar. She knocked, and then pushed it open.

Nobody else was inside; no Arta, their mother, or aunt either. Just two bunk beds that looked as small and comfortable as the ones at the PNP nurse's office—single beds in metal frames with mismatched duvet covers and pillows pushed to either side of the small room.

Merjeme let go of my hand and scurried up the little ladder to throw herself onto the top bunk of the bed that she must have shared with her sister.

Jed and Sam came in behind me, and we three stepped into the room and did a slow spin, until we faced the wall that Merjeme and Arta's bed was against. We could tell it was their bed because they'd tacked the wall with pictures torn from magazines: faces of pop bands and celebrities from the pages of *TV Hits*, *Smash Hits*, and *Dolly* magazine. There was a lot of Spice Girls and Joshua Jackson especially, plus a bunch of the *Home and Away* and *Heartbreak High* cast.

Merjeme flopped down on her bed while we looked at every inch of the room—from their few clothes folded neatly inside two worn suitcases that were open on the ground to the wall heater that was on but not really working considering how cold the room still was.

"Who is this boy?"

I spun around to look up at Merjeme, who was now lying on her side, her brown eyes peeking through the slats of her bunk—looking at Jed.

"Oh yeah, sorry," I said, "um—Merjeme, this is Jed; Jed, this is Merjeme."

"Mer-jeme," Jed said slowly.

"Je-ed," Merjeme copied in a deep voice, and then she giggled.

Sam went over to the ladder and climbed only to the third rung, so he was about level with Merjeme's head at the other end. He hung on to the bars up top as he spoke to her. "Jed's dad brought computers for you." He thought for a second. "Well—not just for *you*—but all of you, to use."

Merjeme sat up. It was lucky she was so short. If it had been me on the top bunk, I would have easily hit my head on the low ceiling.

She frowned. "Computers?"

Sam nodded and swung back a little, while still holding on to the top frame, until I tapped him on the shin and shook my head at him and he straightened up. "Sure—so you can try and find out what's happening back home, email people and stuff. Is your dad still there? Maybe you can look for him. . . ."

At that, Merjeme pulled her legs up and hugged them to her chest, wrapped her arms around them, and I suddenly wanted to make Sam shut up.

"Hey—where's Arta?"

She looked at me and nodded her head somewhere to the left of us. "Painting," she said. And then she must have decided that that was a better place to be, because she crawled to the end of her bunk and waved at Sam to hop off—which he did—so she could get down.

"I show you," she said, and waved us to follow.

We climbed down the staircase and across the grass toward the administration building, from where Luca and Mr. Trần were just emerging.

"Jed, come help me unload!" his dad called, and Jed jogged over to him, the two of them heading for Mr. Trần's white van.

"Come, I show you the rec room," Merjeme said, and then she reached for my hand again, and Sam's too.

The rec room was more like a big hall, with wooden floors, a raised stage down the back, and a little canteen to the side with the roller door shut. Plastic tables and chairs lined the room, as if this was also where everyone ate. But that day only one of the tables was being used, by little kids who were painting on butcher's paper, under the supervision of volunteers in Red Cross vests.

Arta was among the kids and Merjeme ran over, forgetting about us. Instead she fetched a smock from a crate under the table and pulled a chair up next to her sister.

"You must be Luca's kids."

Sam and I looked over at a little old lady in a volunteer vest who was smiling at us. She had short, white curly hair and wore gold-framed glasses.

"Uh—yeah," I said. "He's just outside—I can go get him if you like. . . ."

She waved the idea away. "Knowing Luca, he's probably busy being helpful. I'm Dorothea—one of the grandma volunteers."

I realized then that a few of the volunteers helping the little kids were very old.

"Grandma volunteers?" Sam said.

Dorothea was collecting discarded paintbrushes and dunking them in jars of clean water to rinse. "Of course—Grandparents for Refugee Children. We're a little organization of volunteers whose own grandkids are grown, so we figured we'd give our time to these kids that needed us."

We stayed there for a bit, until Luca came to fetch us.

When we stepped outside there was already a line forming around one of the huts, out the door and connecting to another one—a whole line of people in bulky jackets against the cold, all different ages lining up to get inside.

"Khoa's got two of the computers up and running already," Luca explained, "and they're already in high demand."

We stuck our heads inside to see. Khoa was adjusting a boxy computer monitor, and Jed was standing beside a boy about his age and an older man who was seated at a computer; Jed and the boy were helping him work the mouse and click on browsers.

On the drive home, Sam asked if the computers would really help the refugees connect to their families.

"I don't really know," Luca said, looking at him in the rearview mirror. "There's no way of knowing if people over there have access to computers and the internet anymore, but . . . it's gotta be worth a try, right?"

The drive along Point Nepean Road seemed longer. Through the national park, with nothing but the water of Port Phillip Bay on one side and thick bushland on the other, the whole winding way seemed to go on forever. I thought of how someone like Nora, with a baby due, would cope with being pushed out here. If something like what Anika and Drumlin went through happened to Nora while she was at the haven, I couldn't even imagine how scary that would be.

"They're so far away," I said. Luca nodded.

"That was the idea, Fred."

35

LET THEM STAY

"What's the November deadline?" I asked Luca that night.

He was sitting up at the dinner table with Pop, a calculator and our bills spread out in front of them. They both looked more tired than I'd seen them for a long time.

"Where did you hear about that?"

I leaned against the back of a chair, shrugged my shoulders. "They said it on the news just now, but they didn't really explain. . . ."

Luca nodded. "Well, the deadline is how long our government has agreed to let the refugees stay here in Australia."

"But—what if they can't go back, or don't want to?"

Luca rubbed his eyes with one hand and then gestured for me to come over. When I got close enough he wrapped an arm around my middle and gave me a half hug.

"We've been thinking about that—us volunteers—and we're putting a petition together, asking for the deadline to be extended or rejected entirely. . . ."

I tried to picture Nora returning to a house made of rubble—like the ones that had been on TV. I tried to picture her bringing a baby to a place like that, and then I wondered what little kids like Merjeme and Arta would do.

"Will it work?"

Luca shrugged. "The premiers in Tasmania and South Australia are also asking the prime minister to let them stay, so we'll see what he has to say. . . ."

Pop gathered some of the mail that was spread at the end of the table, and then he pushed a stack over to me. "Here, Fred—if you're going to sit, you're going to help. Look for any addressed to me and sort them into one pile, would you?" Luca patted my back and urged me to take a seat at the table.

We worked quietly, just the sound of rustling paper as my mind ticked over deadlines and rubble houses. I came across a heavy little booklet—all glossy and wrapped in plastic, with an illustration of a village on the front cover and Pop's name stickered on the outside.

"What's the Oliver's Hill Retirement Village?" I asked, reading the swirly title.

Pop looked up and then away quickly when he saw what I was holding. Luca frowned while he stared at the booklet.

"Jeff . . . ?" Luca started to ask, pausing his jabbing at the calculator to turn to Pop, who shrugged in response.

"Look, I don't know—you turn seventy and suddenly you're on all these nuisance mailing lists. . . ." he huffed. "Just chuck it, Fred—straight in the trash."

I turned the booklet back around. "Can't I open it?"

Pop shrugged again. "No skin off my nose."

I started flipping through the glossy pages, looking at line drawings and colorful images of triangle-roofed houses all in a row. There were no photos, just sketches and illustrations.

"I don't get it—what is this place? Is it real?"

Luca paused his calculating again to wave at me to pass him the booklet.

"Looks like it's not built yet," he said, flipping through the pages. "But they're taking offers from those who want to move in from the year 2001 onwards. . . ." Luca frowned down at what he was reading.

"But it's not an actual, real place yet on a map? That you can go and visit?" I asked again.

"Yes, it's a real place—a village, they call it," Pop said.

"But it's not a *real* village."

"It's a community, Fred—that's the point," Pop sighed.

And then he waved his hand in the air, pointing some-where behind him. "Gonna be out Frankston way."

"I thought you were just on the nuisance mailing list?" Luca said suddenly, making me look up at him and frown. "It sounds like you've studied up on this place?"

Frankston was two hours away by bus. It was the closest thing to a city that we had on the Mornington Peninsula, before heading into the real thing in Melbourne. Why would Pop want to move to a place that didn't even exist yet, but would be farther away from us than the RRC was?

"What's the point?" I started to ask, but Pop let out a sigh of frustration and snatched the open booklet right out of Luca's hands.

Luca stared at Pop in surprise. "Jeff! What is your problem?" He said it so quietly it made the skin on the back of my neck tingle.

Pop shook his head angrily, staring at the table. "It's my mail, addressed to me, and I say we're done talking about it, okay?" He shoved the booklet to the end of the table—but he didn't throw it away like he'd told me to.

"*Geez*, Jeff—if you'd just—" Luca started to say, but Pop lifted his head to give Luca one clear shake, and I thought I saw his eyes bounce to me and then away.

Luca sighed and ran a hand over his face like he could smooth his frown away. He turned to me. "Why don't you go and get ready for bed, Freddo? Jeff and I will stay up and finish all this."

I opened my mouth but Pop cut me off. "You heard your father," he said, and I pushed my chair back a little more forcefully than I needed to, then mumbled, "Good night" to the two of them.

Just as I got to my room, I heard Luca roughly whisper, "Is there anything you want to tell me?"

I stood in my doorway, waiting for Pop's reply. But instead he called, "*Good night*, Winifred!" like he knew I was waiting and listening.

When I closed my door, I couldn't hear any more, and never knew what Pop's reply was.

36

PARENTS ARE NOT ALWAYS RIGHT

It felt like we were crawling to the end of July. And, as expected, Aidan's dad forbade him to play in the Albanians vs. Australians soccer game that was coming up, and for all the reasons Aidan guessed.

The more that people around town talked about the possibility that the refugees might stay here past November, the more Mr. McMillan seemed to be stuck in his ways. He even had a letter to the editor published in the local paper, where he said: "Charity begins at home, and Australia has its own less fortunate to put first."

We all thought Aidan had given up on the game, but then Mr. Khouri asked him for his permission slip to play.

"Right here, sir," Aidan said, and he pulled the piece of paper from his backpack.

Mr. Khouri's eyebrows went up as he smiled. "We're

lucky to have you playing for Australia," he said.

We four waited until we were outside the school gates before we turned on Aidan.

"What the—? Your dad didn't sign that!" Jed said.

Aidan looked down at his feet and kicked a stone down the footpath. "No, but I did."

"You forged your dad's signature?" Keira yanked on Aidan's arm to make him stop walking.

Aidan shrugged Keira off. "Don't be ridiculous," he huffed. "I forged my mom's."

"Your dad knows what day the game is on. He just won't let you out of the house—and how do you plan on getting there anyway?" I said.

At that, Aidan looked at me and turned his bottom lip inside out in a puppy-dog pout.

"Oh, no," I said.

"Please, Fred?"

Aidan got down on his knees and Jed shook his head, like he couldn't believe what he was seeing. Sam started giggling as Aidan brought his hands up to me like he was praying.

"I will never ask you for anything else," he said. "Just let me take care of getting out of the house and then ask Luca to give me a lift with you guys? By the time we're out there, the game will be going and Dad won't be able to do anything."

"Since when has this been so important to you anyway?" Jed sneered, and I was surprised at the venom in his voice.

Aidan jumped back up to his feet, dusted off his knees, and stuck his hands back in his jacket pockets. He shrugged, but he didn't answer Jed—he spoke to me. "I dunno, just . . . When I decided that I don't agree with everything my dad says."

He started walking again, and the four of us followed.

"And I don't want it to be like my not playing is the same thing as me agreeing with him, you know?"

Something had been bothering me for a while by then, and that day it finally bubbled over—like I was a kettle on the boil.

"Is that why you still hang out with me and Sam?" I said. "Even though your parents don't like that Anika and Luca are living together and are about to have a baby?"

Sam frowned and looked from me to Aidan and back again.

"Wait, what is happening?" Keira asked, but we all ignored her.

Aidan stopped walking and so did I. I stood in front of him and could see a blush forming on his cheeks and then he finally met my eyes.

"I've never really thought about it like that," he said. "But if I listened to what my dad said, then I wouldn't have you guys as friends, and that would be so much worse. And yeah, it's the same with what he thinks about the haven and those kids. . . . He doesn't know them, but he talks about them all the time. He has *no* idea but he acts like what he thinks is right *just* because he says so!"

Aidan kicked another stone along the path, with a perfectly straight leg like he did when playing soccer. "It's weird, knowing that your parents are wrong about some stuff, you know?"

I sighed. "Okay, I'll get Luca to give you a lift."

"Fred! You don't have to—" Jed started to protest.

Before I knew what was happening, Aidan had his arms wrapped around my middle and was lifting me off the ground and spinning me around.

37

DRUMLIN'S DUE DATE

The town may have been looking forward to August 1 and the soccer match, but in our house Luca had circled August 14 in red on the calendar in the kitchen. It couldn't come soon enough for Anika.

"I am *very* ready to be out of this place!" she said one day when Luca, Sam, and I visited her in the hospital.

"I know, baby, I know," Luca said. "I'm sure Drumlin feels the same way." He stroked her belly, as though greeting him.

"If Drumlin's all healthy and nearly here, then why can't you come home for a bit before he arrives?" Sam asked.

Luca cleared his throat and Anika frowned down at her lap in a way that made my stomach flip. "What, what is it?" I asked.

"It's nothing. . . . The doctors just want to keep an eye

on things. I'm a little older having this baby and they want to make sure things are going according to plan," Anika explained.

I wanted to say that nothing seemed to be going according to plan with Drumlin, but I didn't, and not just because someone interrupted us before I had the chance.

"Knock, knock."

We turned and saw a woman standing at the door, holding two blue balloons in her hand.

"May I?" she asked, gesturing to Nora's side of the room. The curtain was drawn, and Anika told her to go ahead.

When the lady pulled back the curtain, it wasn't Nora sitting in the bed but a redheaded woman I'd never met.

I took a step back and watched as the visiting lady swooshed the curtain closed again.

"Wh-where's Nora?" I asked.

"The Albanian woman?" Anika said. "She went back to the haven—her baby isn't due until November."

"But I thought . . ." I shook my head.

"Are you okay, Freddo?" Luca asked.

I couldn't speak for a second. I was thinking about how scared Nora had been the first time I'd seen her—when she was just the lady in the atrium. And then weeks ago, when she'd cried while watching the TV. She was all alone and having a baby, and all the way out there. . . .

38

GAME DAY

Game day arrived. Sam and I were sitting at Luca's and Penny's desks, waiting for them to finish up a report so Luca could take us. He said he'd get us there in plenty of time for the Under 18s match. Jarman Oval was just a stone's throw from the Quarantine Station and had been built for the army cadets when they used the site.

"Who are you putting money on, old man?" Penny asked, as Luca picked up his bag to go change into plain clothes.

I was keeping my eye on the front doors, waiting for Aidan to come crashing through so he could casually ask Luca for a lift to the haven.

"I don't know. I've been watching the Albanian teams practice these last few weeks, and they're pretty light on their feet. . . ."

Sam was swiveling in Luca's office chair, looking at the clock on the wall to the door and back again, when Aidan came through.

"Um, hello, officers!" he said.

I rolled my eyes.

"Oh, our famous goalie! Shouldn't you be on your way to the game by now?" Penny said.

Aidan scratched at his arm, and then gave a little shrug. "I thought Mr. Khouri would give me a lift, but his car's already full with a defender, two midfielders, and some equipment, so . . ."

"Can we give him a lift?" I asked. "Please?"

Penny and Luca raised eyebrows at each other.

"Your dad is really letting you play?" Penny asked, then Aidan came to lean against her desk. His face went a little pink, but he nodded anyway. "Sure—he'd like to see me beat them."

"His mom signed the permission slip and everything," I said, and very pointedly avoided looking at where Sam was sitting, because I could feel his face going pale just looking at me.

"Do you want a ride?" Luca asked, and Aidan nodded. "Okay then—just let me get ready. I'll be back in a minute."

During the car ride Aidan babbled nervously and constantly about their team's defense and positions, but Luca was only half listening.

"Hey—you okay, Freddo? You're very quiet."

I was looking at the road we were following through the trees, driving off the map and halfway into the national park. I was wondering how quickly an ambulance could get out there if something happened to Nora.

"Is there a hospital at the haven?" I asked.

"Are you worried there might be a brawl today?" Luca asked, a little hint of sarcasm in his voice.

I shook my head. "No, just . . . what happens if people get sick out here? Is there a nurse's office?"

"Sure, there's an infirmary by the administration building."

I had my plan for the day.

When we got to the haven, Luca said there were more cars there than he'd ever seen. It looked like half the town was coming out to support the game. At the administration building we met Mr. Khouri, who was decked out in a soccer uniform and shin guards already.

"You're late, Mr. McMillan."

"You're playing, sir?" I asked, because I honestly couldn't believe it.

Luca and Mr. Khouri shook hands, and then he smiled at me. "Of course I am." He turned to Aidan. "You'd better get to the oval and start warm-ups!"

Sam tugged on my arm and pointed out Jed and Keira, who were sitting with their families, so we walked over.

Luca shook more hands and even got a few backslaps when Khoa pointed out that Anika was due any day now.

"Shame she can't be here today," Vi said.

"That's right, do you have everything you need? All the equipment that comes with babies these days?" Keira's mom asked.

Luca smiled but ran a hand over his head like he always does when he's stressed. I wanted to take his other hand and squeeze it. But before I could, he was pulling away, saying, "I might go and find the volunteers, cheer with them for a bit." I frowned after him.

Vi bumped my shoulder. "It's okay, love—those first-time father nerves seem to be kicking in."

I blinked when she said that. I knew she didn't mean anything by it, but . . . it stung a bit. The idea that Luca was about to be a "first-time" dad when he'd been mine all this time.

And then a siren was sounding, and players were moving out onto the field—the Australian side in green and yellow, the Albanians in red and black. The crowd went wild. The refugees were waving homemade paper flags around: red with what seemed to be a black double-headed eagle in the middle.

I poked Jed in the ribs. "Hey, I'm ducking off for a bit."

"What?"

"There's someone I have to see."

Jed frowned at me and I poked him again. "I'll be right back. I've just got to check on someone. . . ."

And then I was running, back to the haven.

I followed signs to the infirmary, which had a tall smoke-stack sticking out the back, because it was where the quarantine staff used to burn people's luggage and clothes if they were diseased, just like Mr. Khouri had taught us.

It was more like a house, really, made of weatherboard and painted yellow, with a wide veranda that wrapped the whole way around. The double doors were old-fashioned, with windows stuck in the frame. I peeked through and saw a front desk, but nobody around. I pushed the doors open and stepped right in, saw two corridors, and picked the one on the right to walk down.

There were a bunch of empty rooms; some of them had beds and a whole stack of boxes labeled with the Red Cross sign, but no Nora. I thought I'd try the other way, but when I got to the end of the corridor there was another door with windows in the middle. When I looked through, I saw her—down by the little cliffs overlooking the shore.

She was wearing that big brown jacket, except this time she wore tracksuit bottoms and sneakers instead of her hospital gown.

"Nora!" I called, and she turned to me, her black hair out and whipping in the wind.

She looked only a little surprised to see me.

A faint roar of the crowd carried on the wind, and the crashing of the waves in front of us, so Nora turned away from the bay and I waited until she was beside me before walking back to the infirmary.

"You are here for the football," she said, and I nodded. "How did you find me?"

I shrugged. "I didn't think you'd be a big soccer fan, and I figured you'd still need to be resting. . . ."

We got back to the building and stopped at a little two-seater swing chair on the wraparound veranda. It was a rusted thing that squeaked a bit when Nora sat down, so instead I leaned my back against the railing and looked at her.

"So, why aren't you at the hospital?"

Nora threw her hands out as though to say, *Look!*

I rolled my eyes. "I mean the *real* hospital."

Nora closed her eyes. "They say I should come back here, that the baby is still months away. . . ."

I looked behind me at the random buildings dotted all around, and the long stretches of grass that led down to those little cliffs and the beach below. I thought of the drive here, of the winding roads and bushland stretching every way through the national park—I thought of the trip from Portsea to Sorrento, and then the other twenty minutes or so it'd take to get to Rosebud and the hospital. And

I thought of the night Anika and Luca rushed off, when there was so much blood in their bed.

"What if something happens, though?" I asked. "Like before?"

"They say is all in my head," she said, gently touching her fingers to her temple. "They say my bija is okay, no problems."

"Bija?" I said. "Is that *baby*?"

Nora shook her head. "Daughter."

I smiled a little at that. "Do you have a name yet?"

She turned her face toward the wind so it pulled her hair out of her eyes. When she looked back at me I couldn't tell if her eyes were watering from the wind or something else. And I knew she would not answer, so I asked something else.

"Whose jacket is that?"

Like she couldn't help it, Nora ran a hand down the front of it and over her belly, and then pulled it tighter.

"My father's," she said.

I gulped before asking the next bit. "Where is he?"

"He is home, in Rahoveci."

"Why isn't he here? Have you tried to find him? My friend's dad brought these computers in—"

"He is dead."

I swallowed the words that were in my throat, and Nora smiled kindly at me—like she knew I hadn't meant to make her sad.

"He died a long time ago—before the bombings," she said, then looked down at the jacket and shrugged. "I did not think when we left that we might never be back. I do not know why I took this old thing. It was hanging in the . . ." She waved her hand around and I said "Closet?" and she nodded.

I wanted to ask who she left with, and was it her baby's dad? But I didn't think she would answer that either.

"Your baby—your bija—is due in November, right?"

She nodded.

I wondered if she knew about the deadline, and whether the government would let her stay here even if she hadn't had her daughter yet? Or would she be sent home with a baby to somewhere like we saw on the news. All rubble and dirt and rebuilding? But before I could even think about how I'd put those thoughts into words, Nora spoke.

"I am tired now," she said, and she reached out a hand for me to hold as I helped her to her feet.

I walked her back to her room—which at least she had all to herself, even if it was practically empty and seemed lonely.

Nora stood in her doorway and looked down at me. I thought she was going to reach out and tuck my bangs behind my ear, same as Anika would have—and I don't know why, but I so deeply hoped she would.

"It was nice to see you, Winnie," she said.

I startled a little at the name, forgetting that I had

207

given it to her to use—the one my mom called me.

"I do not think we meet again, but it was nice to know you," she said.

I frowned. I wanted to ask her what she meant, and if she even had a home to go back to—let alone someplace her baby could sleep.

But the questions must have been plastered all over my face, because before I could open my mouth, she was waving her hands at me. "Now. You go, back to your games," she said, and dismissed me.

I wandered back toward the oval, following the sound of the crowds and still thinking of Nora and her daughter, and what would happen to the two of them in the next few months as the deadline to leave approached.

I was only a few meters away from where I'd left everyone when I looked up and felt my heart sink down to my knees.

Penny was there—still in her police uniform and with an angry Mr. McMillan. He was standing in front of Penny and Luca, waving his hands around wildly.

Aidan was hanging back behind his dad and Penny, head down and his dirty cleats kicking at the ground. The game wasn't over yet—I could still hear it going on and the crowd cheering from the sidelines—and Aidan was already spattered in dirt and grass stains. Which meant his dad had pulled him out of the match, and I could only imagine how humiliating that must have been for Aidan.

I caught the end of the sentence Mr. McMillan was yelling in Luca's face, the word *kidnapping* cracking in the air like a gun going off.

"Whoa, whoa, whoa!" Penny's hands went up, trying to calm Mr. McMillan down, and at the same time Aidan's head snapped up. "Dad, no!" he said.

I felt a tug on my arm and was yanked to the side by Jed, who was standing with a nervous-looking Sam. I glanced behind us and saw that a small crowd of soccer fans had started turning their heads toward us, but that Khoa and Keira's dad were telling them to enjoy the match, nothing to see here.

But that wasn't the case.

"You carted my son all the way out here without me knowing!" He was practically spitting at Luca, his words easily heard above the crowd. "What kind of cop *are you* that you'd take my kid off without *telling us?*"

Penny stepped between the two of them, and Luca took a step back and seemed to shake himself.

"Now, hold on. Your son came into our station and when we asked him, he indicated that you were aware of where he'd be today and had given your permission," Penny said in her calm and steady voice—and then she looked behind Mr. McMillan to Aidan, who nodded once. "As far as I can tell, Luca—I *mean*, Senior Constable Ricci—was giving his daughter's friend a lift to a game he was supposed to be playing in. . . ."

It was then that Luca looked over and caught sight of me—his eyes seemed to narrow and then he shook his head again before turning away.

I felt my heart crawl even lower, right down to my feet.

"It's true, Dad," Aidan said. "I forged the permission slip, and I thought I'd be back before you got home from work, I didn't think—"

"No, you didn't think!" Mr. McMillan said, and Aidan winced at the words.

"Bill, I promise you—we had *no* idea," Luca tried, but he was waved away.

"We're leaving," Mr. McMillan said. "Now!" He turned around but Aidan held his ground.

"I want to finish the game," Aidan said, his head down and voice so low that we could hardly hear him.

Mr. McMillan reached for Aidan's upper arm, but Aidan shrugged him off.

He lifted his head and stared at his dad with his chin out. "Just let me finish the stupid game!" Mr. McMillan reached for Aidan again, rougher this time. Penny said a sharp "*Hey!*" in warning, and Mr. McMillan reluctantly let his son go.

"This isn't up for discussion," he said, through gritted teeth.

Another cheer went up, and it was so weird hearing the crowds roar with joy and smelling the scent of freshly cut grass on the cold salty air, while watching Aidan and his dad stare each other down. I could see a shine of tears come over Aidan's eyes.

Aidan didn't cry, but he did look behind his dad to Luca, opened his mouth to say something, but couldn't seem to get the words out. Luca gave him a gentle wave anyway, and then Mr. McMillan put an arm around Aidan's shoulders and physically turned him away. The two of them headed toward where the police car was parked, with Penny trudging behind.

"Luca . . ." I started to say, but then an even louder cheer went up among the crowd—someone had kicked a goal and it drowned me out.

39

YOUR OWN COMPASS

"Did you know?"

We were driving home. The Albanians had beaten the Australians 2–0 in both matches. They'd been quicker and more strategic, their crowd seemed to cheer louder, and nobody was that surprised or angry that our teams had been defeated.

And I wasn't surprised at Luca's question during the drive home.

"Winifred, *did you*?" he asked again.

The next day there'd be articles in the local paper about the game, one in English and one in Albanian. There'd be black-and-white photos, and Aidan would be in at least one—the game day pose of both teams lined up before the match, celebrating the community-led outreach.

He told me later that he'd cut the articles out and stuck them in his dresser drawer, underneath his socks and underwear. And when his dad grounded him, and said time and again how disappointed he was, Aidan would pull those articles out just to look at them and remember. He said they made him feel better.

I did not feel better during that car ride home, though. At least, not at first.

"Yes," I said. "We knew that Aidan had pretended to sign the slip from his mom."

Luca let out a long sigh.

"Aidan wanted to play, he—" I started to say.

"His dad's mean!" Sam cut in. "He wasn't going to let him play for stupid reasons, because he doesn't like those people being here, and it wasn't fair!"

Luca looked at Sam in the rearview mirror and shook his head. "You know Bill McMillan isn't the biggest fan of what's been going on here as it is," he said. He meant the haven. "This move may have cost a lot more than you think."

As we sailed past Portsea, Luca looked over at me and then back to the road. "You lied to me."

I felt my cheeks turn red. "I'm sorry."

"Your lie nearly got me into a lot of trouble," he said. "*Serious* trouble, Winifred!"

"I knew too," Sam said from the back seat, and I turned around so quickly that my seat belt locked and nearly choked me.

"Shut up!" I hissed.

Sam ignored me and kept going. "We all knew. Aidan wanted to play because he knows his dad is wrong about the people being here. He wanted to play to prove that he wasn't like him, and—"

"*Enough!*"

Sam and I both shut up.

Luca rubbed a hand over his face and then squeezed the steering wheel so tight we could hear it squeak.

"Do you know what a moral compass is?" he asked.

Sam and I were quiet.

"It's when a person knows deep down the difference between right and wrong. Even when other people tell them otherwise. Your moral compass kind of points the way that you know you need to go and what you need to do in order to head in the right direction."

Luca pulled into the driveway, cut the engine, and turned to look between Sam and me.

"Does that sound like what happened here?" he asked, and we both nodded.

Luca seemed to hold me in a stare I couldn't break away from. "Then I understand, but what you did was still reckless and foolish. You should think very carefully about how far off course you'd be willing to tread, just because you think you know what's best."

Sam and I didn't say anything. It was like we didn't need to. I can't say how exactly, but part of me thought

Luca wasn't just talking about what we'd done that day, in covering for Aidan to go against his dad.

Or maybe it just seems so to me now, because I'm further away—looking down at this memory from the map of my story, I'm so much further away from the time when this happened, but I can still see how all the little paths fit together to lead the way. . . .

40

BORN FROM DUST

We asked Mr. Khouri once why the Earth spins at all, because it's amazing that it does.

"What keeps us moving?" Jed asked.

Everyone else thought Mr. Khouri's answer seemed kind of silly, but not me.

"Because there's no restrictive force trying to slow the Earth down, it never does. In a way, the Earth rotates now because it rotated before—back when it was just a ball of interstellar dust that was spinning around in the galaxy, gradually adding more layers and becoming more solid."

And it made perfect sense to me that we can't see what keeps the world turning. And that maybe we would never know why, if one day it all just stopped.

Mr. Khouri showed us a plastic globe of the world with a segment cut out like it was an orange, showing the oozing core in the middle and the Earth's guts . . . and then on the outside it was like a regular globe with maps of countries and oceans and things.

"Fred."

I thought of Drumlin like that, ever since we first learned about what formed our planet.

"Freddo."

Like he was this little speck of dust, and then as the months went on and Anika's stomach grew, I figured it was like him getting his core and crust and mantle too.

"Winifred."

And then the day came when he was ready to be the world, I guess.

"Winifred, wake up."

I was in bed so I groaned and rolled, then blinked my eyes open to find Luca hunched over me with a hand on my shoulder.

"Wha—"

"The baby's coming," he said.

41

DRUMLIN

Me, Pop, and Sam stayed home. Luca said it could take two hours or twenty for Drumlin to arrive, so there was no point in all of us sitting on the hard plastic chairs in the waiting room.

Pop said that was fine, that he'd already had enough of hospitals to last a lifetime, but that we'd all be sitting by the phone, waiting to hear the news.

Sam lasted two hours, but after drinking the hot chocolate Pop made for us, he ended up curled on the couch, his head hanging over the armrest and his curls in every bed-head direction.

Pop had the TV on with the volume low. It was *Rage* on ABC, the music coming out soft and tinkling as a bunch of people danced on the screen to a song I didn't know.

I must have fallen asleep, too, because suddenly I was

opening my eyes to light the color of freshly spread butter coming in through the windows, and Sam's croaky voice yawning and asking, "How long has it been?"

Pop shifted his arm and shifted me, too, since my head was resting on his chest. He pulled his sleeve up and checked his watch.

"Eight hours, thereabouts."

Who knew waiting for a baby could take so long? But then I thought of Drumlin like he was the Earth again, spinning and forming and still making oceans and rainforests, and I figured it would take as long as it had to.

"When will we name him?" Sam asked.

"Oh, as soon as we meet him, I suppose," Pop said, and then he shifted to make me more comfortable. "Honestly, though, Drumlin has grown on me."

"Me too," Sam said.

"Littlest ridge," I said, and then I yawned too.

The next thing I remember was the scream of the telephone, and Pop saying, "Here we go!" as he hoisted himself to standing.

Sam and I looked on from the couch, fizzing with excitement as we listened to Pop's cheery "How many fingers and toes?" as soon as he answered the phone.

But then his face fell.

I sat up.

Pop turned his back to us and put a hand out on the

kitchen counter as though to steady himself while he spoke in a low hum.

"Luca, oh, *Luca*. . . ."

Sam stirred, raised his twisty curly head, and scooped up his glasses from the coffee table. "Is he here yet?" he asked.

My mouth felt as dry as the desert, and I couldn't get any words out as I watched the phone go back in its cradle.

Pop turned to us then. His face was gray and he was already crying.

"Pop?" I said.

He ran a hand over his head. Like he was scrubbing something away.

I got to my feet. "Pop?"

42

HE WAS STILL

was wrong.

Drumlin wasn't spinning and forming like the Earth; he was still.

Stillbirth. That's what the grown-ups called it.

He was born without a heartbeat, with the cord wrapped around his neck.

They said it was an accident. Nobody could have predicted it.

Pop couldn't drive, but Sam wanted to go see his mom.

"I know, mate. I know," Pop sighed.

Sam tried to kick at him. "I want to see her!"

Pop shook his head and tried to explain. "She's okay, she's okay—but she needs to stay in the hospital for a bit, and Luca is with her. . . ."

Sam kept kicking and then trying to hit Pop. I stood

back and put my hands over my ears; like if I couldn't hear what he was saying, then none of it was really happening.

"Come on, come on!" Pop said and tried to grab Sam's flailing limbs. Eventually his big hands got hold of Sam's shoulders, squeezed him tight, and gave him a little shake. "Sam, stop! Stop it!"

And then he was just holding him, Sam's head on Pop's shoulder, and Pop's big arms wrapped around him and both of them crying.

I stayed where I was, though, in the space between the living room and the kitchen. I couldn't go to them, there was no room for me—Drumlin was gone, and he'd been more Sam's brother than mine.

He'd been a part of Luca, Sam, and Anika.

But not me. Never me.

43

STOP THE SPINNING

We stayed home from school that Monday. Pop watched us, even though Sam barely left his room. When I went into mine that afternoon, Drumlin's crib was gone. I didn't know where Pop had put it, but my desk was still pushed up against the window to make room and I didn't put it back. I couldn't.

Anika called late in the day—I heard Pop murmuring gentle words into the phone, and then he was waving at me to go and get Sam.

"Your mom's on the phone," I said.

I watched Sam adjust his glasses, use his sleeve to wipe his nose, and shuffle out of his room to take the phone from Pop. When he had it pressed to his ear Anika started talking right away, and Sam started shaking. Pop went over and put a big hand on one of his bony shoulders as it shook from crying.

"When are you coming home?" Sam asked.

As they said their goodbyes I put my hand out, sure that either Anika or Luca would talk to me next.

But then Sam was hanging up and turning toward Pop and accepting his big arms coming around him in a hug.

I clasped my hands behind my back, leaned against the wall, and tucked my chin into my chest, not wanting to look up.

"Sam's asleep," Pop said later, when it was just him and me in the living room.

I watched him gently lower himself onto the sofa, then put his head back as he closed his eyes.

"What will they do with him?" I asked. "Drumlin, I mean."

He seemed to wince before he said, "I don't really know, Fred—I'm sure they'll take care of it, but maybe best not to think . . ."

"You know, the Earth only spins because there's nothing stopping it."

"What?"

I shrugged. "Mr. Khouri told us—he said because there's no restrictive force trying to slow the Earth down, it just never does. The Earth keeps spinning because it always has."

"I . . . I did not know that."

"What do you think it'd take to stop the spinning?"

Pop rubbed his eyes again. "I don't know, Fred, but it's getting late."

He didn't understand. And suddenly Pop looked so tired to me, sitting there rubbing his face and looking older than I'd ever seen him. Older than he'd looked when Mom died, the day I came home and found him crying.

I said I was going to bed, but I only stayed in my room until I heard the screen door slide shut and then I counted to one hundred, guessing how long it'd take Pop to go down the garden path to his apartment.

When I gently pulled my door open, our house was dark and quiet. And when I peered around the corner of the living room to the sliding door, I watched Pop's light in his apartment go out and then the backyard was dark too.

I'd put shoes on and a jacket over my pajamas, had the flashlight from the kitchen drawer in one hand, and I was just reaching to unlatch the lock on the front door when—

"Where are you going?"

I spun around and Sam was standing there, squinting at me in the dark and rubbing one of his eyes with his pajama cuff.

I opened my mouth to tell him to go back to bed, but other words came out instead: "To see Jed."

Sam held his palm out to say *wait* and then turned around and went into his room. I stayed where I was, listening to the hush of the house until Sam came back out—this time wearing his sneakers and his glasses.

"Get a jacket," I said.

We didn't talk as we went out the front door and around to Jed's side of the house, where only his bedroom was. I lifted the flashlight and clicked the button on and off four or five times as it shone right into his room. I'd seen it done in one of my favorite movies, called *Now and Then*, when these best friends wanted to reach each other in the middle of the night. I didn't know if it would work in real life until I saw Jed's face appear like a moon in his window. He rubbed his eyes a few times and then finally made a sign for us to stay where we were.

Once he'd snuck out and joined us, we walked to the corner of our street and the quiet, empty road that joined ours. Without saying anything, we took a seat on the curb and hugged our knees to our chests, with me in the middle and Jed and Sam on either side.

"Did Vi tell you?" Sam asked, and I felt Jed nod.

"I'm sorry," Jed said.

"Mom says she'll be home in a few days, she doesn't know when exactly. . . ." Sam's words drifted off. "I wonder what they'll do with him. I mean, Drumlin."

"Pop says we shouldn't think about it," I said.

Sam didn't say anything else. None of us did for a bit—until I couldn't keep what was in my head quiet anymore.

"You know how Mr. Khouri told us that the Earth spins because it does?"

I felt Jed nod again. "Because there's nothing stopping it."

"Yeah, I . . . I keep thinking about that." I turned to Sam. "And Drumlin, too—I can't stop thinking about him either."

I took a deep breath.

"I had this idea that he was this little world being made. And then something comes along that just stops everything. This force that stops the spinning."

Jed reached a hand out, and without thinking I put mine in his and he squeezed it back.

"What do you mean, Fred?" Sam said.

I tried to breathe, but it was like the words were crowded in my head and trying to push their way out of my mouth and I had to get them out or else.

"She was driving along the same road she did every day, and I didn't even say goodbye to her that morning because she was just going to work. She'd started at the council office, do you remember?"

I looked to Jed, but he just kept squeezing my hand and I kept talking.

"Pop was home but Luca was still at work, and it was

227

school break and I just wanted to go play at your house—I ran out and didn't even tell her goodbye or to have a nice day or anything. . . . And sometimes I remember waving to her from your backyard when she got into her car, but I can't really remember—do you know? Did we wave to her?"

Jed still didn't say anything, but he didn't really need to.

"She would have gone the same way she did every day, down Hotham Road and onto Point Nepean. She must have known that road so well—but then someone else was coming and maybe she just didn't see them? She braked so hard, and must have missed them because she was the only one, the only one . . ."

I'd started shaking.

"Luca was on duty but he wasn't the first one there; Penny was." And then Sam put his arm around my middle. "And she had to tell Luca, y'know? I think about how she had to do that, sometimes. And then her and Luca having to drive home to us, and Pop being there all alone because I was at your house." I turned to Jed. "Do you remember? We were pretending to be Power Rangers in your backyard?"

Jed nodded.

"And we noticed Luca's police car and came running over. We went through the back way—I remember there used to be a hole in the fence that we could squeeze through and I remember hearing Pop crying. I'd never heard him cry before."

And then I was leaning my head on Jed's shoulder and I could still feel Sam hugging me around my middle. I thought I could hear sirens, but it was just my imagination—remembering the day when Luca had come roaring up in his police car a few weeks later, because I'd climbed onto Jed's roof, wanting to get closer to Mom.

"So maybe it's me," I finally said.

And Jed kept squeezing my hand, and Sam kept hugging my middle.

"Maybe I'm like the force that stops everything, even the Earth from spinning?"

And then finally—finally—I said why.

"I didn't want Drumlin to come."

Sam's arm slid away from me.

"I didn't want you here in the first place, Sam—and then Drumlin didn't feel like anything to me," I said. "And I didn't want him here, not really. And now he won't be."

"You don't mean that," Sam whispered.

"Not now I don't. But I *did*!"

I pulled away from Jed and turned to Sam, wanted to scream to make him see and understand. But my throat wouldn't go above a whisper now—it felt like I'd scraped it raw.

"I thought those things—maybe just for a second!—but

I still thought them, and then it really happened, so what if it's me?"

"You didn't wish that he would die," Jed said.

No, I didn't wish that.

Never that.

"My dad doesn't want me either," Sam said suddenly. "And sometimes I'd think, if my mom ends up loving Drumlin more than me, because she's with Luca now—who would have me?"

He hugged his knees to his chest again, put his chin on top of them, and then kept talking.

"Maybe I thought the same thing, Fred. Does that mean I did it, that I made him die?"

"No!" I said, straightaway.

Jed nudged me, and I turned back to him. "So why would you think it was your fault?" he said. "Or anyone's?"

I shook my head.

"The world hasn't stopped spinning, Fred."

No, no it hadn't.

And I remembered something Luca had told me not too long ago—that the world doesn't really stop just because there's tragedy happening in one part of it.

"It just feels like it did," Sam finally said.

And none of us knew what to say to that. We sat there for just a little while longer, on the freezing cold curb in the middle of a world turned silver by the moon.

44

HIS BIRTHDAY

Anika and Luca came home on what was meant to be Drumlin's due date. His birthday.

Pop was sitting with us in the kitchen waiting for them to arrive when Sam spotted the calendar—and the big red circle around the date.

He jumped up and ripped that page off in one go, the tearing so loud it made me jump. Then he jammed it deep into the garbage and sat down again.

When we heard the front door unlock we all stood up—and then didn't know what to do. We waited while Anika came slowly in, with Luca following after.

She was still round; that was the weird thing. I thought she'd be like a deflated balloon, but she still had the big bump where Drumlin had been.

Pop was the first to move.

He took his cane and limped right up to Anika, so much taller than her that he had to bend a little to plant a quick kiss on her forehead. "All right, love?" he said, and she reached up to lay her hand flat on his chest for a second, then nodded and stepped away from him.

"I think I'm going to go lie down," she said, and then she turned to head to their bedroom.

Luca reached a hand out to help her, but she waved him away.

It was mostly Sam, Pop, and me in the days and week afterward—doing our homework, eating dinner together, and then most evenings watching TV. Anika stayed in her room that first week she came home, and Luca went back to work, and Sam and I went back to school.

It felt like we were living in a house with ghosts—hearing Anika moving around in her room but hardly ever coming out. The sounds of Luca leaving late at night for the graveyard shift and coming home too early in the morning. The two of them in their room whispering; and then sometimes the sound of Anika crying.

"This can't go on," Pop said one evening, when he didn't know I was listening. "The two of you need to speak to someone—privately and together. For the sake of Sam and Fred, you can't stay this way."

I was in my room, where I'd been reading under the covers with Luca's flashlight. I hadn't been able to sleep lately. I'd listen to the sounds of Luca leaving for work in the middle of the night and toss and turn until I heard his car cutting out and the door slamming, keys jingling in the lock and then his heavy footsteps coming into the house. Once I knew he was back it was like I could breathe properly again.

But that night I'd also heard the back door slide open, Pop's voice whispering, and Luca's footsteps stopping. Then I'd snuck out of bed and opened my door a crack, had seen them both in the kitchen—Pop leaning against the counter and Luca sitting on one of the breakfast stools, with his head in his hands.

"Believe me, if anyone knows what you're going through . . ." Pop started to say.

"No offense, Jeff—but you have *no idea* what it's like to keep losing family before you can even get started."

I had to cover my mouth with both my hands when Luca said that, to stop from crying out—and then I had to squeeze my eyes tight against the tears when I heard a cry rip out of Luca's throat, a cry he couldn't keep in.

And then Pop was pushing off from the counter, laying a hand on Luca's shoulder and squeezing it. "Take it from someone who's been to hell and back more than once: talking lightens the load—not by much, but enough so you can at least breathe again." And then he just held Luca a little bit longer, his heaving shoulders making Pop's hand move up and down.

45

SUGAR THIEVES

I can hardly remember that last week of August. And trying to is like catching a dream after you've just woken up,
when you can already feel it slipping away.

One day stands out, though, because it's when Sam and
I saw the sugar thieves for the first time.

It was the weekend, and Pop had given us money to
bike down to the shops on Ocean Beach Road and buy
some bread and milk. He still wasn't driving, Anika had
stayed in bed, and Luca was working odd hours. He hadn't
been back to the haven since Drumlin.

Sam and I were putting the groceries in our baskets
and were about to snap our helmets back on when we saw
Merjeme and Arta on the other side of the street.

I elbowed Sam, and we both stood there and stared as
the two of them were joined by a few more haven kids.

"What are they doing?" Sam asked.

Merjeme, Arta, and their friends had stopped right beside Mr. McMillan's Pram Stop café, all of them on rented bicycles from Mac's. As we watched them, Merjeme and a boy about her age hopped off their bikes while two of their friends kept hold of them and waited.

Merjeme and the boy crept toward the Pram Stop and then ducked into a crab walk once they got to the big front windows, so nobody inside could see them.

It was a cool August day, with the sky a constant gray and looking like it might break into rain clouds at any minute. Mr. McMillan had set up his steel outdoor furniture, but all his customers were sitting indoors just to be safe.

As we watched, Merjeme and her friend crab-walked past the windows—the boy went to the glass front door and peered in, then he waved at Merjeme.

We watched her creep toward the tables, until—

"Is that allowed?" Sam said.

"I guess it's not technically stealing, if they're free?" I replied.

Merjeme reached a hand up to the little canister in the middle of the first table. It was filled with thin blue packets of sugar. She grabbed hold of it, then hid under the table as she emptied the canister into her hand. She did this to every table, until by the end she had a fistful of sugar packets and each café table had empty canisters placed back.

Then we watched Merjeme and the boy crab-walk back to their friends, who seemed to be fizzing with excitement as they waved at them to hurry back on their bikes.

Merjeme dumped her sugar into the basket on the front of her bike, and it was only as she took hold of the handlebars that she thought to look around—and then she saw us, the only people on Main Street to have seen them.

When she threw her arm in the air and waved at us, Sam and I could only give a little wave back, probably with both our mouths hanging open. And then she was on her bike and all five of them were turning around and racing up Ocean Beach Road, their long hair whipping and tangling behind them in the wind.

"Let's follow them," I said.

"Jeff said to come straight home from the shops. . . ."

I kicked my kickstand back and got on my bike, and then looked at Sam over my shoulder. "What's waiting for us at home?"

Sam's face told me he knew exactly what there was—Anika in her room crying, and Pop getting tired from limping around the house trying to do all the grown-up chores by himself while Luca was off at work and not back until late again.

With the click of Sam's helmet, we headed off.

* * *

They rode away from the main beach that faced Port Phillip Bay and down Ocean Beach Road to the other side of the peninsula strip and the beaches on the Bass Strait side.

I don't know if they knew we were following behind or just didn't care—but they had little Arta with them and another younger girl, so they weren't pedaling fast enough to outpace us.

After ten minutes or so, we reached Sorrento Back Beach. In summer it's so popular with locals and tourists that you can hardly fit your towel on the sand.

Merjeme and her friends stopped. As we watched, Merjeme dipped into her bike basket and passed a sugar packet to each of them. They tore them open, tipped their heads back, and trickled the sugar into their mouths.

The group let out a burst of giggles, and Sam and I smiled too. Once the sugar rush hit, Merjeme turned around to look straight at us, and her friends followed her gaze.

"This way!" she yelled, and then she scooped the air with her arm—inviting us along as they all kicked off and pedaled again.

Sam and I looked at each other. It had been ten a.m. when we'd left to get the groceries, and we were meant to come straight back. . . .

"Hello!" one of Merjeme's riders yelled as they raced away.

"Hello! Hello! Hello!" Arta and the others echoed.

I shrugged. "Don't you want to see where they go?"

Sam nodded, and so we followed.

"But it's too cold to swim," Sam said as we pedaled past Coppins Lookout.

We were headed away from the popular Sorrento Back Beach and onto the dirt track that ran alongside the coast. Down that way wasn't as popular with tourists, so there was no easy access for cars—only bike paths and walking trails.

We bumped along the uneven ground, keeping the five haven kids in our sights. They stopped by a long stretch of wooden railing, got off, and leaned their bikes there. Then Merjeme scooped the rest of the sugar from her basket and led the way down a long wooden staircase to the beach below.

"It *is* too cold, right?" Sam said again as we skidded our bikes to a stop right by theirs.

"They shouldn't—it's not patrolled until December," I said. "But besides—it'll be low tide now anyway."

Sam and I hung our helmets on our bikes' handlebars and raced to the top of the staircase.

"What is that?" Sam sounded just a little amazed.

"*That* is the Sphinx Rock," I said.

The Sphinx Rock is exactly like it sounds—a rock

formation jutting out low from the coastal cliffs that looks just like Egypt's Great Sphinx of Giza. It has paws outstretched and a face with a slightly broken nose pointing toward Bass Strait. It's separated from the shore by those jutting cliffs, and a little out of the way, but it's a good place to go exploring, which is what Merjeme and her friends did that day.

All along the beach are beautiful limestone arches and stone walkways, formed by old cliffs that have fallen into the ocean. At low tide you can walk all around them and peer into the rock pools to see the shallow worlds the ocean traps there by day.

But when king tides hit, it all gets washed away—the whole place goes back underwater and even the Sphinx Rock is drowned.

"It's nicer in summer," I said, just as a gust of wind slapped us in the face. I lifted the hood on my sweatshirt to cover my head. "We'll all come down here and hang out."

Sam turned to me and gave a little lopsided smile. "Even me?"

"Course," I said.

He looked back down to where Merjeme, Arta, and their friends were darting around the rock pools and throwing their heads back to pour sugar down their mouths.

"Do you want to go down?" he said.

I remembered what Mr. Khouri had said about the

haven kids thinking this place was paradise. I could see how where we lived must have seemed so magical and perfect to them, compared to the conflict and destruction in their country. But right then, even though this place was like paradise, Sam and I weren't really in the mood for exploring or playing.

"Nah, let's leave them," I said. We watched for a few more seconds as two of the boys balanced on slippery rocks to make their way to a wide tide pool that was probably full of starfish. Merjeme and Arta looked up at us, but we pointed behind us to explain that we had to get going.

"Mom would like it here," Sam said suddenly. "Next time we come back, we'll bring her—yeah?"

"Yeah," I said. "We'll bring Anika—Pop and Luca too."

My nose and cheeks were starting to tingle from all the salt and wind. As I sniffed and brought my sleeve up to rub my nose, Sam said something I couldn't quite hear. I had to turn and ask him to say it again.

"I said, it wasn't too bad today, for my birthday."

I stared at him, my mouth hanging open. "What do you mean, *your birthday?*"

"Today is," he said, and shrugged. "Twenty-ninth of August."

I thought back to the night before and this morning—to Anika staying in her room, and Pop doing chores and

Luca at work and Sam not saying a single thing. Not one word about today being his birthday.

What just-turned-eleven kid does that? What kid can hold it in and not make a week-long event out of their birthday?

And then I had another sinking feeling.

"Did . . . did your dad ring you yet? Is he coming down?"

Sam adjusted his glasses and brought his sleeve up to wipe his red nose. "Nah, Mom would have had to remind him. He's bad with stuff like that. . . ."

Sam didn't need to say any more. We both knew why Sam's birthday had slipped Anika's mind.

I looked at the haven kids jumping over the rock pools down below, and then back to Sam. "We could go down if you wanted to hang out for a bit . . . ?"

But Sam shook his head. "It's okay, let's just ride back." He put one foot on a pedal, ready to kick off, and then looked over his shoulder at me. "But, Fred?"

"Yeah?"

"Don't say anything to my mom about forgetting—okay?"

I nodded.

"It's just a silly birthday."

I winced when he said that but followed after him when he pushed off the ground and started pedaling.

I didn't say anything when we got home either. Anika was still in her room, Pop in his apartment, and Luca not yet back from work. Nobody asked us where we'd been, because they didn't even know we'd been gone.

And nobody wished Sam a happy birthday. Not once, not all day.

So I knocked on his door that night.

"Yeah?"

I went inside and closed it behind me, keeping my hands behind my back. He was lying on his stomach in bed, playing on his Game Boy Pocket.

"Pretty crap birthday, huh?" I said.

He sat up and shrugged. "At least it's nearly over now."

Just as Sam predicted, his dad hadn't called either, so I could see why he'd rather just forget the whole thing.

"Well, before it is over, I just wanted to give you this. . . ." I pulled my hands out from behind my back and thrust the parcel at him. It was covered in newspaper, the closest thing to wrapping paper I could find around the house.

Sam got up off his bed to take the parcel from me. I hadn't even used sticky tape, so I watched as Sam unfolded the newspaper to reveal the two books within.

He read from the covers: "*A Series of Unfortunate Events: The Bad Beginning,* Book the First and *A Series of Unfortunate Events: The Reptile Room,* Book the Second. . . ." Then he turned the books over and over again, looking at the covers with mysterious drawn-figures and ornate borders. Even the author's name was strange and otherworldly: Lemony Snicket.

"They're brand-new, promise! I got the first one ages ago but never read it, and the bookstore had the second one in when Pop took me there a few weeks ago. . . ." I bit my bottom lip, watching Sam turn the books over again and trace the lettering of the name with his fingertip. I worried that he'd think it was silly or maybe he'd get even more upset that I was gifting him books I'd bought for myself and was passing off to him. . . .

"Look inside!" I said, and then instantly regretted it, in case he wasn't the type of person to write in books.

"'To Sam,'" he read, "'Happy eleventh birthday, Love Fred—1999.'"

I also blushed when he read the "love" bit, but I wrote it in the first one without really thinking and then just did the same for the second book too.

"See? They're properly yours! And because my pop has this idea that books should look loved and have, like, marks in them to remind you of when you first read them. Does that make sense? He always writes that in the top corner of the books he gives me for birthdays and Christmas and it always makes me happy to remember how they came to me, and to see his writing when I open them again. . . ."

"Fred?"

I took a deep breath. "Yeah?"

"Thank you."

"You're welcome, Sam," I said. "Happy birthday."

46

HAIR LIKE HERS

Not much had changed by September, except that Anika had started coming out of her room. Her stomach wasn't a round reminder either, but that might have been because she only ever picked at her food.

The strangest thing was that nobody said Drumlin's name anymore. Not Pop or Luca, and Anika didn't say much of anything anymore. It was only when Sam and I were talking in private that we mentioned the Littlest Ridge. His brother.

It reminded me of being Winnie—Mom's name for me that nobody else used, and how I'd started missing that part of myself. Until recently, when I'd given it to Nora.

"You have hair just like your mother's," Vi said one day in late September when I went to her shop for a haircut.

She gathered my hair and twirled it atop my head, the

246

way Mom had worn it on her wedding day.

"Really?" I said, a little shyly.

I saw her nod her head in the mirror. She'd told me a couple of days ago to stop by after school because I needed to get my bangs out of my eyes.

She bent down and rested her chin on my shoulder, looking at me in the mirror. "Just like Maria," she said. "More and more each day."

I loved when Vi cut my hair. She'd been doing it all my life and my favorite part was at the end when it was straight and brushed and she'd run her hands through it like it was water.

"What do you think, boys?" she asked, and spun me around in the chair to face Sam and Jed, who were waiting on the couch for their turn.

Sam barely looked up from his Game Boy Pocket. But Jed's cheeks went red and he mumbled that it looked all right. Vi signaled at him, so Jed jumped up to sweep my hair away, ducking his head until his cheeks went back to normal.

Then Sam got his hair trimmed so we could see his eyes again, and Vi kept scrunching his curls until they bounced. "I love this hair, Sam the man!" she said.

Jed came back and sat next to me on the couch. He nudged my shoulder and offered me a turn on the Game Boy Pocket, but I shook my head.

"I wish more of the haven kids would let me play with their hair," Vi said. "So many of them have hair just like yours, Sam, so lovely and curly. . . ." And then she snipped one or two on Sam's head, pulled them straight, and let them bounce back up.

"Mẹ is volunteering at the haven," Jed said. "She's been going there with another hairdresser to give free cuts."

I sat up a little straighter. "Since when?"

Vi caught my eye in the mirror as she turned Sam this way and that, looking at his head from different angles. "Just the last couple of weeks . . ."

"Can I come the next time you go out?" I asked, and Vi's face changed as she shook her head.

"I don't think that's a good idea," she said. "It's very bad there now."

"What do you mean?" Sam caught Vi's eye in the mirror, but she busied herself choosing a different pair of scissors.

Jed piped up. "You didn't say anything, Mẹ—I thought you liked cutting the kids' hair?"

Vi came back to Sam and ran her fingers through his hair. "I do it for those poor kids," she said, sighing, "but it's very bad there now. The little girls want their hair all cut off—"

"What! Why?" I snapped.

"Sometimes they come to us or their mommies bring

them in." Vi placed her hands on Sam's shoulders, and we watched her in the mirror but she seemed far away. "They ask us to cut their hair short so the girls look like boys, for when they go home."

"Why would they do that?" Jed asked.

"To protect them, of course." Vi turned around and frowned at Jed, then reached for his hand and squeezed it. "War ends, but bad things still happen—you kids are so lucky living here, you've never had to know. . . ." Then she shook her head again and let go of Jed's hand. "Now, Văn, help me clean up!"

But Vi's words had made the hair on the back of my neck stand up.

47

THE ANNOUNCEMENTS

That night over dinner, Sam brought up what Vi had said.
"She's been volunteering at the haven, cutting kids' hair," he started, "but the way she talked, it sounded so different from the last time we were there."

Luca wasn't working that night, and Anika had joined us for the first time in days, although she only picked at the gnocchi that Pop had made.

"She's going there again tomorrow," I cut in. "I thought maybe we'd ask if she'd take us with her."

"No," Luca said, quick and hard.

I blinked at him.

"But why not? You let me and Sam go before."

"Because I'm saying no now."

Sam and I looked at each other, and I tried again. "But I want to see. . . ."

Pop started to say, "Fred, leave it—" but Luca cut him off before he could finish.

"You don't want to see!" he snapped, and even Anika jumped a bit at the crack of his words.

There was silence around the dinner table, except for the sound of Luca's fork scraping the bottom of his bowl. He shook his head. "We're in September now, and the November deadline is fast approaching. The haven is . . . different."

"What do you mean, *different*?" Pop asked.

I frowned and added, "Plus you said people were talking about changing the deadline, letting them stay longer—"

"It's not happening," Luca snapped. "And we've been getting reports at the station of the haven kids acting out—skipping class and taking off during the day to who knows where."

"Why would they do that?" Sam asked quietly.

Luca scraped his chair back and took his empty bowl to the sink.

"Luca. . . ." Anika's voice was soft and a little croaky, and I realized that she hadn't spoken to us in such a long time. "What do the kids say when you speak to them? What do their parents think?"

He kept his back to us, and it was only when Anika said his name again that he turned around, drying his hands on a tea towel.

"I've stopped volunteering there."

"What? Since when?" And then she took a deep breath, and her eyes went a little glassy as she asked, "Not because of Drumlin . . . ?"

It was the first time I'd heard her say his name, since.

Luca winced. "No, no," he said. "I stopped when they started the announcements."

He took a deep breath as we all stared at him.

"They have these speakers all around the haven to make announcements. They've been broadcasting this message. . . ." He threw the tea towel behind him, crossed his arms, and continued. "Every hour during the day, they play this recorded message in Albanian—a voice telling them it's safe to go home. Saying peace has been restored, Australia can't help them anymore, and encouraging them to come forward and sign consent forms allowing our government to send them back."

"Geez," Pop whispered.

"Some of the elderly didn't really know what was happening, they just blindly followed the instructions. Went to the front office and signed a bunch of papers and were shipped home within days. They didn't know. Didn't have a clue what it really meant, what they were signing away."

My heart was lodged in my throat, and I could taste it like metal. I wondered if Nora had signed those papers—if she'd already been sent home to a house of rubble and a

252

country torn apart. And what that meant for her baby.

"Why . . . why would our government do that to them?" I asked.

"They want them gone," Luca said.

"They play that message every day?" Anika asked, and Luca nodded.

"Like clockwork. In the rec rooms and dining area, the computer lab we set up and their dorm rooms. Every hour, on the hour. And the kids hear it"—at the word *kids*, Luca's voice seemed to crack—"telling them to go home, that we can't help them anymore. Meanwhile, their parents are scared out of their minds—hearing stories from home that soldiers are still all around, and entire cities have been bombed out. . . ."

"That's why you don't want to go back there anymore?" Pop asked, and Luca nodded.

"How can you do that?" I whispered.

Luca rubbed a hand over his face. "I gave my time there and now it's all wrapping up, there's nothing to be done."

"It's meant to be a haven!" I said. "That's a port in the storm, a place to stay that's safe—and they're making them go away."

"Those who have a reason to stay, will," Luca said, and then he raised his hand before I could speak again. "I am sorry that you feel that way, Winifred—but there's nothing we can do. Trust me, we tried."

I shook my head.

"Anika," I said, and she looked at me with sad eyes. "You said that we have two hands—one to help ourselves and one to help others. So why can't we—"

"Stop!" Luca snapped, louder than I think he meant to. He rubbed his face again.

"In case you haven't noticed, we can *barely* help ourselves right now."

My eyes began to water, and Sam fidgeted nervously in his seat next to me.

"There is just too much tragedy and awfulness in this world, Winifred—and some of it is just *too big* to bear if we don't have to."

He came to me then, cupped the back of my head with one of his big hands, and bent down to kiss my forehead. When his hand fell away, he said, "We're done here."

48

CHANGING THE LANDSCAPE

Keira stopped hanging out with us by October and around the time that I discovered Nora hadn't been sent home yet, and Mr. Khouri appeared in the local paper.

We were sitting at our usual spot on the rocks. Ever since Sam and I told our friends what Luca had said about the announcements, we'd been scouring the paper for news of the haven.

That day, the paper said NATO had dropped a bunch of cluster bombs months ago, and that thousands of the tiny bombs were lying undetonated. They could go off and kill people if they were disturbed. At the safe haven, refugees were being taught how to detect and avoid the bombs for when they eventually went home.

"Little kids are learning how to find bombs?" Aidan asked, horrified.

Jed nodded. "My dad says it's wrong that they're teaching them to avoid bombs instead of keeping them here, where it's safe, until the bombs are all gone."

Jed turned the page and his eyes widened. There was a photo of Mr. Khouri standing at the gated entrance to the haven; he was staring at the camera, his arms crossed and a serious expression on his face.

"'Ferman Khouri, a volunteer teacher from the haven, speaks out,'" Jed read, and we all leaned in. "'These last few weeks the children have been exhausted, distracted, and prone to violent outbursts or crying fits. The adults are distressed and the children can feel a shift in their mood and spirits. Some children wander aimlessly around the school buildings or else disappear during the day completely. . . .'"

We were all quiet for a bit, and then Jed continued.

"'Nora Ramusa works as an English teacher back home in Rahoveci,'" Jed started, and I sucked in a breath. "'She has been working with Ferman Khouri as his teacher's aide and translator. . . .'"

"What else does it say?" I blurted, feeling like I would jump out of my skin if Jed didn't hurry up and finish reading.

"'Ms. Ramusa expressed her deep sadness that in her opinion the refugee children have been unfairly used in political games. She says their world had been turned upside down and they were just starting to find their feet again, but any good work is now being undone.'"

"Nothing else?" I asked, wondering if they'd mention that she was pregnant and unsure if she'd be sent home too.

Jed shook his head.

By that same week, Keira had stopped sitting at our table in class, and Sam took her spot instead. Pretty soon she'd also stopped hanging at the rocks with us during lunchtime too. And I knew that we'd probably never again eat chocolate crackles on her bedroom floor or stick cootie catchers under each other's noses to predict our fates.

It wasn't just because we probably wouldn't go to the same high school next year. We were already in a composite classroom because there weren't enough students to make up single grades, so our sixth grade had to be smooshed together with our fifth grade. Sorrento was so small that they made us older kids travel a couple towns over to attend one of the bigger high schools. And there we'd stay for seventh to twelfth and all that next phase of our school lives. No wonder it felt like this chasm between us was slowly turning into a gorge. She'd moved on to a new group. I wasn't mad, but I still felt sad. I knew it was probably because of Sam and me, and how upset we'd been. If moving on to a new group of friends meant I wouldn't have to think of Drumlin ever again, or worry about Nora learning how to find bombs, then I'd move on too.

But I couldn't. That wasn't a choice for me.

And then something happened in the first week of October that would change everything—those contour lines spreading out and rippling, changing the landscape again, and this time maybe forever.

49

A HIDING PLACE

Merjeme, Arta, and their friends had started stealing more. Not just the sugar packets, but anything left out on restaurant and café tables—napkins, cutlery, salt and pepper shakers too.

Aidan told us that Mr. McMillan had even called the police to report them and told the local paper.

Sam and I hadn't told Luca what we knew about seeing Merjeme and other haven kids stealing that time, so he wasn't sure who from the haven was guilty until one weekend when me, Jed, Aidan, and Sam had spent the morning and afternoon at the Sorrento Back Beach.

Spring had come, and the warmer weather brought tourists every weekend. And on that particular weekend it was warm enough to take Sam down to the Back Beach. We chucked our towels on the sand and dared each other to sprint into the still-chilly water and back.

I figured being at the beach was better than being at our house. Anika was out of her room more often by then, but still not herself. Luca was at work as usual, and Pop just wanted to stay in his apartment and read.

That afternoon we were riding back up Ocean Beach Road and to the center of town. We'd shoved our towels into our baskets and flip-flops into our backpacks, because it was easier to ride our bikes barefoot, even if the metal pedals stung for a bit after being in the sun so long.

"Would you rather eat toe jam or drink garbage juice?" Aidan asked.

"Depends," Jed said. "Toe jam if it's only a day old, but garbage juice if it's been sitting there a week."

Sam laughed but I pretended to gag. "You're disgusting," I said.

But really it was nice that we'd gone back to normal, for a bit.

Jed shrugged and weaved his bike between me and Sam. "Nah, it makes sense—toe jam after a day wouldn't be too bad, and garbage juice sitting there for a week would start to go all hard, so you couldn't drink it anyway."

"You're so gross!" I said, then I lifted my butt off the seat to get my legs to pump harder. "And you've already got garbage juice for brains, so you may as well drink more of it!"

We were coming up to the bend in Ocean Beach Road,

and I meant to race off ahead of them, let the wind rush by and cool my hot face down a bit. But then three bikes came around the corner, going so fast down the little slope that Aidan had to swerve to avoid being hit by one of them.

"What do you think you're doing?" Aidan yelled.

When I saw and heard the three bike riders squealing to a stop, I was off my own bike in a second, letting it crash to the ground as I stormed up to the three of them. I repeated something I'd heard Luca say often, after he'd had a day working the speed camera: "You're a menace on the road!" And then I heard Sam, Jed, and Aidan let their bikes go, too, to come stand behind me.

"Sorry, sorry, sorry!" one of the bike menaces said, planting feet on either side of his bike to keep balance. Except when he spoke he was all out of breath and it came out more like "sorry!"—huff—"sorry!"—huff—"sorry!"

I didn't recognize the two boys or girl, who all looked older than us—more like teenagers, and definitely out-of-towners. They were riding fancy mountain bikes, the kind with gearshift dials on the handlebars, and wearing these slick silver helmets that made their heads look like they were in constant whooshing motion, even when they were still.

"What's the hurry anyway?" Aidan asked.

"There's this kid," said one of the boys. "He's stuck on some rock."

"And he's about to drown!" the girl chimed in excitedly.

The first menace had regained his breath and put one foot back on a pedal. "We were just coming out of the movies and this woman in a car pulls up next to us, asks if we know where the ambulance station is—"

"—because there's this kid stuck on a rock, and the tide is coming in!" the girl interrupted again.

"What? Did you tell them where the station is? What about the police?" I hurried over to my bike and picked it up, ignoring the little pebbles pressing painfully into my feet and ready to pedal like mad into town.

"No need—someone walking by told her the directions," the girl said, "and the police probably already know, since they were looking for him."

"What do you mean?" Jed said.

The girl huffed. "It's one of those haven kids who've been stealing things—this guy from the café found him and chased him away, but he got on his bike just as the police pulled up."

I saw Aidan's hands tighten on his handlebars as they said that.

"And apparently he thought he could hide out at the beach," the first bike menace added.

Sam and I looked at each other. I could feel the flush draining out of my cheeks just as I watched Sam's face turn white too.

Jed piped up. "So you're going off to do what? See if

some kid will die?"

The second boy tried to sneer, but it didn't look so tough since he had so much sweat collected on his upper lip. "Whatever kills time in this town."

Even his two friends looked a little sick at that.

"Do you even know where you're going? What rock is he on?" Aidan asked. Then he put a sneer on his lip that would make even Lily Trần proud. "There are a lot of rocks around here, you might want to be more specific."

The girl shrugged. "The one that looks like a cat or a . . ."

"The Sphinx Rock?" I said, and all three of them bobbed their whooshing helmet heads.

"Come or don't," the sneering second boy said. He put his foot in position back on a pedal. "But you never know—he could get rescued, and then it'll be a miracle!" And then they pushed off and started pedaling, back the way we'd come.

Sam ran over and righted his overturned bike. "It might be one of Merjeme's friends, Fred—come on!"

Aidan looked between me and Sam. "It's who?"

There wasn't time to explain, so all I said was "Someone we might know," and then I hopped on my bike.

And even without needing to turn around, I knew Jed and Aidan would be right behind us.

50

SPHINX ROCK

The steep wooden staircase leading down to the beach was crowded with gawkers when we pulled up. People were hanging over the railing and looking out toward the Sphinx. Sure enough, a little lone figure was huddled near the head; the rock was already half-submerged, but the path back to the shore was already completely underwater. The kid was hugging their knees and looking out to the gray sky and horizon.

The three menaces we'd followed had already ditched their bikes and were racing down the wooden stairs, joining a bunch of other kids.

"I don't see the lifeguards or ambulances anywhere," Jed said, removing his helmet and running his fingers through sweat-wet hair.

"There are no lifeguards around—not until December,"

I said, and felt my heartbeat kick up with the words and what they meant.

There were so many people standing around and staring, but no one was doing anything to help.

"How long do you think before he's under?" Aidan asked, a waver in his voice.

I could feel Sam shiver beside me.

"Dunno—maybe an hour?" Jed said. I leaned against his shoulder, feeling as though I might fall over from his words.

While we were watching that huddled little figure, the tide seemed to get higher still—the waves crashing against the Sphinx's hind legs.

"It's Merjeme," Sam said, and I turned to look at him.

"It is. She's cut all her hair off, but . . . it's her."

When I looked again, I knew it, too—it was Merjeme down there. She'd come to the beach she knew when she'd been caught thieving.

Aidan stepped back as though to get a better look at the problem. "I reckon if I hug the coastline, I can walk and swim to where the rock meets the cliff, then climb up and get to them. . . ." But his voice faded as he came to the same realization I had: there was no way. Aidan was just a kid himself, and the waves were crashing harder and harder.

And then a roar sounded somewhere behind us,

followed by a siren whoop, and we all turned around to see a motorbike coming down the dirt track—blue-and-white checkered pattern on the front shield, and blue light flashing on the back.

Luca!

By now some of the crowd on the staircase were making their way back to the top to see. Luca dismounted from his motorbike, pulled off his helmet, and instantly glared at me. Tourists weren't meant to be at this beach because of the king tide, and neither were we.

"We were just . . ." I started to explain as he came over.

"Later" was all he said, before his radio crackled. It sounded like Penny on the other end, saying, "ETA fifteen minutes, this road's a mess!"

Luca came to the ledge and looked over.

Aidan sidled up next to him and pointed to where the Sphinx Rock met the cliff face, in a craggy bit of low granite that was only just above the tide. "There's still sand left along the backshore. I think you can walk and swim out to the rock, then climb up and get to him."

"*Her*," I said, and Luca looked over at me. "It's Merjeme—one of the girls from the haven."

The radio on Luca's lapel crackled again, but I couldn't make out what Penny said this time, or Luca's coded reply. My heart was pounding, and I squeezed my shaking hands together.

"Where are the lifeguards? The ambulances?" I asked, once the voice on the two-way stopped.

"The ambulance nearly hit a pothole on the road in. Only my bike could get down that track easily," Luca said. "And we've had to put the call out for volunteer surf rescue since they're not on duty, but they wouldn't be able to get a boat close enough anyway—because of those rocks." And then he seemed to remember we were just kids, maybe because Sam had started to cry a little bit. "Don't worry—they're on their way."

Just then a collective gasp went up from the crowd on the staircase, and we looked over the railing to see what was happening. Merjeme—in her sopping wet tracksuit and worn-out runners—had stood up and was slowly trying to walk back toward the tail end of the Sphinx. But the rocks were so wet, and she misstepped and slammed down hard on one knee. When she stood up again her pants were torn and bright-red blood dribbled down her exposed white leg.

"*Whoa, whoa!*" the crowd started to almost chant at her when it looked like she might start walking back again toward the shore, even though that end was clearly submerged. She looked up at the staircase—at all of us—and even from that far away I could see she was crying. But either the pain in her leg or the warning chants of the crowd made her plant her butt again and not try to walk back to shore.

Luca seemed to shake himself, and as I watched, his eyes gained focus.

He quickly started stripping down until he stood in just his white T-shirt and boxers.

"You are to all stay up here, *no matter what!*" he said, looking at each of us. "Is that understood?" He looked between me and Sam, and it wasn't until we both nodded that he turned away.

He went to the top of the staircase.

"I am Senior Constable Ricci," Luca's voice boomed. "Any minors are to come off the staircase *immediately*, remain *behind* the railing up top, and leave a clear path for rescue services!" It was pretty amazing that he managed to sound like a policeman who meant business, even in just his boxers.

A murmur began up and down the staircase, until Luca bellowed, "*NOW!*" and suddenly at least a dozen of the onlookers—the three bike menaces among them—straggled up and came to stand near us. Luca walked a little farther down the stairs, and we could just see the top of his head as his voice continued to blast. "We need to get that child off the rock, and we don't have much time," he began. Sam whimpered beside me and I put an arm around his trembling shoulders as Luca continued, "Those of you who are willing and able, I am going to ask for your help—and I'm sorry, but it's going to mean we all get a little wet!"

Uneasy laughter rippled down the staircase, and a couple more people straggled up to come stand with us kids.

"We all have to work together, and you need to *trust me!*"

By the time the ambulance pulled up twenty minutes later, along with two bright-yellow surf rescue vehicles, Luca had organized his volunteers to form a human chain from the bottom of the staircase to the base of the low jutting cliff that connected to the Sphinx Rock. They were standing in water up to their waists, with their arms hooked together against the waves that continued to lap and crash around them.

As we watched, I had Jed on one side, squeezing my hand, and Sam on my other side, burrowing his face into my shoulder while Aidan gently rubbed his back in comfort.

The paramedics stayed up top while three lifeguards barreled down the stairs. We watched as they pulled themselves along the human chain—they grasped at shoulders and waists to slug through the rising tide until they got to Luca at the end of the chain. And then those lifeguards linked arms with him and each other until the last one—a young man wearing a wetsuit—managed to scramble up the craggy rocks and walk, then crawl, along the back of the Sphinx to Merjeme.

By then, Penny had arrived in the police car. A woman

sprang out of the front passenger seat and raced to the railing, and a paramedic had to hold her back from going farther. I recognized her as Merjeme and Arta's mother.

The lifeguard had Merjeme on his back and was crawling along the slippery Sphinx and connecting up with the human chain, which slowly started coiling back toward the staircase.

I could hear Merjeme's mom—her mëma—whimpering as she watched all those people pull one another along, and her little girl clinging to the rescuer's back. The waves swallowed her legs, and her arms looked so tight around the lifeguard's neck, I wondered how Merjeme wasn't choking him.

Click click click click click.

I looked around and saw a tall man close to the top of the staircase. He had one of those fancy black cameras with a long lens pointing down at the scene and was taking pictures of all those people strung out along the backshore to save Merjeme.

When the first of the human chain came up the stairs, the clicking got louder and quicker—the man took pictures of the paramedics and Penny patting people on the back and offering them foil thermal blankets.

And then a huge cheer went up and the crowd surged nearer to the top of the stairs to watch as Luca staggered up, followed by the three lifeguards, including the one with Merjeme on his back.

The photographer went into overdrive, running around as everyone clamored to pat Luca and the lifeguards on their shoulders, shake their hands, and keep clapping.

It was Luca who started bellowing again. "Get back! GET BACK! LET THEM THROUGH!" He threw his arms out, clearing the way for the paramedics.

Everyone went quiet again and started stepping away, until all we could hear was the *click click click* of the camera. We watched the paramedics rush up to Luca and the lifeguard, who were talking in low murmurs to Merjeme. She only whimpered in reply.

Eventually the paramedics eased her off the lifeguard's back, leaving a streak of glistening blood on the wetsuit where her gashed leg had been resting. We could all see she was trembling and hiccup-crying, and her short hair was a matted mess on her head. Her eyes were wide and wild as she looked around until they landed on someone who was pushing her way through the crowd—her mëma.

And all the while the *click click click* of that camera.

51

WAVES CRASHING

The photos of the rescue didn't just appear in our local paper—they were in the big national papers and on the evening news. It got to the point where I looked at them so much, I started to imagine I'd been there with Merjeme—I knew how she felt to be stranded, and to wait for Luca to come save us.

For weeks after the rescue, I dreamed of being back on Jed's roof, between the gutter and the window, wanting my mom—and in my dreams I could hear waves crashing.

On the day of the rescue, Penny had insisted on driving Luca to the hospital to be checked over, and she took Sam and me too. Pop and Anika met us there, and when Anika saw Luca sitting up in the hospital bed, her face just sort of melted.

He opened his arms and she fell into them, both of

them heaving with tears as he stroked her wild hair.

"I'm okay, I'm okay, I'm okay," he said, again and again and again.

Pop came over and squeezed my shoulder. "How about you, Fred?" I nodded, even though I wasn't sure I meant it.

Anika pulled away from Luca to cup his cheeks in her hands as she said, "I don't know what I'd do if I lost you too."

"Not gonna happen," Luca said, and then they kissed, and me, Pop, and Sam looked everywhere else but at them.

"Anika and I will get the car, bring it around," Pop said, and then he went up to Luca and laid a hand on his shoulder. I was surprised when he bent over and placed a kiss on Luca's forehead too.

Anika nudged my shoulder and said, "You stay and keep him company while we get things sorted."

And then it was just me and Luca in the room. But it also felt like it could have been just the two of us in the whole world, it felt so quiet and still.

"What are you feeling, what's in your head?" Luca said to me, and I could have cried right then.

"Come here, Fred."

When I was beside his bed Luca folded me in his arms just like he'd done to Anika. He patted circles on my back the way I thought only mothers knew.

"What if you'd died?"

Luca eased me off him and looked into my eyes. "I'm sorry I scared you."

I kept shaking.

"Fred, I'm—"

"I stopped calling you Dad."

"What?"

"I thought . . ." But then I couldn't say any more, and Luca had to rest me back on his shoulder while I shook with the words in my head.

"Tell me, Freddo, just tell me," he said.

"I thought I loved you more than her." And then I whispered who I meant. "Mom."

He must have felt my shaking, because he squeezed me just a little bit harder to him.

"You've been here for longer, and I thought she'd know that I loved you more than her, even though you're not . . ."

I couldn't say it, because that at least wasn't true—he *was* my father.

"I get so mad at her for dying, for not being here anymore, and I think she must hate me for that . . . and I thought you'd love him more than me too." Before he could ask, I added, "Drumlin."

I started to cry then, and I couldn't stop.

"That's not the way love works, Fred."

He cupped his hands around my cheeks, the way Anika had done to him, and really looked at me. "There's no more or less about it, there's only love—do you hear me?"

I nodded.

"And I don't care what you call me, because I know exactly who I am," he said, and his eyes turned glassy with his own tears. "I am your dad, the same way I was Drumlin's. The same way you are still Maria's daughter. None of that ever changes. And I promise you this: just like I'm still so proud to have been his dad, your mom still has the same pride and love for you. And so do I."

He gently ran his thumbs underneath my eyes to wipe away the tears. "They may not be here anymore, your mom and the baby, but the love for them still is. That's just how it is, Fred—and I tend to think that's probably what heaven is. . . . We go on loving them, even after they're gone."

And then I laid my head down on Luca's chest and I cried, because I knew it was true.

52

THEY JUST CAN

Days after Merjeme's rescue made the evening news, the volunteers were told to stop going to the haven.

We heard about it first on the radio, and the next day at school I waited with Sam, Jed, and Aidan outside the teachers' lounge for Mr. Khouri, to find out if it was true.

"I'm afraid it is, yes," he said, and then he walked with us to our classroom.

"I was told to go there and pack up the equipment that I'd brought." Mr. Khouri took a seat at his desk and we all crowded around. "I was also told not to speak to any of the children at all. The other teachers were instructed to do the same."

I could feel myself about to cry.

"What about Merjeme?" Sam said. "Did you see her—is she okay? The papers said she was out of the hospital."

Mr. Khouri looked at each of us, and my heart plummeted toward the ground.

"They told her mother and aunt that she was in a lot of trouble for what she'd done." I didn't think he meant to, but Mr. Khouri's eyes seemed to stay on Aidan. "Some of the shop owners said they intended to press charges, and so while she was sitting by Merjeme's bedside, the government officials had her mother sign the voluntary consent forms, allowing them to be taken home."

I must have made a sound, because Jed reached for my hand and squeezed it.

"They never came back to the haven. They were taken directly to the airport."

Sam shook his head. "How can that be allowed? How can they . . ."

"They just can, Mr. Murray."

And then he said it was nearly time for class to start, and we had to file out and wait for the bell to ring. But while Jed and Aidan went, Mr. Khouri waved at me and Sam to hang back.

"My friend and colleague Ms. Ramusa told me—"

"Nora! You spoke to Nora?" I interrupted. Mr. Khouri's eyes widened, and I felt Sam looking at me oddly too.

"How do you know Nora?" Mr. Khouri asked.

"She . . . she was sharing the same hospital room with Anika, for a little while," I explained, and I watched as

Sam's jaw dropped.

Mr. Khouri nodded slowly, like he understood. "Well, Ms. Ramusa told me that she'd been at the hospital for her checkups and saw the family there. She said that Merjeme's mother can barely speak English, let alone read it, and may not have had a clue what signing those papers meant."

I bit my lip to stop from saying the angry words that were in my head.

"She also spoke to the girl, who admitted to stealing various paraphernalia from Mr. McMillan's and other cafés, along with her friends, but . . ." Mr. Khouri paused, and rubbed at his forehead before he continued. "She said they were gathering supplies."

"Supplies?" Sam said.

Mr. Khouri nodded once. "For when they would run away from the haven."

My mouth opened in shock.

"Tell your father, Winifred, that I intend to come see him about these matters tomorrow. It's something his station should be aware of."

I couldn't say anything. I could only nod my head and wonder at what Mr. Khouri had just said, and what it all meant.

53

DETENTION CENTER

Luca hadn't been back at work since the rescue. The station said he needed rest and had to take some sick days. He was home when Sam and I got back from school, after a whole day of us thinking on what Mr. Khouri had said.

"Merjeme and Arta got sent back to Kosovo."

Luca looked up from where he was sitting on the couch, and without saying a word he opened his arms and I crawled into them.

"I know, I know," he said.

I heard a noise and looked up. Anika had come out of her room. She had Sam's face buried in her middle and her arms wrapped around him, one hand running through his curly hair.

"Dorothea called," Luca said. "She told me what happened."

"Can we do anything?"

He shook his head.

"They must have been so scared," Sam said.

I felt the couch dip as Anika and Sam sat beside us.

"What can we do to help?" she finally asked, and I felt Luca shrug.

"There's nothing we can do. They're here on temporary visas, and unless they present a compelling case for why their lives would be in danger if they went back, or the minister personally grants them leave to seek permanent asylum . . ."

I lifted myself out of Luca's arms and looked between him and Anika. "But what about Nora—she's pregnant!"

I heard Anika's sharp intake of breath, just as Luca shook his head.

"That may be enough of a medical reason to keep her here for a few months past the deadline." He sighed. "But she *will* get sent back. The baby too."

"Can't we go and visit her? Make sure she's applying and writing to the minister?" Anika asked.

Luca leaned forward and looked at each of us. "We have no way of knowing, since we can't get back in." And then he said, "You have to understand. The place is no longer a safe haven. It's a detention center now."

54

HE WAS OURS

Jed and Aidan walked ahead of Sam and me on the way home from school. Aidan had been coming over to both our houses more often since he and his dad hadn't been getting along so well. His dad didn't like the way Aidan's opinions were shaping up, but Aidan thought what he really didn't like was that they were his own opinions and not his dad's.

"Do you think we should become a republic?" Sam asked me as we crossed the road from school. The idea had been on the news a lot, and adults were going to vote on it soon. "I mean—if you *could* vote, what would you choose?"

I turned a little to look at him. "Republic, for sure."

"How come?"

I tried to raise one of my eyebrows the way Mr. Khouri would, but Sam just laughed at me. "Because I think it's silly that Australia's *all the way over here*, and England's *all the way over there*, and we hardly ever see the queen, but she still rules over us."

We walked and I talked. "And because maybe if we were completely independent, we could go back to calling things what they were meant to be."

"Like what?" Sam asked.

"Like Uluru instead of Ayers Rock, and Wonga for Arthurs Seat . . . and all the other places that got renamed just because certain people controlled all the maps around here."

"I never thought of it like that." Sam nodded and we both looked up ahead to Jed and Aidan, who were trying to trip each other by stepping one foot in front of the other's leg.

"I like how Mr. Khouri says that lines on a map can't contain people," Sam said suddenly. "And maybe people know deep down where they belong—even if they can't point to it on a bit of paper?"

I looked at him out of the corner of my eye, at his too-big backpack and his unruly curls, just like Anika's, and the glasses that were always halfway down his nose.

"Hey, Sam?"

"Yeah?"

"You know you're my brother, right?"

He nearly tripped over his own feet, and I smiled but we walked on.

"Hey, Fred?"

"Yeah?"

"You know Drumlin was too? He was both of ours. . . ."

I didn't know what to say to that, so instead I threw an arm over Sam's shoulder and squeezed him to me, fast and hard—then I stuck my leg out in front of him and tried to trip him, holding him up by his backpack strap when I nearly succeeded.

And we laughed so loud that Jed and Aidan turned around to see what we were doing, and they joined in so our laughter became a rumble—like a low growl. And then I realized the growl wasn't us, but a shuttle bus coming up Main Street.

Our laughter petered out as we saw the logo on the side of the vehicle. It was a haven bus—something we hadn't seen in weeks. Without saying a word, we all started walking slowly up the hill toward the shops. We watched as two security guards got out.

Women from the haven came out next and went straight into the supermarket, while the two men in their bright-yellow "security" vests hung back and waited for them.

"Why do they need security guards to go shopping?" Sam asked, but none of us had an answer for him—not until he and I got home, and told Luca, Pop, and Anika what we'd seen.

"Penny said other havens have been reporting runaways," Luca said, shaking his head. "They've all been told to tighten security, so I doubt it'll be long before excursions into town are stopped altogether."

"Then what?" I asked. "They'll just be locked up there until . . . ?"

"They're sent back home," Luca finished.

55

THEY COULDN'T STAY

The next day, Sam and I told Aidan and Jed the real reason Merjeme and her friends had been stealing. And the reason there were always security men with the refugees when they came into town now.

It was a sticky, warm day in early November, when everything had started to smell like summer again—of ocean salt and pine trees, the smell of my birthday.

We were heading to the rocks, where a bunch of other sixth graders were eating their lunch, including Keira.

We hadn't talked in such a long time—not since she'd started hanging out with Stacey and Katie. But when I sat down, Keira smiled over at me and I smiled back. We didn't have anything to say to each other, but it was something, at least.

Pretty soon, though, everyone went off to play an epic

game of four square, and my friends were the last ones sitting in the shade of the rocks.

"Not very good supplies for an escape plan: salt and pepper shakers and packets of sugar," Jed said after Sam and I had told them everything we knew.

"It's like when my sisters promise to run away and then only pack their Barbie dolls," Aidan said.

"What do you mean?" Sam asked.

Aidan shrugged. "Whenever Rachel and Rochelle get so angry or upset that they want to run away from home, Mom always says to let them go through the motions. They plan and pack to run away, getting all emotional; sometimes Mom even lets them get as far as the end of our street. But by then they're so exhausted, and all they really wanted to do was say they were going without actually doing it."

"But they wanted to stay," I said. "The haven kids wanted to run away so they wouldn't be sent home, so they could stay here in Australia."

We sat in silence for a little bit after that, just listening to the rolling of the ocean.

Jed broke the quiet. "My parents still miss Vietnam," he said, his head down. "They were only kids when they left, but they still talk about it like they miss it, and how none of their family really wanted to leave, but they couldn't stay."

Jed looked up and caught my eyes for a second, and

then he turned to Sam and Aidan. "Home wasn't safe any-more, but it was still their home, y'know?"

We didn't, not really—but I figured it was like when Pop said it's possible to be both happy and sad at the same time, or to take the good with the bad. "They had to leave, but they still miss what they left behind," I said, and Jed nodded.

And I was just about to learn that something could be both illegal and the right thing to do at the same time.

56

GET VERY FAR

It was close to my birthday when the escape happened.

It was another hot day, with our heads heating up underneath our helmets as Sam, Jed, and I rode our bikes to school.

Halfway to town we heard the faint sound of a siren in the distance. We didn't think anything of it until we turned onto Ocean Beach Road and the main drag of town. Jed was in front and screeched to a stop at the corner of the footpath.

"What d'ya think that's about?" he said, when Sam and I came to a stop on both sides of him.

Up ahead were two police cars and the haven shuttle bus parked haphazardly in the parking lots that ran down the middle of the main shopping strip.

"No idea," I said.

We hopped off our bikes and walked them toward the commotion. As we got closer, we could see men in security vests standing around with a bunch of Sorrento police officers, including Penny.

I waved at her, and she squinted against the harsh morning sun until she recognized me and made her way over to us.

"Hey, Fred," she said, then nodded at the boys. "Hey, kids."

"Is something wrong?" I asked.

She gave me a tight smile. "It's nothing, probably just a mix-up by the rent-a-cops."

That was what Penny called the security men who worked at the haven; Luca had said she wasn't their biggest fan.

"What kind of mix-up?" Jed asked, and Penny trained her gaze on him.

"Nothing to concern you guys with," she said. "One of the refugees they thought they accounted for yesterday may still be in town."

Sam and I glanced at each other, like we were sharing one brain and a single thought.

"Is it one of the kids, or—" Sam started to ask, but then someone called out to Penny and she waved at them before turning back to us.

"Like I said, nothing to worry about." Then she smiled

at me. "Tell your old man I said hi, and ask him if he's got around to buying himself a cape yet?"

After the rescue and all the media attention, Penny had bought Luca a Superman T-shirt and told him to start assembling the rest of the costume.

"I will," I said, and then waved as she jogged back to the other police and security guards.

"You think one of them escaped?" Sam asked as soon as Penny had gone away.

"Wouldn't matter if they did," Jed said, nodding as another patrol car pulled up. "They wouldn't get very far."

57

THE BROWN JACKET

We were in class when we heard the sirens again. This time they were loud, screaming past PNP's front gates.

Mr. Khouri told us to keep our heads down. The school day was nearly over and we were in the middle of a spelling test.

"Don't worry about what's going on out there. Think about what's happening up here." And then he tapped his head and asked us to spell the word *impressive*.

But the heat had turned my memory to mush, and the sound of that siren had scratched at my brain until I couldn't concentrate.

The bell rang, so we put our pencils down and handed our tests in to Mr. Khouri. While we packed up our chairs, everyone started doing that thing where they talk about every little part of the test until I could feel myself break out in a sweat as I tried to remember where exactly I'd put an *a* and an *o* in the middle of *memorable*.

"Stop worrying," Jed said, tugging once on my backpack strap and then again until I smiled.

Aidan and Sam were walking and talking behind us when the four of us stepped out into the beating sun and the pickup rush. The bike shed was jam-packed, and we had to hang back until other kids had gotten their bikes out first. Car horns were honking, kids were yelling, the school crossing guard was blowing his whistle, and underneath it all were the sounds of the bay across the street, where pine trees lined the Esplanade footpath.

"Are you coming back to my house?" Aidan was asking Jed.

The whistle blew again and another car honked twice to get some kid's attention. I lifted a hand to block out the sun and half listened while Sam asked about the homework Mr. Khouri had given the fifth graders.

Up ahead, something got caught in my vision. I kept my eyes trained across the way, at someone standing on the footpath in the shade of a tall pine tree, the blue of Port Phillip Bay behind her and kids walking past in groups or on their own, not even looking at her as they passed.

"You guys," I said, but so quietly they must not have heard me.

Maybe she wanted me to see, but I couldn't be sure.

"*Hey*, you guys. . . ." I said again, a little louder this time.

It was odd. Odd that she was wearing that big old brown jacket on a warm day like today, and she seemed to be hugging herself to the wide shadow cast by the pine. . . .

"Guys!" I yelled. Jed, Aidan, and Sam—even a few of the last kids left in the shed—turned to look at me and frowned.

I hefted my backpack higher on my shoulders and tugged on Jed's and Aidan's packs, pulling them with me to the side of the shed—Sam followed.

"What?" Jed said, "Fred, what is it?"

"It's Nora."

"You don't know it's her they're looking for," Jed said, as the four of us peered around the bike shed to where she was standing across the street.

Sam and I both gave him a look, and Jed nodded a little reluctantly. "But it probably is," he agreed.

"What are we going to do?" Aidan asked, once we'd pulled our heads back. We'd told him at lunchtime what Penny had said about someone being missing from the haven, and then we'd all heard the scream of those sirens. . . .

I looked at each of them staring back at me but also

waiting for me to say something. To make a decision. To lead the way.

And I can't describe it exactly, except to say that Luca had been right—about the compass inside us that points the way. It was like that needle spun on my heart, and from one breath to the next, I knew what I had to do. I just hoped the boys would help me, that their own compasses would point the same way.

"She's here to see Mr. Khouri," I said. "She has to be. They've been working together and it's the only reason that'd make sense! Sam, Aidan, you need to find him and tell him, somewhere private where no one else can hear, and then get him to wait in the Skeleton room for us."

Sam and Aidan nodded, and I told them to go—*hurry!*

Then it was Jed and me.

"We can't make this a big deal. We have to act totally normal." I said. And then we were heading toward the crosswalk, and the crossing guard blew his whistle for us, and by then Nora must have spotted me because she'd turned her back to us and wandered over to the other side of the footpath.

"Çkemi," I said when I came to stand beside her.

Nora had her arms wrapped around her middle, but when I said that she eased them a little and turned to me, smiling sadly.

"Hello," she said, and I could see she'd been crying.

"Are you here to see Mr. Khouri?" I asked, and Nora nodded. I could feel Jed shuffling his feet nervously behind us, then the crossing guard blew his whistle again in two sharp bursts that made Nora jump.

"They're looking for you, aren't they?" I asked. She took a deep breath and nodded her head again.

I put my hand out—palm up—and Nora looked down at it, blinking back more tears. "Falemenderit. *Thank you*," she said, and took it.

Everyone must have thought that Nora was another mom because none of the last few people left at after-school pickup paid much attention to us.

When we got inside the school building, Jed ran ahead, peering around hallway corners, hand waving to say it was safe to keep going.

And then we got to the Skeleton room, and Jed pushed the door open and held it for me to walk through, followed by Nora.

Mr. Khouri got up from his desk quickly, looked between the three of us and sighed, then rushed to her side.

Jed and I went to stand by Aidan and Sam, watching as Mr. Khouri and Nora spoke quietly until she lifted her arm to wipe her eyes on her sleeve. Then Mr. Khouri sort of leaped into action again and steered her toward his desk—where he offered her his box of tissues.

"I can't go back," Nora finally said, blowing her nose and then taking a deep breath. "I cannot, Ferman—you understand? They will keep us locked away somewhere and when the time comes, they will send us back with no one knowing." Mr. Khouri nodded.

It was quiet in the classroom then, with just the sound of Nora breathing deeply and trying to stop crying, and Mr. Khouri saying soft, soothing words to her under his breath.

"What's going to happen now?" Aidan asked.

Mr. Khouri looked up at us, blinked a few times, and then frowned. "You are all going home, *immediately*."

"We can't do that," Sam protested.

I felt the needle of my compass spinning again, and figured Sam's must have been too.

"That is admirable, Mr. Murray, but you've all done more than enough."

I shook my head. "What about the baby?"

Nora's head snapped up and she looked right at me.

"That's what this is about, right? The baby's nearly due, and you don't want to have it *there*—and you're afraid they'll send you both away when we're not looking. . . ."

Nora closed her eyes.

Mr. Khouri said, "Ms. Ramusa is applying for permanent asylum and is afraid she'll be rejected—not right away, but a few months after the baby is born. You're right, Winifred, she's afraid that they'll both be sent back." Then, a little more quietly, he added, "I'm not sure this situation is going to help your case either."

"Can't she just go back now, to the haven? Say it was all a mistake, she got lost, and she wasn't *really* running away?" Jed asked, but Nora shook her head violently and Mr. Khouri put a hand on her arm to settle her.

"Even if Ms. Ramusa were so inclined, I do think they'll use her"—Mr. Khouri raised one of his brows, as he searched for a word—"*absconding* as a reason to deny her application completely and immediately. They will make an example out of her."

Absconding was another police officer word I knew because of Luca.

Which gave me an idea. "Come with us."

"Winifred—" Mr. Khouri started to protest.

"No, think about it! Take her to our place, Mr. Khouri."

But he was already shaking his head. "That is *not* an option, Ms. Owen-Ricci."

"She's right," Sam said quietly. "Nora needs somewhere safe to have the baby, right? Where's safer than a policeman's house?"

"Well, the hospital for a start. . . ." Mr. Khouri sighed.

And then Aidan jumped in. "But they're looking for her, right? The hospital is the first place they'll look for a pregnant lady—and she just needs someplace to hide until she knows for sure she'll be safe and they'll let her stay, right?"

Mr. Khouri and Nora looked at each other, seemed to have a whole conversation with just their eyes, until he finally said to her, "We could force their hand, use my contact from the local newspaper to tell your story, plead your case to the media. . . ."

Just then the sound of sirens rang out again—we all fell silent as we listened to them go past the Esplanade and up Ocean Beach Road.

"Come with us," I said again, stepping forward a little bit.

And then Sam stepped forward, too, to stand next to me. "We want to help," he said.

Mr. Khouri tilted his head and frowned. "And how do you suggest we transport Ms. Ramusa to your house? I ride my bike to work, and unless one of you happens to have a car waiting in that bike shed. . . ."

Sometimes I wonder what we would have done if Pop hadn't been home. If he hadn't picked up the phone when I rang from the teachers' lounge.

"Fred? Why aren't you and Sam home yet, is everything okay?"

Or if Pop wasn't my pop and he didn't trust me the way

he does, when I asked him to please drive to school and come get us—even though he hadn't driven for months, and even after I refused to tell him why I needed him.

"I'm coming," he said, and hung up.

He arrived quickly, and Sam met him out the front and led him to our classroom—where he opened the door and dropped his jaw.

"You're the one they're looking for?" Pop asked, and Nora nodded. "You know they're walking up to people and pulling cars over on Main Street to ask everyone if they've seen a pregnant woman around town."

Then he turned to me and said, "I hope you have a plan, Fred." I gulped but didn't say anything, so then Pop added, "And you'd better hope that Luca gets onboard with it."

It's so easy to know the right thing to do after it's already happened, but just then none of us could have predicted the future as we took our places and started following this path.

"I have an idea." We all turned to Sam. "All we need is a distraction, right?"

58

RIDE LIKE MAD

t was that time of early evening when everything had a kind of orange and pink haze, like the sky was a snow cone you could bite into.

"Are you sure about this?" I asked Aidan and Jed, and they both nodded as they clicked their bike helmets into place. I walked up to Jed's handlebars, lightly touching the cool metal as I spoke to him. "Vi's going to be so mad if she finds out what I made you do."

He frowned. "You couldn't make me do anything I didn't want to." Then he shrugged his shoulders. "Besides— Mẹ would understand, because it's you. . . ."

I was about to ask him what he meant, but Aidan started bouncing on his bike seat, so I shook my head and stepped back to clear a path for them.

"Remember—it's Route 787," I said, and they nodded again.

Then Sam and I watched as Jed and Aidan pushed off and started pedaling, their legs pumping fast as they sped out the front gates and took a hard left, heading toward Ocean Beach Road and Main Street.

"Will they get in trouble for lying to the police?" Sam asked.

I knew the real answer, but I shrugged instead. "Only if *we* get caught."

But Sam still looked worried. He pushed his glasses up his nose roughly, which I knew meant he was fidgety and nervous. I took a deep breath and turned to him.

"I'm glad you were here this year," I said. Sam's eyes widened, and I half smiled at him. "I just . . . I don't know what I would have done if you hadn't been around for everything."

"Even the bad stuff?" he asked.

I nodded once, and hard. "*Especially* for the bad stuff." And then I laughed because I couldn't believe my eyes felt shiny, and my throat felt a little raw from the emotions that wanted to come bubbling up. "I don't think I can do this without you, because I've kinda gotten used to you being around and helping me."

Sam didn't say anything; he didn't need to.

We made our way back through the doors, down the corridors, and to our classroom. We stuck our heads in and Sam said, "The ghost is clear!"

"*Coast*, Mr. Murray," Mr. Khouri said, as he put a hand

under Nora's elbow and helped her stand. They followed us out the corridor. "The *coast* is clear—an idiom that was used to describe a vessel that had safely cleared the coastline. . . ."

Pop chuckled as he limped after us. "I see you like to enlighten when you're nervous," he said to Mr. Khouri.

We went down another corridor and out the back doors to the teachers' parking lot. The cleaners wouldn't come for another half hour, which was when the building would be all locked up. The lot was clear except for Pop's old pickup truck.

Mr. Khouri knelt down and made a little cradle with his hands for Nora to step up to the truck bed. Pop and I steadied her until she could crawl to the middle of the bed and lie down.

"You all set?" Pop asked, and she nodded—then he and Mr. Khouri pulled a black tarp over her.

"You two ready?" Pop asked, turning to Sam and me.

When we both nodded, Pop said, "We'll see you at home then."

We watched as he and Mr. Khouri climbed into the truck.

Then it was just me and Sam.

As soon as Pop's truck pulled out of the parking lot, we ran around the side of the building and back to the bike shed. As we started riding toward Ocean Beach Road, the whole town was covered in this kind of pink-golden light, as the clouds came out to streak the sky goodbye.

We rode side by side and as fast as we could, just managing to keep Pop's white truck in sight. We could see the faint glow of blue and red police lights atop the hill.

"It didn't work," Sam puffed, his legs still pumping.

"It'll work. . . ." I said, even though I wasn't sure.

But those lights kept flashing, and Pop's truck was heading right for them.

"They didn't believe them," Sam said.

As soon as Sam said that, one of the police cruisers let out a whoop of their siren, and I swallowed down the dread that was rising up from my stomach as another whoop rang out, followed by another and another—whoop, whoop, whoop. . . .

And then the police cruisers started moving. Just as Pop's truck sailed past them, they pulled out from their parking spots and went racing back down in the direction we had just come from, down Ocean Beach Road, away from us, and toward route 787.

"What if Luca says no?" Sam asked, the words coming out between huffs of breath as we came to the home stretch.

"He won't," I said.

"But how do you *know*?"

We turned onto our street and watched as Pop backed the truck into the driveway, so the nose was facing the street and we could sneak Nora in through the back door.

Sam and I rode over the curb, dumped our bikes and helmets on the front lawn, and raced to the side of the house, where Pop and Mr. Khouri were helping Nora down from the truck bed.

Then Pop was opening the back door and I could hear the scrape of chairs inside, in the kitchen, as Luca and Anika stood up suddenly.

"Where have you been?" came Luca's voice. "We got home and nobody was here. Where are Fred and Sam?" And then he stopped as we watched Mr. Khouri walk through our back door.

"So sorry to intrude, Senior Constable."

"Ferman?"

And then it was Nora's turn. Sam and I each took one of her elbows to help her up the stairs. I heard the reaction to her right away.

"Oh, oh no . . ." Anika breathed, and then Sam and I were coming in behind Nora. Luca and Anika were standing in the middle of the kitchen with their jaws hanging open. Pop was hobbling to take a seat at the dinner table while Mr. Khouri rushed to Nora's side.

Luca's eyes landed on each of us, then swung back

around to Pop. "Jeffrey—what is this?" he asked as we shut the door behind us.

"This," Mr. Khouri said, as he walked Nora to our couch, "is a very bad idea."

59

THE RIGHT WAY

"Mirëmbrëma," Nora said. "Good evening."

Mr. Khouri turned to Anika and Luca as soon as Nora was seated. I'd never seen his eyes look so wild and worried. "Ms. Ramusa has left the haven," he said.

"I can see that," Luca sighed.

"We saw the police looking for her, and then we spotted Nora across the street at school and knew she must have been looking for her friend—for Mr. Khouri!" Sam said, nodding over at the two of them. "And then Fred said we should help her, and . . ."

I felt the blood drain from my face as Luca turned to me. "So, you've aided and abetted?" he said.

I knew what that meant—someone who helps a person commit a crime.

"Flee," Mr. Khouri corrected. "We have—each of us—helped Nora to flee, which is the very purpose of a haven." He paused before adding, "Or at least—it *should* be."

Luca ran a hand over his face. "Aside from that explanation not holding up in a court of law, have you all failed to notice that she's *pregnant*?"

"She is right here, and she knows," Nora said quietly.

I saw Anika's jaw drop open again when she heard Nora's words, in perfect English; and then Anika seemed to shake herself, closed her mouth, and walked over to stand before her.

"Hello, Anika," Nora said.

Anika nodded. "Your English is . . ."

"As it was," Nora said. "I am sorry. I was . . . I could not talk then, I had nothing I wished to say."

Anika looked between her and me, and I felt myself blush. She must have figured out that I'd known and had been speaking to Nora for a while.

"Your baby is due now, in November," Anika said, and Luca let out a string of curses as Nora nodded.

"You'll need a hospital, you will have to go back, we can't just . . ."

Nora firmly shook her head.

Anika sighed.

Luca turned to Mr. Khouri. "Ferman, whatever you think is going to happen here—"

"It's already happened," Mr. Khouri interrupted. "She has written a letter to the immigration minister that will now almost certainly be rejected. As soon as her daughter is born—or perhaps after a small extension until April—they *will* be sent home!"

"Well, maybe they *should*!" Luca suddenly exploded, slamming his hands down on the kitchen counter so we all jumped in shock.

He bowed his head, hands splayed, as he whispered, "You don't get to decide—*none* of us do! Some things are just out of our control."

"Luca. . . ." Anika walked toward him.

"We don't all get what we deserve!" he said, as Anika gently laid a hand on his back. He looked up at her, and then stared down at Nora. "And this plan certainly isn't going to help you get what you want."

"What is it you think I want?" Nora asked, so gently I didn't know if everyone else had heard her.

Luca shook his head. "You think they'll just let you stay? Make you a citizen, give you a nice big house somewhere and a pension to live off?"

"Don't talk to me this way!" Nora snapped, and I knew everyone in the room heard her then—because they were all suddenly looking at her, as she struggled to stand and face Luca.

"I don't want *any* of this," she said, waving one hand

around while bringing the other one to rest on her high, round stomach. "I had no say, *no say* in any of this! I did not want my country to tear itself apart or ask for those bombs to be dropped in the name of *peace*! I did not want to leave my home, to be chased to the border and squeezed into that camp and . . ." She sucked in a deep breath that only seemed to rattle in her lungs. Mr. Khouri made a move like he would go to her, but she waved him away. "*None* of this is what I want, but it is where I am—I have nothing to go back to, and if it was just me . . ." She shook her head and placed her other hand on her stomach. "But it is not just me anymore—I know there is nothing for us, no home back there—but maybe forward."

Nora looked between Anika and Luca and back again. She said, "You know, you know—if it was your bebe right now, would you let them be taken to so much danger?"

There was silence, and I watched as Anika sucked in a breath and lay a hand on her own stomach, Nora's eyes following the movement. Luca swore under his breath, and Pop said something about how she wasn't to know.

Nora looked around the room again, this time her eyes landing on me and Sam.

"Our brother died," I whispered.

Her face went white and she shook her head once. "Më vjen keq," she said. "I'm so sorry."

Nora and Anika held each other's gaze for what felt

309

like a hundred years, until Luca's voice cut through the quiet.

"Whatever chance you had for that child is *gone*— they'll never let you stay now, it's pointless to even try."

"I can't believe that!" Mr. Khouri said back. "You should know as well as anyone that morality doesn't always equal legality."

That sounded so much like what Luca had said about our own moral compass, that I was sure he would listen to Mr. Khouri and help us.

"*I* can't do this," Luca said, and then he scrubbed at his face again. "I am an officer, I could lose everything. . . ."

"She already has!" Mr. Khouri snapped.

A bad feeling crawled along my spine with icy fingers.

"Is that why you brought her here?" Luca asked, but he wasn't looking at Mr. Khouri anymore—he'd turned to Pop. "Because who'd come knocking on a police officer's door, looking for an escaped refugee? Was that the plan, Jeff?"

I heard Sam inhale quickly, and I felt the weight of Pop avoiding my gaze. "Who indeed?" he asked, not breaking contact with Luca's hard stare.

"Do you know what you've done?" He made a move toward Pop, and Anika took a firm hold of Luca's arm, squeezing it so tight I saw her knuckles go white.

"Please," I whispered.

"Why do you even *care*? Where have you been this year, Jeff?" Luca spat, while Pop slowly stood up to his full height. "You've brought this mess to *my* family's doorstep. Are you even sticking around for the fallout?"

"What's that supposed to mean?" Pop said. "And *your family*, is it?"

"Please . . ." I said again, and Sam reached for my hand and squeezed.

"You can't save everyone!" Luca suddenly yelled, and I felt myself stepping forward.

"Yes you can!" I must have screamed it, because suddenly everyone went quiet, all their eyes turned to me.

"You can, I *know* you can!" I said, staring up at Luca. "You saved me, once—you got to Merjeme in time." I looked from Nora to Luca and back again. "You can save her, too, I know you can!"

Luca started shaking his head.

"Why won't you even *try*?" I yelled.

He opened his hands out to me, but then they fell by his side again and he just kept shaking his head.

"It was our idea," Sam said behind me, quietly. "It wasn't Pop—*I mean*, it wasn't *Jeff's* idea to bring Nora here," he corrected, and Pop gave Sam a little nod, telling him to go on. "It was mine and Fred's, because this *is* the safest place for her, and Fred's right—it's what you do."

This time it was me reaching for Sam's hand, and

311

squeezing while he said one last thing. "You said deep down inside we all know the right way and what it looks like, and . . . this is the right way, we know it."

Just then, there came a knock at the door, and everyone froze.

60

A DIFFERENT PATH

Nora doubled over from the shock of the sound until Mr. Khouri and Pop rushed to her side and took her hand.

"Quickly, my room!" I said and pointed wildly to my open doorway. They rushed inside and shut the door quietly.

Three sharp knocks came again.

It was Anika who shook herself, who looked up at Luca and cupped his cheek in her hand and nodded once, and then walked to the front door.

Two more sharp knocks before she got there and swung it open to reveal police officer Penny McNeal standing there in her blue uniform—which looked a little more creased and wilted than it had when we'd seen her at the start of the day. Even her tightly bobby-pinned bun had wisps of red hair escaping at the neck.

Anika stepped aside and Penny came into the house, the sound of her leather shoes squeaking and her duty belt jangling as she looked around the room at each of us, frowning.

"Ah, sorry, folks—have I interrupted something?" she asked.

I held my breath, and I figured Sam and Anika did, too—all of us waiting for Luca to say something.

Because it felt just then like we were standing and looking at two different paths, and Luca was the one who'd have to choose which we took.

"You've just caught us in the middle of a big decision, Penny," Luca said, and I felt the color drain from my face.

I wanted to run over to him, throw my arms around his middle, and beg him to please, please, please not tell her about Nora. Beg him to save her. Choose the better way.

But I was steady and unmoving as a mountain.

"Oh?" Penny said, quirking one eyebrow and smiling nervously at all of us. "How's that?"

Anika slammed the door shut, which made me and Sam jump. Then she strode back into the kitchen, went to stand beside Luca, and crossed her arms while smiling tightly at Penny and flicking her eyes to us. "We're in the middle of a grounding," she said. "These two were late home from school, trying to get in on some excitement happening around town this afternoon. . . ." Anika glared at us, and Sam and I bowed our heads, doing our part.

"You happen to know anything about that?" Luca asked, and I looked back up. "Would that be why you're still in uniform when your shift ended hours ago?"

Penny's face finally broke into a real, weary smile, and she nodded. Her shoulders seemed to sag and it was just the signal she needed to come deeper into the kitchen and pull out one of the bench stools and take a seat.

"You would be correct, old man," she said, and Luca pulled out another stool and sat beside her.

"Tea?" Anika asked, and Penny thanked her as she started making up mugs.

"There's been a breakout at the haven," Penny said. "Some nine-months-pregnant woman went into town yesterday afternoon and hasn't been seen since."

"Pregnant?" Luca said. "Can't imagine she's gone far then."

"Nine months? It's hard to even walk in that condition," Anika added, her words coming out hard, and then Penny seemed to remember us—me and Sam standing still as mountains between the living room and kitchen—and she raised her eyebrows at us.

Luca looked over his shoulder at Sam and me, and then gently tipped his head toward the kitchen table. "This is what you two were so interested in being grounded for, you may as well hear," he said.

Penny opened her mouth like she was about to protest but Luca continued, "It'll probably be all over the evening news anyway, but you both know not to repeat what's said in this room, understood?"

Sam and I nodded, and we sat side by side at the table and listened as Penny continued.

"Well, she's not the first of them to flee a haven—apparently dozens around the country have been broken out, suspected to be hidden by civilians."

"That so?"

Penny nodded, and then looked over at Sam and me. "Your little friends said they might have seen her hopping on the 787. . . ." I held my breath, until Penny shook her head. "But that was a bust, and we've had no other sightings." I could feel Sam exhale beside me.

"So I thought I'd come here and see if you had any ideas about who it is we should start looking at," Penny said, turning back to Luca.

Sam started jiggling his leg underneath the table, and then pushed his slipping glasses roughly back up his nose. I gently pressed my knee against his to get him to stop fidgeting.

When Luca looked confused, Penny went on. "We figure it's one of the volunteers, right? Who do you think would be most likely to have helped her out?"

Luca ran a hand over his face, then looked at Penny and smiled a little bit. "You're going to think I'm paranoid, but one of the little old ladies there. . . ."

I sucked in a breath, but Penny didn't seem to notice as the kettle came to the boil and Anika poured water into two mugs before her.

"I think her name was Dorothy or Dorothea? Something like that. She's a Portsea local, part of some Grandmothers for Refugee Children grassroots organization, and honestly—I'd start with her."

"Really?" Penny said, and Luca nodded.

"Oh yeah, her name will be with the Red Cross—she volunteered nearly every day, and I imagine she grew very close to most everyone. . . ."

Penny stayed and drank her tea, then thanked Luca for the tip-off and headed out. I tried smiling at her as she waved goodbye, but my guts felt like they were about to heave out.

"How could you do that to Dorothea?" I said, turning on Luca.

He put his hands in the air. "Trust me, I *know*! But we also know she has nothing to hide—which is exactly what Penny will find, and then she'll be right back at the start again with no leads."

"Smart," Sam said.

"Thank you, Samuel. I am a police officer, I know how we think."

As soon as we heard Penny's car pull out of our driveway, my bedroom door swung open. Pop, Nora, and Mr. Khouri emerged, looking a little more frazzled than before.

"You get all that?" Luca asked, and it was Pop and Mr. Khouri who nodded, after which Luca added, "So I guess we're doing this."

"Thank you." Nora's voice came out strong and steady, and she touched her belly as she looked to Luca, and then Anika. "Thank you."

"What *is* the plan?" Anika asked, "I mean—*if* we manage to not get caught, what's the plan for Nora having the baby, and after . . . ?"

Mr. Khouri spoke up. "Call an ambulance when the time comes, but someone must stay with her at all times—in case the officials—"

"—make me sign away," Nora interrupted, and Mr. Khouri nodded.

"You know they will. They did it to Merjeme and her family. That poor girl." Mr. Khouri shook his head. "I know someone at the papers. I'll call them and make sure they come—if we make a big song and dance about a mother and her baby being turned away and made to go back. . . ."

"You're hoping to turn the tide of public opinion?" Luca said.

"It worked before—didn't it? To bring them here in the first place?" Mr. Khouri replied.

"You're basing this rescue on a lot of long shots and slim chances."

"What happens if we do nothing, though?" Anika said, coming back to stand in front of Luca. "What happens to that baby if Nora is made to go back?"

He shook his head. "This isn't a do-over, Anika—this isn't . . ."

"But what if it was us? What would we do in her situation?" Luca leaned down, pressed his forehead against Anika's so the two of them looked like they were sharing one breath. And then, so quietly, we heard Luca as he said, "All right, *all right.*"

61

IT'S YOU

We had to tell the Trâns what was happening.

There are just some things you can't hide from your neighbors, and especially those who are more like family. And especially not after I'd gotten Jed to lie to the police for me.

The next day Nora's face was all over the morning paper, and then on the evening news. They said she was "absconding" from the safe haven and had last been seen boarding the 787 Sorrento to Safety Beach bus—which meant authorities were looking for her all the way up and down the Mornington Peninsula.

And that night, we invited the Trâns over for dinner— and only three of them got the shock of their lives when they walked through our door and saw Nora sitting at the table.

Vi slammed her plate of Pop's favorite spring rolls onto the table, and instantly turned to Jed. "You knew! You lied to me!" she whisper-shouted.

I guess she knew because Jed wasn't wearing the same look of shock and horror as his sister, and the fact that Penny had visited their house yesterday, too, following up on Jed and Aidan's not-too-accurate eyewitness sighting of Nora. . . .

"Kids, go and play outside," Anika sighed, and so Jed, Sam, Lily, and I trudged out to hang in Pop's apartment, which had become Nora's hideout.

I remembered months ago, when Aidan had explained to Sam that a conspiracy was like a secret. And I thought of that again as we walked into Pop's place, Lily collapsing on the couch, folding her arms and raising an eyebrow at us before narrowing her gaze at Jed. "How does it feel to be a criminal, Văn?"

When Jed didn't say anything, Lily kept prodding. "You've really gone and done it now. Mẹ is going to kill you!"

I spun around and pushed the screen door open, banging back out into the night. I plopped myself down on Pop's ramp, my legs dangling through the railing, and listened as Jed spat, "Get lost, Huệ!" and came out to sit beside me.

"You okay, Fred?" he asked.

I was, and I wasn't. Which I guessed was the way you

felt when you were doing the right thing by doing something illegal.

"Vi's gonna hate me now," I said weakly, "and you will too. I shouldn't have asked you and Aidan to lie for us."

Jed reached over and tugged on my T-shirt sleeve. "Mẹ won't hate you," he said.

"No, she'll think I made you—her good boy—" I started to say, but Jed shook his head.

"She'll know I had to, because it's you."

I turned to him then, remembering what he'd said by the bike sheds the day before too. "What does that mean? Am I so scary?" I nudged his shoulder, thought he'd smile back at me and maybe laugh. But instead Jed turned his head and looked at me.

"No. It means that she loves you, and I . . ."

I thought Jed was going to say something else, but he didn't. Instead he shrugged and looked down at his feet, and then back up at me. And when he did, he was blushing.

I went red too. I was just about to speak when we heard the door to the big house open, and voices making their way down the garden to us.

It was Anika and Vi, walking on either side of Nora and each with a hand on her arm to steady her as she waddled along the path.

"Get in the apartment!" Vi said when they were closer,

and Jed and I stood up and did as we were told.

Sam and Lily were still sitting on the couch, but Anika waved them away to make room for Nora and her big belly.

Nora made a *whoosh* sound as she sat and started rubbing her stomach. When I saw Anika watching the movement, I went to stand beside her. Without saying a word, she wrapped both her arms around my shoulders and planted a kiss atop my head. I reached my hands up and held on to hers, both of us clinging to each other.

"We're going to help," Vi declared, and I saw Jed let out a deep breath.

"Isn't she, like, on the run from the police?" Lily said, and Vi shook her head at her daughter.

"It's more complicated than that. . . ." Vi started to say.

"Is this a Vietnam thing?" Lily butted in. "None of this is like the war, Mẹ."

"This is a decency thing!" Vi snapped, holding a hand up before Lily could say more. "I believe we have right on our side, and your father does too. Same with Anika and Luca."

"They do," Jed said, and Vi's eyes swung around to where he was leaning against the wall on the other side of the room. "It's why I—"

"Not now, Văn!" Vi snapped again.

"I will never be able to repay all of you," Nora said, and Vi went to her, bent down, and held both her hands and stared up into Nora's face.

"People helped me and mine once, when we needed them . . . when they probably didn't have to." Vi nodded and squeezed Nora's hands. "This is how the world heals, I think. One small act at a time."

62

CALL ME WINNIE

News of the haven fugitive was blasting out all night from the radio. *Fugitive* was another policeman word. I guess it applied pretty accurately to Nora.

All the grown-ups were sitting around the dinner table with the radio on quietly in the background as they planned. Vi and Khoa had sent Jed and Lily home, and Pop had given up on trying to convince me and Sam to go to bed and get some rest.

But then Nora stood up and said she couldn't listen anymore, so Anika and Vi helped walk her down to Pop's apartment.

A little while later Vi came back and approached me. She reached out and ran a hand through my hair and I felt my chest untangle a little.

"Go down, see if they need anything else," Vi said

quietly, and I started down the garden path.

Even before I got inside, I could hear them.

"A-donny-tel-ker-soni?" Anika said.

"A doni të kërceni?" Nora corrected.

I stood in the doorway of Pop's bedroom to find Nora sitting up and Anika cross-legged in front of her at the end of the bed, resting her hands on Nora's stomach.

"A doni të kërceni?" Nora said again.

"What's that?" I asked, and Anika jumped a little and snatched her hands back. She turned around and looked relieved when she realized it was only me.

"Would you like to dance?" Anika said. "A doni të kërceni?"

I smiled as I came in, and Anika scooched over and made room for me on the bed.

"I am asking Nora's daughter to dance," Anika explained, "and she replies. . . ."

Nora leaned forward and put her hand out. I placed mine in hers so she could put it on her belly—where I felt her daughter kicking and fluttering.

Exactly the same as Drumlin had.

"I talk to her always," Nora said, smiling down at the place where my hand was on her belly, and I remembered Anika telling me once that babies would seek the warm spot.

When Nora gave a big yawn, Anika said we'd head

back and leave her be for the evening. She said I should be getting to bed too.

"Is it hard?" I asked, when Anika came to the doorway of my room a little while later to say good night. "Feeling Nora's baby like that . . ."

Anika looked behind her—Mr. Khouri, Khoa, and Vi had all gone home, but I could still hear Pop's and Luca's low voices coming from the kitchen. She stepped into my room and I turned on my bedside lamp.

Anika came to sit on the edge of my bed, where I could see she was smiling a little sadly.

"It is," she said, "but I'd rather be reminded and think about Drumlin than forget him, y'know?"

I nodded, because I did.

"That's what I tried to do at first. Just sit in my room and try not to cry—try to empty my brain of thinking about him. . . ." Anika reached out, tucked my bangs behind my ear, and said, "But grief is an expression of love, and I loved him *so much*. He changed everything for me, the same way you did."

I looked down at my hands, but Anika gently lifted my chin until our eyes met. "I love you, Freddo—you do know that, don't you?"

I couldn't speak, because I didn't know. It wasn't too long ago that I'd felt like Anika and Sam were coming in and rearranging all my family's borders and leaving me off their new map. And without needing to explain any of that, I think Anika suddenly saw it all.

"Oh, Fred—I love you, and I didn't want to worry you with that. I know you miss your mother something fierce, and Luca told me that you were scared of forgetting her, so I didn't want you to think I was replacing . . ."

"Luca says love doesn't work like that."

Anika smiled. "Well, Luca is a very smart man."

I closed my eyes and heaved myself out from underneath the covers so I could crawl over to Anika, and let her arms wrap around me as I leaned into her and did the same.

"Anika?" I said.

"Yes, Fred?"

"Do you think you could call me Winnie from now on?"

She squeezed me a little tighter and said, "I think I can do that, yes."

63

NAMED FOR A PLACE

That night when I fell asleep I dreamed of Drumlin; he had Luca's eyes and Anika's curls. He was such a happy, bouncy baby and we all loved him.

But then I blinked my eyes open and thought I could still hear him, even in waking. It was then I realized that the sound I heard was coming very faintly from down the garden path, and I wasn't dreaming—there really was a baby screaming.

Nora's daughter had arrived.

I got up and opened the back screen door, walked down the path just as pink morning light was breaking, and when I came through Pop's door and stood at the entrance to his room, I found Anika and Vi on either side of Nora, all three crowded on the bed, and a wriggling bundle wrapped up in a towel sitting on Nora's chest.

"Come, come," Nora said when she saw me.

Anika reached out a hand and I climbed into her lap. Nora peeled back the corner of the towel and I saw her daughter's wet, red, scrunched-up face—she'd stopped crying for now and her lips were making a gentle sucking sound, her eyes shut tight.

Vi came around to Nora's other side and pressed a damp hand towel to her head, and it was then I noticed that Nora was still flushed and sweating. Giving birth must have been exhausting.

"What now?" Vi murmured.

I felt Anika shift next to me. "There's nothing else we can do."

I frowned, unsure what they were talking about. The baby was here, and that was all that mattered—surely? Then I had an idea.

"Shouldn't we call Mr. Khouri?" I whispered, so Vi and Anika got up to do exactly that, back at the big house, but not before I thought I saw them exchange worried glances with each other.

Then it was just Nora, me, and the baby.

Nora, with her hair in a loose braid with wisps stuck to her face, and I didn't know how she could look so lovely and drained at the same time. Because she did; both glowing, and also red-hot with a fever sweat that the cool towel hadn't wiped away.

"What will you call her?" I asked, watching as the baby burrowed deeper into her mëma's chest, her little head with a mass of black hair and tiny fists pulsing delicately.

"I was thinking to give her a place," Nora said, and then she whispered her name, and the baby stirred.

"Rose," I repeated, and just then she opened her little mouth to make a soft, whimpering sound.

"For Rosebud," Nora explained, and that made me smile.

I reached out to stroke a finger very lightly along her chubby arm to the curl of her fist that opened a little, like a flower.

"Winifred," Nora said, "we can't stay here."

I nodded and gave Rose my finger, which she wrapped her whole hand around. I didn't know babies were so strong right away.

"Mr. Khouri will take you away somewhere, and once everyone's stopped looking, you'll come back. . . ."

Nora shook her head, and the movement made Rose grumble and start to cry, so Nora started rubbing her back gently.

"No, no. Vi and Anika are worried. I have something inside that is meant to come out after the baby, but it hasn't. . . . They don't know what to do; it is something for hospital and doctor to help me, I know."

Nora shifted again, and this time I saw her wince as

she rearranged Rose slightly, and I pulled away—afraid I was hurting her.

"And I won't put Rose or any of you in danger," she said. I looked up at her and saw that she had started to cry. "I give her this name to remember a place that is special in our hearts—from when I start to feel safe again."

Nora bent her head a little to nuzzle Rose's mane of black hair and when she looked back to me her eyes were filled with tears, but she was trying to smile too. "One day I will tell her what it took for us to come here, everything left behind, and why I give her this name to hope that we come back again."

I started shaking my head. "Just stay," I said. "What if we could find a doctor, one who'll promise not to tell. . . ."

Nora gently lifted a hand to my face, cupped one of my cheeks, and rubbed my tears away with the pad of her thumb. "I need to get strong, for my baby. I need to be strong for her now, too, because she's here, and I realize hiding is not living, and it is no way to make a home.

64

WHAT CAME NEXT

The police and an ambulance were coming.

Nora told us to call them, Vi and Anika said it was the right thing to do, too—that Nora could get very sick if we didn't call for help—but that didn't make it any easier. I stood with Sam in front of me, my arms around his chest while he cried into the sleeve of his pajama top. I couldn't even promise him that it would be okay, because I wasn't so sure myself.

"I could lose my job over this," Luca said. We were all crowded in the small bedroom by then.

Pop stood up. "No, you won't," he said, "because you didn't know about any of it."

"Jeffrey. . . ."

Pop waved a hand. "No, you listen to me—this is my property, and it was me and Ferman who helped her escape and hid her away, not you—you and Anika just came in at the tail end, literally, when all you were doing was saving this young woman's life, and that of her baby."

Luca started to shake his head again, until Mr. Khouri interrupted. "They know a volunteer likely aided Nora—that's my connection accounted for—and Mr. Owen . . . he was just picking the grandkids up from school, in the right place at the wrong time, that's all."

"This is insane!" Luca said, throwing his hands out. "I can't let you."

Then Pop did something I'd never seen him do before. He went over to Luca, reached up, and held his face in his hands so they looked eye-to-eye. "It is entirely possible to do the wrong thing for all the right reasons." Then he leaned forward a little and placed a kiss on Luca's forehead. When he pulled back he said, "I love you, but you have everything to lose and I have this to give—so take it."

Not long after that we had police cars at our door. Not too unusual for a policeman's house, except when the lights are flashing blue and red and the siren whoops a warning.

Even more unusual is to be standing on your front lawn in pajamas, watching as your pop and favorite teacher get taken away by your dad's partner in the back of her cruiser, while you hold your brother's hand and can't do anything.

Then to see an ambulance pull up, and you watch a woman you met in a glass atrium—who changed your life completely—getting wheeled out on a gurney, holding her baby girl and trying not to cry while you're left wondering if you'll ever see them again.

But that's what happened.

And I play it over and over in my mind, like retracing my steps. I keep trying to see if there was another path we should have taken—a different way from the one where we all ended up.

65

POINT OF VIEW

t was a quiet, stay-at-home birthday for me, with just the family. Pop was home, but he was still in trouble—just like Luca said—for aiding and abetting Nora to flee the haven.

Mr. Khouri was in trouble too. As Luca had said, it looked like he'd lose his job for his role in helping Nora.

All in all, it was a pretty rotten birthday.

Except for when Sam had given me a present, wrapped in newspaper—a book called *My Sister Sif* by Ruth Park.

"I know you liked that Beatie Bow time-travel one because of the book report you gave, and the bookstore person at Farrells said this other one by her was really good, even though it's old now. . . ."

It had a beautiful blue-green cover with this girl in a red bathing suit swimming with dolphins.

"I wrote inside too," Sam said.

I opened it up, and there in Sam's neat handwriting it said: *To Fred, Love Sam on your twelfth birthday. 1999.*

That had been good.

It also hadn't been entirely rotten when Jed came over and ate sponge cake with whipped cream and fresh fruit that Vi had made for me. Or when I walked him back to his house afterward, until the last ten steps to the front door, when he suddenly reached over and held my hand in his.

That was really good.

And I was thinking about all of that when I rounded the curb back to my house and saw Mr. Khouri at my front door, speaking with Luca.

I ran up to greet him. I wanted to throw my arms around his middle and hug him—but that would have been weird, and impossible anyway, since he was holding something large and square and wrapped in brown paper in front of his chest.

"You want to come in, Ferman?" Anika shouted from somewhere inside the house, but Mr. Khouri looked between Luca and me and shook his head.

"You mind if we just chat here for a bit, Winifred?" and he pointed down at our front steps.

"Take your time," Luca said, and he let the screen door close, but not before I saw him hustling Sam back inside.

"Ah, your pop and I have had cause to spend a bit of time together lately, and he mentioned once or twice that it was today . . ." Mr. Khouri said, and he handed me the brown parcel. "Happy birthday."

I knew from the weight what it was, and from the shape too—I'd spent one whole term balancing Mr. Khouri's personal copy of the ninth edition of *The Times Atlas of the World* on my lap, so of course I knew exactly how it felt, and I wasn't the least bit surprised when I opened it up to find exactly that.

"I can't take this," I said, and tried to hand it back to him.

"Nonsense, I insist," he said, holding his hands up, "and besides—I'm not your teacher anymore, so it's perfectly appropriate. A proper present for a gifted former student."

I snorted at that. And then I ran my hands over the image of the Earth on the front cover, the continent of Africa in partial view.

"You told us once that maps lie," I said, still tracing the continent that I remembered Mr. Khouri said was three times the size it's often drawn on maps.

"You know why they have to, though, don't you?" Mr. Khouri said, and I turned to him.

"Maps are designed to appeal to our human nature. The Earth is imperfect. It's not even a perfect sphere, it's all lumpy landmasses and constantly moving oceans and atmosphere. It's impossible to capture all of that on a map, so we lie and simplify, and have been for hundreds of years."

"So . . . none of it's real? There's really nothing solid that we're standing on? The whole world is a lie?"

Mr. Khouri leaned forward and placed his elbows on his knees. He looked out past our front yard to the end of our street, over the rooftops and past the trees and somewhere down there was the ocean stretching out.

"*People* lie, which is why geography is such an interesting study of them, of *us*." He brought his hands together and threaded his fingers through each other. "But no, I don't think the world is a lie, Winifred. . . . It's just our perspective of it that could use some work. Do you know what that means—*perspective?*"

I shrugged.

"It's everything we did in geography—it's the art of representing three-dimensional objects on a two-dimensional surface, so as to give the right impression of their height, width, depth, and position in relation to each other. . . ."

"So, mapping?"

He nodded. "It's that, but it also means your unique point of view; the way you see things. Most people, their point of view is very narrow. It's either what's right in front of them, or else only what they want to see, regardless of the facts.

"And what I think is very important, and truly rare, is to try to gain a different point of view . . . a little more perspective of the world, which usually entails stepping out from your little corner of it and seeing through someone else's eyes."

With that, Mr. Khouri unlaced his hands and reached over to tap the atlas. "Page two hundred and fifty-three," he said, and I opened to that.

Tucked in the middle of the Oceania maps was a photo.

Except it wasn't printed in blurry black ink like some I'd cut out of the newspaper. This was an original photo, one that a journalist friend of Mr. Khouri's had taken, when they'd come over to Pop's apartment before the police arrived.

It was in full color: Nora and her baby Rose, sitting up in Pop's bed and with Nora staring right into the camera with her pleading eyes, black hair all a mess.

"Nora gave you that—a little more perspective— and you shouldn't underestimate how valuable it is." Mr. Khouri slowly stood up, raised his hand against the sun, and kept talking to me. "It's like everything has been redrawn, and you see the world as it actually is. Hold on to that, Winifred—hold on to them—and I will too."

BACK TO THE TOP

An article with the photo of Nora and Rose ran in the local paper . . . and then in the national ones too. The headline read, "Let Them Stay."

The whole piece still gives me chills, but the last little bit was the best part—and I'd practically memorized it:

Nora Ramusa's case is now before the immigration minister, and this newspaper would like to urge Mr. Ruddock to show compassion by offering permanent protection instead of temporary asylum to Nora and her daughter, Rose—named after the township of Rosebud, where her mother spent much of her convalescence upon arrival in the country, and where she says she first met and made some of her most important friendships while in Australia. Friends who are currently campaigning—along with dozens of other representatives from Kosovar communities—to let those brought here under Operation Safe Haven remain, instead of returning to an unstable and volatile homeland.

We add our voices to their campaign.

We've boundless plains to share, Mr. Ruddock—and we urge you to let them call Australia home.

It was weeks later, and I was still asking Luca if there was any news on them, and he said that as soon as he knew, I'd know—because he'd tell me ASAP, which meant As Soon As Possible.

And I told him that waiting was the hardest part—waiting to hear if Nora and Rose were allowed to stay, how much trouble Pop and Mr. Khouri were in, and that the war was really over.

"But, Winifred," he said, "life isn't like a map you can follow—these things take time, and there's no clear starting point or *X* marking the spot at the end. . . ."

And I was about to tell him that proper maps weren't like that either, but then I suddenly had a thought. A clear direction, in my head.

Which was how we came to be snaking our way back up Arthurs Seat—what the Boon Wurrung people called Wonga—and which is actually just a hill, but feels more like a mountain when you're making that climb squished in the back seat between your pop and your brother on a bright hot day in December, watching as Anika was reaching out and Luca was, too, bringing their clasped hands to his lips for a kiss before the next bend.

And then a few moments later, it was Sam and me standing side by side, waiting for the chairlift seat to touch the backs of our knees.

"Ready?" I said.

Sam pushed his glasses up his nose, and kind of gulped. "I guess?"

I reached for his hand and squeezed, and then the chair came and we both folded into the seat and it swayed a bit with the weight of us—but carried away just fine.

I looked over and saw that his eyes were closed behind his glasses, his hands gripping the metal bar and turning white.

But I didn't tell him to open his eyes, or that he was missing out.

Instead I gripped my own hands to the bar and told him what I was seeing. My perspective.

"We're past the parking lot and kiosk, Sam—it's Port Phillip Bay now, and it's all water like sky and little flecks of sailboats, the sand hugging the blue, and trees and houses sloping all the way out to the city that's just this jagged line."

I stopped, feeling myself blush and thinking I was being silly. Until Sam's shoulder bumped mine and I looked over—his eyes were still closed, but his hands were a little looser on the bar.

"Keep going," he said.

And so I did.

"Point Nepean is in the other direction, but it's just this kind of blur on the horizon, this speck of land that looks so small and far away. . . ." Because it was, I suppose. "We can't see it, but there's a whole world past the peninsula where the water stretches out—beyond the Indian Ocean to the west, Pacific Ocean in the east, and the Southern Ocean down here, down south. . . ."

"Now you're just showing off," he said, and I looked over to see he was smiling, eyes still closed.

"Everything looks smaller, Sam." And I wondered if that's what Mr. Khouri meant. "Even though it's just the same as it's always been—it feels smaller too."

Or maybe I just got bigger.

ACKNOWLEDGMENTS

Kate Stevens—I had for so long admired your passion and dedication to eclectic storytelling that it was very easy to trust you with my own. It has been an honor to create something so deeply personal and meaningful with you, and the entire Hachette team. Thank you!

To my US publisher, Alyssa Miele—I cannot thank you enough. Book people are my kind of people, and fellow Melina Marchetta fans are in a different league altogether. Thank you for letting me share Fred's story a little farther with Quill Tree Books—an imprint I so admire.

Karen Ward and Kimberley Bennett—editors extraordinaire who made me sound far more coherent than I really am. Thank you both!

John Hendrix—a thousand times *thank you* for my gorgeous cover full of light, stars, and my beloved Fred. You made this big moment so beautiful.

Astred Hicks—thank you for my beautiful map; it makes me smile and I always go in for a closer look.

Jacinta di Mase—you completely changed my life the day you tapped me on the shoulder at the Wheeler Centre. I will never be able to thank you enough, or fully explain how wildly I appreciate and admire you; but I do. You're one of my favorite people in the world.

This book took—all up—about five years to write. To that end, I'd like to figuratively tip my hat to some of the people I met along the way during my research:

Jill Coombe—whose report I read in the *Australian Journal of Emergency Management* (volume 15, issue 1, 2000) back in 2013, and who generously answered my questions when she got a very random email asking her to recount events that happened some fourteen years ago.

Photographer Emmanuel Santos—he documented the lives of Kosovar refugees seeking temporary asylum in Australia, and kindly chatted to me about his time spent with the refugees at Point Nepean that resulted in some beautiful and empathetic photographs.

Two books greatly aided in my initial research of this story: *Kosovo: War and Revenge* by Tim Judah (Yale University Press, 2002) and *Borderline* by Peter Mares (UNSW Press, second edition 2002).

The quote from Ursula K. Le Guin at the beginning

of the book is taken from her Bryn Mawr Commencement Address, 1986.

Mr. Khouri's sentiment for the class—"Not all those who wander are lost"—is a line from the poem "All That Is Gold Does Not Glitter," written by J. R. R. Tolkien for *The Lord of the Rings*.

Librarian Sharon Muir—from the Singleton Public Library, who kindly spoke to me about her memories, and then went through the archives to aid my research. Singleton kept wonderful and meticulous newspaper records of their own "Operation Safe Haven," and this was a good reminder that public libraries can be the keeper of community conscience, history, and memory—and that librarians really are superheroes.

The photograph mentioned in the chapter "Worldly possessions" is real. It was taken by Carol Guzy for *The Washington Post*, with the caption: "Family members, reunited after fleeing Kosovo, pass 2-year-old Agim Shala through the barbed-wire fence into the hands of his grandparents at a camp in Albania." The photo was taken on March 3, 1999.

In 2014 I won the Ray Koppe Young Writers' Residency through the Australian Society of Authors (ASA), which provided me with a week-long stay at Varuna, The Writers' House. I remain incredibly grateful to Varuna, the ASA, and particularly the Koppe Family—who established the Residency in memory of their mother, Ray, who managed the ASA's business affairs for many years. Let me also take this chance to encourage every creative reading this (because I know serious book people read the acknowledgments, the same way film buffs read the final credits!) to join their local, national, and/or state associations, who have your best interests at heart by providing you with advocacy, support, and advice.

Early readers Sally Rippin, Suzie Bull, Danielle Carey, Emily Gale, and Angela Crocombe—thank you so much for your enthusiasm and endorsement.

My invaluable authenticity readers—and a blanket statement to say that anything not quite right or entirely wrong is all on me. Danielle Carey—who was a teenager in 1999, and living just outside the Singleton Army Base when it was part of Operation Safe Haven. Danielle kindly read a *very* early draft of this manuscript to give me her impressions of living through this period and in a similar capacity to Fred. Her early encouragement and praise also buoyed me considerably and made me feel less afraid.

Diem Nguyen—for helping me properly bring the Trần family to life; for reading my clunky draft attempts and offering invaluable feedback, strategies, and insights. I've known Diem for a number of years now, and she continues to be an exciting and ever-evolving spark in Australian publishing. I am forever grateful that she was willing to give her time and thoughtfulness to this story of mine.

Natasha Solomun (and Ratko!) gave their insights and memories of the NATO bombings, and wider international implications. I'm especially thankful for Natasha's keen understanding of packing and tempering all of the above into a story for children. I am incredibly lucky to call her a friend and colleague; that I was also able to tap into her compassion and knowledge so close to home was incredible.

Farrells Bookshop and the entire team who continue to make that bookshop as magical in my adulthood as it was in my childhood: Suzie, Indy, Eleesa, Romy, Kate—and especially the original owners (the Farrells!) and current owners (the Hortons!). Local and independent bookstores and booksellers are the lifeblood of literature in Australia, and the world over.

My friends Carly Findlay, Tessa Meehan, and Adele Walsh—their cheerleading over the years has meant so much. Thank you.

Murray and Bella—you were both at my feet or receiving distracted ear scratches and head pats as I wrote a lot of this. I love you both, and I miss you, Bella—very good writing and editing companions and 11/10 doggos.

I can't thank the dogs and then not the rest of my family. So, Laura, Adam, Harry, Lisa, Claire, Andrea, Carl, Helga, and Don, thank you for constantly asking when the book was coming.

Omi—I have loved sharing books with you all my life. One of my favorite quotes is from Emilie Buchwald: "Children are made readers on the laps of their parents." I am a reader today because my mom was one, and for that we both have you to thank. My whole life is books now, and any tiny dent my writing and agenting may have on literature can be traced back to you, forever more. Another quote I love is a riff from Lin-Manuel Miranda's *Hamilton: An American Musical*: "What is a legacy? It's planting seeds in a garden you never get to see." Omi, I love you and I thank you—everything you planted in me is starting to grow.

I took creative license with some descriptions of towns, buildings, general locations, tides, and travel times, etc. Ironically enough, I had to accept that oceanography and geography are not necessarily story and I adjusted the grid accordingly. But please know that I love the Mornington Peninsula (Victoria, Australia)—it's my home, and I meant no disrespect by straddling the line between cartographer and storyteller, to make the map work for me.

Likewise, I had to accept that this is a story inspired by true events, and not a strict recounting of those times. Certain historical and political events may be imprecise; I again take on that responsibility as a fiction storyteller and encourage you as reader to go forth and read more about this time in Australian and world politics.

Mom and Dad—thank you for your patience. By now you've also probably realized that there's a lot of our family and my childhood within these pages; thank you for that too. I love us, to the moon and back.